EAGLE AT TARANTO

Mark saw the cone of fire that was Taranto,
sixty miles away, but he watched it for
another minute before he realised what it
was. The sky was clear ahead, and the cone
stood on the horizon, shaped like a Red
Indian teepee and made of a patchwork red,
white and green light: brilliant, scintillating,
shifting colours. He spoke into the Gosport
tube, "Did you ever see the like of this?"

"What?"

Mark did not answer but waited for Tim to
put aside his chartboard, stand up and peer
around the overload tank.

Then Tim said, "Good God!"

"It's a barrage."

There had never been any hope of having
the advantage of surprise, they knew that.
Just the same – Mark said, "Right bloody
welcome."

Tim did not answer and Mark could guess
at his thoughts: was it possible for any
aircraft to survive such a barrage?

**Also by the same author,
and available from Coronet:**

AUDACITY
DEED OF GLORY
SEEK OUT AND DESTROY
SHIP OF FORCE

About the author

Alan Evans is a highly talented thriller writer
who vividly and evocatively re-creates the
atmosphere of the First and Second World
Wars, he is also the author of three children's
books. Born in Sunderland, he was a member
of the Royal Artillery (Volunteers) for many
years, and has served both at home and
abroad. For two years he was a gunner
and he later went on to be a survey sergeant
in various R.A. units. Married with two sons,
the author lives at Walton-on-Thames in
Surrey where he is working on his next novel.

Eagle at Taranto

Alan Evans

CORONET BOOKS
Hodder and Stoughton

Copyright © 1987 by Alan Stoker

First published in Great Britain in 1987 by Hodder and Stoughton Ltd

Coronet edition 1988

British Library C.I.P.

Evans, Alan, *1930–*
Eagle at Taranto.
Rn : Alan Stoker   I. Title
823'.914[F]

ISBN 0 340 48918 9

Printed and bound in Great Britain for Hodder and Stoughton Paperbacks, a division of Hodder and Stoughton Ltd., Mill Road, Dunton Green, Sevenoaks, Kent TN13 2YA.
(Editorial Office: 47 Bedford Square, London WC1B 3DP) by Cox & Wyman Ltd., Reading.

Acknowledgments

I have received help from many sources while researching this book and I am grateful to:

Clare Hollingworth, a war correspondent in 1940.
(The ranks of the following are those held at the time.)
Capt. O. Patch, R.M., H.M.S. *Eagle*.
Cdr. C. L. Keighley-Peach, R.N., H.M.S. *Eagle*.
Douglas Clare, Signalman, H.M.S. *Eagle*.
Lt. Cdr. J. W. Hale, R.N., H.M.S. *Illustrious*.
Lt. F. M. A. Torrens-Spence, R.N., H.M.S. *Illustrious*.
R. Murphy, Telegraphist Airgunner, H.M.S. *Illustrious*.
C. Horrocks, R.A.F., Sgt. Armourer, H.M.S. *Illustrious*.
Capt. R. F. Chance, King's Royal Rifle Corps.

My thanks also go to:
H. Jacob, P.O., Air Mechanic (A), F.A.A.
Lt. Cdr. K. Patrick, R.N., and the R.N. Historic Flight for taking me over, and up in, a Swordfish.
Neil Ewart, who gained his B Licence as a commercial pilot in 1937.
Chris Ellis, for telling me about the song-publishing business in the thirties.
Adrian Cruft, who took me around the Royal College of Music.
Public Records Office, Fleet Air Arm Museum, National Maritime Museum, Imperial War Museum and the Performing Rights Society.
I would also like to gratefully acknowledge Don Newton and A. Cecil Hampshire for using their map from *Taranto*

(published by William Kimber, 1959) on which the diagram in this book is based.

But, as always, any mistakes are mine!

Among other accounts I read that of Lt. M. R. Maund, R.N., who took part in the raid on Taranto but was sadly killed in 1941. In particular I have quoted his simile of 'four-poster beds' on page 189 because I think it cannot be bettered.

Since this book was set I have learned with regret of the death of Cdr. J. W. Hale. He, also, was a hero of the attack at Taranto, indeed one of the leaders, and kind, courteous and helpful to me.

Contents

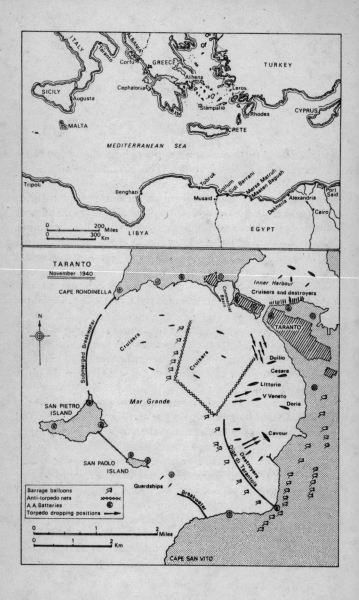

TARANTO
November 1940

CAPE RONDINELLA

Inner Harbour
Cruisers and destroyers

Commercial Basin

TARANTO

Submerged Breakwater

Cruisers

Cruisers

Mar Grande

Duilio

Cesare

Littorio

V Veneto

Doria

SAN PIETRO
ISLAND

Cavour

SAN PAOLO
ISLAND

Destroyers

Diga di Tarantola

Guardships

Breakwater

| Barrage balloons |
| Anti-torpedo nets |
| A.A. Batteries |
| Torpedo dropping positions |

0   1   2 Miles

0   1   2 Km

CAPE SAN VITO

ITALY

Taranto

Corfu   GREECE

TURKEY

Athens

SICILY   Augusta

Cephalonia

Leros

Stampalia

Rhodes

CYPRUS

MALTA

CRETE

MEDITERRANEAN SEA

Tripoli

Benghazi

Tobruk
Sollum   Mersa Matruh
Sidi Barrani   Maaten Bagush

Dekhela   Alexandria

Musaid

Port
Said

Cairo

0   200   Miles

0   300 Km

LIBYA

EGYPT

Overture

Sarah woke to the murmuring of the radio alarm, a soft burst of music and a cheerful voice: "This is Capital Radio . . ." Her fumbling hand found the switch and pressed it. Silence. Morning sunlight gleamed through the curtains swaying to the breeze from the open window, that also let in the distant rumble of London's traffic. Rob lay still beside her, breathing evenly but awake. He always woke at the slightest unusual noise, instantly alert like a cat. She knew he was a soldier but he had told her little more of his profession. She had a strong suspicion about what kind of soldier he was although she had never seen him in uniform and his red hair grew down to his collar.

He was not wearing a collar now, nor anything else. He reached for her but let her push away his hand. She pushed away temptation, too. "Oh no you don't," she told him, slid naked from the bed and stretched, tall and slender. "This is a busy day for me."

She padded away to the bathroom, and standing under the shower, she thought of the day ahead, planning. Articles and interviews were her business and she was good at them. She believed in hard work and preparation, had no use for the slipshod, hope-for-inspiration approach of some other journalists she could name. She thought now, nervous, that ordinary showbiz interviews were one thing – she found most stars willing to talk, though maybe some had made an exception on account of her eyelashes or whatever – but Mark Ward was different. He was a giant. He had written the scores for a succession of block-busting musicals and he never gave interviews.

Sarah had told Rob: "I've tried and so have plenty of people, big in the business. He always sends a polite letter saying he thinks he has answered all the questions already, and no, thank you."

Rob had grinned down at her, "Mark Ward? No problem. He's a relative of mine – umpteen times removed, but just the same I think I can fix it."

And so, incredibly, she was going to see him. Out of the bathroom now, wrapped in a towel and passing the kitchen where Rob was cooking breakfast, she called, "Will you be here tonight?" Sometimes he went away for weeks on end.

"I'll be here, and waiting. You can tell me all about it." Rob's voice carried across the passage to the bedroom where Sarah was dressing quickly: "I go back to regimental duty soon. Life will be a little more stable."

Sarah stood still for a moment then and said from her heart, "Good." She selected a pair of shoes from the row at the bottom of the wardrobe and slipped them on. Her notes were already in the shoulder-bag hanging by the door of the flat. She had done her homework and was ready.

She sat down at the breakfast-bar opposite Rob. He had washed but not shaved. A tee-shirt was pulled on over his solid shoulders and stuffed into faded blue jeans. He poured orange juice and coffee, then stretched a long arm to fetch scrambled eggs from the grill. He buttered toast and said, "This'll be your first introduction to my family – or one distant branch of it."

Sarah had been based in Paris for the last year, and had met Rob Dunbar there. Over the year he had visited her frequently, sometimes when he was on official business. He said vaguely that he was "a sort of adviser and odd-job man". Whenever she returned to England he was away on duty so they had neither of them met the other's family, but a week ago she had come home for good. Sarah was wary of his relations, knew his father was a lieutenant-colonel (retired) and his grandfather another. Starched shirts and formal dinners, horsy women. God!

Sarah said, "This will be a professional visit." Anyway, Ward was only a distant relative, hardly family at all.

"You'll have to meet them all sooner or later," Rob pointed out. "You can hardly stop on our walk down the aisle and say: 'Pleased to meet you,' to mother and the old man."

Sarah knew she could not. And that walk down the aisle might not be far away. She wanted this man, was sure about him, would have to bear with his family as every bride must, but she also wanted to put off the moment as long as she could. She put it off now, kissed Rob hard, grabbed the shoulder-bag and left the flat.

In the Mini she sped quickly through the streets of London and out onto the motorway. She had no doubts about her own family in Northumberland, was sure her truck-driving father would welome Rob as his kind of man, and her mother would dote on him. Mother who had worked hard through the lean years to help bring up her kids, who suspected Sarah was living with a man and disapproved, but accepted she had to move with the times.

The Ward house was deep in the country and Sarah had to map-read her way to it, but she had allowed time for that. The last stretch of narrow road wound between high hedges so that she came upon the open farm gate suddenly but was able to read the name on the post as the Mini rolled past. She stopped at a track a furlong further on and reversed into it then looked at her watch. She had timed it exactly: was ten minutes early. She spent five of those minutes skimming through her notes once again then drove back down the road and in at the open gate.

A gravel drive ran up to the house; built of old, red brick it looked warm, wide and solid. As she let the Mini drift gently in, muttering softly under its breath, she remembered to turn off the stereo. The cassette was music from "Tiger!" the first of Mark Ward's big successes, and if she turned up playing that he might think she was creeping.

He came around the corner of the house and strode to meet her, a man of seventy but walking briskly, thick iron-grey hair above black brows. A labrador, lean and golden, trotted at his side and stood, tail wagging, through the handshake and greetings. Sarah thought Ward was taller than Rob and better-looking than his photographs. He pushed open the front door, sat down on a bench inside and pointed: "My study – last door on the left. Please make yourself comfortable. I've been walking the dog so I'll just change my shoes first." He stooped to tug at muddied laces.

Sarah walked along the slate-floored hall, her footfalls muffled on a thick carpet down its centre, and into a room at the back of the house. A chesterfield and two deep chairs were spaced around a fireplace laid with logs, unlit in the summer's heat. A desk stood in the window, beyond it a view of distant hills and a nearby meadow with brown cattle moving lazily in the green. The dog followed her and sprawled by one of the chairs. Sarah guessed why that chair was chosen: it was Ward's. A tall clock stood like a sentry against a wall, a long, slow-chunking pendulum swaying in its glass-fronted case.

There were two photographs on the desk and Sarah stooped over them. They were old monochrome prints in worn leather frames. One showed a young woman standing beside a small pick-up truck. She wore a shirt and trousers, both baggy, and was smiling at the camera. The other photograph was of an aircraft in flight, a big biplane. A registration number was painted on the side: E- ? Sarah leaned closer to read it.

"Looking at Ethel?"

Sarah started, "Yes." Mark Ward had been standing at the door. And as he crossed to her side she pointed at the girl: "She's very pretty."

Ward grinned, "Ethel is the other one, the Swordfish."

"Oh?"

"However . . ." That meant: down to business. And he had not mentioned Rob. Sarah asked herself if, since Ward had probably been heavily persuaded to give this interview, he was now regretting it. She sat down opposite him where he lounged with one long arm reaching down to stroke the dog. She marshalled her thoughts, wished that bloody clock wouldn't join in making Ward seem so silent and withdrawn.

Then he used his other hand to pull a magazine clipping from the pocket of his shirt. He flipped it open and read aloud, his tone neutral: "'There is a raw energy to the music, a drive and a passion, but at other times a haunting loneliness. There are passages that leave the listener feeling suspended between heaven and earth, lost and remote. What fashions a man that he should write such music?'" Ward's eyes lifted and looked across at her.

Sarah was caught off guard, had not expected this, but claimed, "Yes, I wrote that." A year ago, when she had asked to talk to him and been refused. So she had worked up the article on the man's musical career using what she could learn from others – and from listening to his work.

Ward asked, "That's what you want to know?"

"Yes, I –"

"Um." He frowned now as he tucked the clipping away, the black brows lowering, coming together.

Sarah thought, Not encouraging, but keep plugging, girl. Begin with "Tiger!". She said, "It all started for you in the early sixties with that first big musical –"

"No." Ward's head moved in a slow negative.

So he had changed his mind now he had heard what she was after, and wanted to back out. Sarah persisted, "Mr. Ward, I will let you see the completed article and if there is any –"

He was looking beyond her, remembering: "It started for me twenty years before that, when I was about your age."

BOOK ONE

The Innocents

1

Ward

Katy Sandford was twenty-one years old in that fine summer of 1940 and Mark Ward was her senior by a year. To each other they were strangers, and to the bad business of war, reluctant apprentices. That war, after a bitter winter of sub-dued rumbling, had erupted in the spring. German tanks crashed through to the coast of France; the wreck of the British Expeditionary Force was salvaged from Dunkirk; and German armies were close to Paris. Then on the tenth of June Italy joined the battle on Hitler's side, dragged in by her own dictator, Mussolini, greedy for his share of the spoils.

Sub-Lieutenant Mark Ward of the Fleet Air Arm had a hollow feeling at the pit of his stomach. He was tall like all the Ward men, folded now into the open cockpit of the Swordfish. He wore khaki flying overalls and despite the rush of the slipstream was warm enough under the Mediter-ranean sun. The leather flying-helmet, earflaps clipped to-gether under his jaw, hid the black hair that lay thick and close on his head. His dark eyes were masked behind the goggles. What showed of his face was sun-browned, the jaw clamped shut and mouth set in a straight, determined line.

He did not feel determined. He looked down over the side of the cockpit at the wrinkled surface of the sea below as the hiccuping Pegasus engine faltered and died then coughed and caught again. The big, slow, old-fashioned biplane, a torpedo-bomber-reconnaissance aircraft, was usually re-liable, but when the engine of a single-engined aircraft gives up then you go only one way. He spoke into the Gosport tube, the rubber pipe that ran back inside the fuselage and was his intercommunication with the two other cockpits: "I think you two had better jump. I'll try to land her on."

Tim Rogers' voice squawked back at him, "Right!" Ward wondered what Tim, the observer, and Campbell, the telegraphist airgunner, were making of things. This was their first flight together and it was ending abruptly, maybe disastrously, only ten minutes after take-off. Mark and Tim had joined the aircraft-carrier only weeks before. They had flown separately with more experienced men and only today, the tenth of June, had been deemed fit to be teamed in this operational Swordfish.

In fact Leading Airman Doug Campbell was mouthing curses as he reached for his parachute. In the airgunner's cockpit that looked back over the tail, his words were torn away on the wind. "A real good old ship, a carrier full o' regular officers, and I have to wind up with two bloody amateurs." Campbell was a regular. "I was a boy seaman when these two were still farting around at their private schools. A flaming piano–player for a pilot and an observer who's supposed to navigate for us but he can't even find his own Stringbag on the flight-deck!"

Tim Rogers had come out onto the flight-deck from the briefing for this, his first patrol on active service, his mind juggling with details of courses and speeds. Unthinkingly he had gone to the wrong Swordfish of the two ranged aft, waiting to fly off on the patrol, and had had to be pointed to the right one. His embarrassment over that error was forgotten in his present terror.

Campbell glowered at Rogers and saw him swallow nervously, Adam's apple bobbing below the leather straps of the helmet. But at least he'd got his parachute from the stowage at the front of the cockpit and clipped it onto his harness. He's ready, or thinks he is, Campbell thought, glancing down at the sea. Wish I was. Don't fancy this, but here goes.

Mark watched them fall away, one after the other, and winced as he saw their parachutes jerk open. He did not want to make the terrifying jump but wished he was out of this mess somehow. People who thought of him as a pianist were not correct. Though he'd had to demonstrate some competence on that instrument when gaining entrance to the

Royal College of Music, he didn't really think of himself as a musician at all. He'd studied composition because his mother's half of the Ward family were artists or musicians (the other half made money, like his father) and she thought he had some of her talent. And because there was nothing else he wanted to do. He had London, music, girls and was happy. But now, instead, he was trying to fly a Swordfish that had gone bad on him. He thought, I should have stayed with the music. Nobody ever crashed in a piano.

The Pegasus engine hiccuped once more, cut out for a second then stuttered into uncertain life again. Mark looked to his left over the side of the cockpit. He was flying in a gently banking circle down the port side of *Eagle*, where she cut a white furrow in the sea below. He surveyed the long, fearfully narrow-looking rectangle of the flight-deck, with the two funnels and the towering island structure housing the bridge out on the starboard side. She was out of Malta, bound for a rendezvous off Alexandria to join the rest of the Mediterranean Fleet now based there, under Admiral Cunningham who had taken his ships to sea on this first day of the war with Italy to hunt the Italian Fleet. Cunningham needed to destroy or cripple the Duce's ships because so long as they existed intact they posed a threat to Britain's control of this eastern end of the Mediterranean. This first patrol of Mark's had been intended to search for the Italian Fleet – if it was at sea.

Eagle was sliding astern of Mark now, but turning into the wind for him to land on. He could see the steam jet in her bow trailing a fine, white straight line down the six-hundred-foot length of her flight-deck that ended at the round-down of the stern. He held Ethel in the gentle, banking turn to bring her round above *Eagle*'s wake. He had called his Swordfish after an elderly, amiable aunt of fond memory. Ethel had never let him down before, but as he straightened her on course astern of *Eagle* and steadily losing height, the engine spluttered yet again.

Mark swore, but mildly, "Hold up, blast you." He had been an awkward adolescent, rebellious, quick-tempered, no sooner the word than the blow and often seeming surly with his heavy black brows. But that glower had been only shyness, and now he was a grown man, a good pilot. He knew Ethel's trouble had to be a blockage in the fuel supply. There was plenty of fuel, too much. The hiccuping had started soon after flying off from *Eagle*, and Mark wondered how big a fire you would get with a hundred and fifty-odd gallons of aviation fuel aboard. By ducking his head he could look under the cockpit cowling and through the cut-out in the instrument panel to the fuel gauge two feet ahead of him on the engine. It showed close to full.

He was sliding in towards *Eagle*'s stern and now the engine was coughing more than running. He was losing height as he should but his airspeed was down below seventy knots and still falling. He had seen a crash during training: the aircraft had burned and the fire-fighting team was too late to save the pilot. The only way it might have been in time was by trundling along beside the aircraft when it struck – and even that was doubtful.

There'd been the smash and then the explosion of blazing fuel, following as quickly as the *flash-bang!* of a gun. Mark and his brother officers had carried the coffin on a bitterly cold winter day. It was his first experience of the solemn ritual of a military funeral with the flag-draped coffin, bugle sounding the "last post" and the rifles firing a volley over the grave. The young pilot's widow stood at the grave-side. Mark had seen the body, now in the coffin, but she had not. Identification of the charred corpse was only possible because the pilot had been the only man in the aircraft.

There would not be any doubt in identifying Mark either, and for the same reason. He saw one of *Eagle*'s escorting destroyers had raced in to pick Tim and Campbell out of the sea. He thought they would be all right, barring accidents, though they were neither of them expert or enthusiastic parachutists. What a bloody shambles.

He wanted desperately to bring Ethel home. She was wobbling in towards the round-down now. He had just enough height to clear it and he eased the stick forward to sacrifice a little of that precious height for airspeed. The batsman stood out on *Eagle*'s port quarter by the first arrester wire strung across the deck, his round, white bats held up at arm's length like the hands of a clock at ten to two – so the approach looked all right to him. But he wasn't sitting up here in this bloody thing and sweating it out.

The round-down was sliding under Mark so close that he was certain he felt the wheels rub. He eased the stick back gently and this time when the engine died, he cut it. Ethel plumped onto the flight-deck on all three wheels, lumbered on until the hook dangling below her belly caught on the first arrester wire – and she stopped.

The deck-handling party came running to manhandle her along the deck to the forward lift, right in the bow. When they halted Ethel there Mark unclipped his harness and stood up in the cockpit, swung his long legs over its side and climbed down, feet finding the cut-out steps in the fuselage. He stood on the deck, tall enough to look out clear over the heads of the other men. But even so, Ethel towered above him. She was nearly as tall as a double-decker bus. He reached up and patted her because she had got him home. But he muttered, "For Christ's sake, don't do that again!"

Ethel's fitter and her rigger were in the crowd; at that time each Swordfish had its own maintenance crew, and these two were Royal Air Force personnel, as many were. The Fleet Air Arm had become part of the Royal Air Force in 1918, reverted to the Navy only in 1937, and the Navy had not had time since then to train enough of its own crews.

Mark thought of Ethel's two as Laurel and Hardy. They were not comic, but Hardy the fitter had a barrel of a body set on short, thick legs that strained his oil-marked white shorts and a round face burned brick red, while the rigger was shorter, thin and wiry. At sea or ashore they were always together, Laurel's high-pitched Cockney voice rising and falling, interspersed with Hardy's flat Yorkshire monosyllables.

Laurel, the rigger, asked now, "Are you all right, sir?"

Mark did not answer but continued to stare over their heads out to sea. "How about Mr Rogers and Campbell?"

"Destroyer picked them up," Laurel reassured him. "We got a signal; they're O.K."

"Good." So that was all right. Mark edged out of the crowd. Laurel glanced at Hardy and muttered, "He's taking it cool." They followed. The handling party were pulling out the retaining pins that held the wings out in their full spread of forty-six feet, folding the wings in along Ethel's sides and securing them with the clamping bars swung out from under the tailplane.

Mark turned to the two men. "She cut out on me, kept dying and coughing, running ragged then dying again. A fuel blockage. Not a good start."

Hardy answered, "No, sir. I'm sorry."

Mark eyed him, "Was it your fault?"

The fitter met his stare. "No, sir. She was serviced and fuelled thorough and regular, like she always is. I'm just sorry it happened."

Mark nodded, hiding his edginess. "Very good. We'll try again."

Hardy said, "I'll strip the fuel system and clean it right through.

"Do that." He smiled wryly. "Still, it was an experience."

"Yes, sir. Suppose it was." Laurel's face was expressionless.

Mark stepped from the lift to the deck as the hooter sounded, warning that the lift was about to descend. "I think I'll try that line on Messrs. Rogers and Campbell. It should provoke some interesting comments."

The lift sank, taking Ethel down to the hangar deck, Laurel and Hardy riding with her. The rigger waited until they had sunk from Ward's sight, then burst out, "Bloody cheek! 'Was it your fault?' he said." Hardy flapped a meaty hand in a forget-it gesture but his incensed friend continued with his tirade: "And him a flamin' weekend sailor!" Laurel, like Campbell, was deep into a twelve-year engagement. "And he's goin' to tell Doug Campbell it was 'an experience' after Doug's had to swim home spittin' and swearin'!"

Hardy said stolidly, "Shut it. He asked me, I told him, he believed me. I reckon he's all right. He could ha' copped it today and he knew it. If it had been me, I'd have asked some questions, an' all." The lift settled on the hangar deck and he turned to Ethel, squatting, wings folded, like a huge settled bird. "Now, you old cow, we'll sort you out."

Mark stood for a moment on the flight-deck after the lift had gone down, leaning against the wind that swept in over *Eagle*'s bow. Then he turned and walked aft along the starboard side, headed for the island. He would make his report to the Commander (Flying), could see him up on the compass platform now. He considered his team of Rogers, Campbell and himself in the air, Laurel and Hardy in the hangar, and knew he had to get them working more effectively together.

Another Swordfish was ranged aft, engine bellowing, waiting to fly off to take over the patrol Mark had been forced to abandon. The flight-deck officer stood in front of it, hand circling in the "wind-up" signal; the pilot of the Swordfish had obediently opened up its engine. The Commander (Flying) signalled with his flag from the bridge, the F.D.O. waved the Swordfish away and it rolled along the deck, picked up flying speed and lifted neatly off.

Mark thought, Nice work. He watched it climb away, banking onto its course. The sun was sinking and there were perhaps two hours of daylight left. He wondered if they would find the Italian Fleet – if it was at sea even. If not, then the Italians would be lying safe and snug in the harbour of Taranto. He knew little of that harbour, only that it lay in the heel of Italy, big and heavily defended.

He passed the two four-inch anti-aircraft guns, pulling off his helmet, the tension easing, combing his long fingers through his hair. Landing on had been a risky business but he could grin about it now.

Taranto. He thought it sounded like a bugle call or a ruffle of drums. Ominous. A challenge. Taranto.

Leading Airman Doug Campbell dried out after his dip, then went hot-foot and hot-headed to his petty officer. "Here! I want to fly with somebody else up front."

The P.O. raised his eyebrows, "Ho, do you? Well, Sunny

Jim, maybe you were put there for a reason. Maybe the Commander (Flying) thought you were the best man for the job."

Campbell retorted with bitter sarcasm, "Because I can swim?"

"Very droll." The P.O. tapped Campbell with a thick finger. "You're not the first matlo *that*'s happened to and you won't be the last. What did you expect? The admiral's barge waitin' out there for you? Look, we're not running five-bob joy-ride flights. You stay with those two. And cool off."

2

Katy

Katy Sandford was day-dreaming – she saw the Italian Fleet in the great harbour, but it made no impression on her. Bert Keller, on the other hand, could hardly take his eyes off the ships. The two Americans walked along the wide, tree-lined promenade at Taranto with all the other strollers in the cool of the evening. The sun setting out over the Mediterranean sparked light from the glassy surface of the harbour, but this made no impression on Katy either, for she was dreaming of Jamie Dunbar. Meanwhile the men among the strollers glanced approvingly at this slim, sun-tanned girl in her thin cotton dress that set off her figure. She was not tall; even in the tapping high heels her head with its blonde mane did not quite reach to her companion's shoulder.

Keller shambled along at Katy's side, long and thin, an inch or two over six feet, loosely and awkwardly put together. He wore a good suit but he had bought it off the peg and no peg was Bert's shape. The suit looked dragged on carelessly; even as if he had slept in it. At times, he had. He admitted to being in his fifties, which meant he was nearly out of them. The Camel stuck in a corner of his mouth was as much a part of his face as his nose. He squinted through its smoke at the ships anchored in the great bay and said, "Boy! That's an impressive sight."

They looked out over the huge, circular harbour. It was three miles across from where they walked to the islands of San Pietro and San Paolo. Those islands were linked by a submerged breakwater and another such connected them to the northern shore of the bay. A third breakwater, this one standing up from the sea like a great wall, ran out from the

25

southern shore of the bay. The gap between its tip and San Paolo was the entrance to the harbour from the Gulf of Taranto, and the whole complex made the harbour unassail-able from the sea.

Five battleships – floating steel fortresses, grey and mass-ive – were anchored in a long, spread line a quarter mile from the promenade. Cruisers and destroyers were scattered beyond them and launches running on errands between the ships carved white tracks on the blue mirror-like surface.

"Impressive? Yeah . . ." Katy's agreement was restrained. "I suppose so."

"You *suppose* so!" Bert glanced at her. "With your old man you have to know something about ships."

"No, I don't."

"He's a captain in the United States Navy."

"So what?" Katy shrugged. "I knew a girl whose father was a gynaecologist but she still got pregnant at college."

Bert shook his head. "I don't believe it."

"Well, she did."

Bert growled irritably, "I didn't mean that."

"I know you didn't . . . Look, Bert, my father went to sea the way other girls' fathers went to the office. I loved him, I always knew what ship he was in, I'm proud that he's at Annapolis now and a success in his job. But it's not my job and I never dug into it. All right, I know something about ships but an expert! Never. Those five big ones are battleships, right?"

"Right."

"That's it. End of knowledge."

They strolled in silence for a time, Bert peering at the distant grey monsters. Katy believed that although she was proud of her father she was entitled to her own opinions, and one of these, held by many other Americans, was that the money spent on defence by Congress was mostly wasted. America had the Atlantic on one side, the huge Pacific on the other. Who was going to attack her? The war in Europe was none of her business. True, she had allowed herself to become embroiled in the last European bloodbath but that must not be allowed to happen again.

Thinking of home and her father's profession led her back to her day-dreaming. As the daughter of a naval captain she had met a succession of young officers, invited to her house for dinner. They were polite, very correct and on their guard in the presence of their senior. She thought they were like so many wind-up toys – except for Jamie Dunbar. He was English – or Scottish? Well, British, with the drawling accent of the British officer class. It was not just that he was handsome. She had overheard her mother say, "That Dunbar man is a ladykiller."

And her father's reply: "Don't let that fool you. He's a tough professional soldier."

Maybe. But when Jamie Dunbar looked at a girl . . .

She was jerked back to the present by Bert's slow drawl. "Well, they're big, newish, and faster than any of the four battleships Admiral Cunningham has. And now Italy's in the war that means he has a problem."

Bert's knowledge of warships came not from a casual interest but was part of his stock-in-trade. He was a war correspondent, had covered the Russo-Japanese war, the 1914 War and the Spanish Civil War and those were only the high spots.

Now he went on: "You see, Cunningham has to sink at least some of them before he can call the shots at this end of the Mediterranean. And if they won't stand and fight and he can't catch 'em, then Egypt and the Suez Canal look pretty shaky. That's what Mussolini's after: the gateway to the east, and the oil."

Katy said, "But the British have an army in Egypt, don't they?" She knew there were British soldiers in Cairo, and one British soldier in particular. "And there's the French."

"Oh, sure," Bert's reply was off-hand.

"You don't sound very certain."

"Let's wait and see."

Katy thought: 'Wait and see, or go and see? And if the latter, then the sooner the better.'

A group of sailors passed them and ogled her appreciatively. Bert said drily, "You've filled out some in the last two years."

Katy knew Bert too well to blush. "Don't be a dirty old man."

He grinned at that. He was an old friend of her father and had watched her grow up over the years, but the last time he'd seen her was in Boston in 1938 when he was on a brief visit from Spain while covering the Civil War there. It was because of his friendship with Captain Sandford that Bert had got her the job as a photographer attached to him. Katy wanted it because she needed professional experience and it was a way of getting her name and her work known, but she had no intention of making a career out of pictures of this or any other war, and so she had told Bert. She had a contract for six months. It was a way of making a start – and what had decided her was that Bert's assignment was to Italy and the Middle East, which included Egypt and Jamie Dunbar. But she had not told him this.

Bert was silent again. He flicked away the stub of the cigarette and did not light another. She thought he was working up to saying something. Well, so was she . . .

They came to their hotel and Katy asked, "What are we doing tomorrow?"

Bert halted, and she paused with one foot on the wide steps that led up to the big glass doors. He said, "France is going to fall."

Katy asked, puzzled, "Fall?"

"Surrender."

She could not believe that. In the last war France had fought for four years, and won.

Bert said, "Fact is, I think Egypt could be the place to see some action. So tomorrow I'm going to clinch a passage on a ship to Turkey and from there on to Port Said and Cairo."

Cairo! Couldn't be better, thought Katy. "All right," she said non-committally.

They walked up the steps and pushed through the glass doors. Bert halted again, glanced in at the bar off the foyer and then: "I said 'a passage' because you don't have to come.

28

I've been thinking it over. To tell you the truth, there were plenty of guys against your getting this job. Nobody ever took a woman photographer to a war."

Katy eyed him suspiciously. What was he leading up to? She said, "There's always a first, for everything."

Bert agreed quickly. "O.K. Sure. You're dead right. Only what I was trying to say was, I know how you feel about this war and I reckon it's going to be rough out there from now on. So if you'd like to call it a day and head for home, well, that's O.K. by me. I can handle a camera. I'll get some sorta pictures."

Head for home? To her own country, at peace? The idea appealed to Katy, but at the same time Cairo lay ahead. And perhaps Jamie Dunbar.

Bert saw the colour rising to darken her cheeks. He started, "Nobody's going to think any the worse of you because –"

Katy almost barked an answer, her strong streak of proud independence getting the better of her. "Look here, Mr. Keller!"

He stared. "What's all this 'Mr. Keller' stuff?"

She ignored that. "Mr. Keller, I took on this assignment and I was glad to get it. I took it because I believed I could do a good job and earn my money. What's more, if I said I'd do it, then I will, right down the line!"

Bert fumbled another cigarette from a crumpled pack, and said evenly, "O.K. I heard you." He struck a match and drew on the Camel, took it out of his mouth and examined its red tip.

Katy demanded, "Was there anything else?"

Bert looked up at her, picked tobacco from his tongue, and began gently. "Yeah, Miss Sandford, something else there is. You can get down off your high horse. I was in this business before you were born. So you call me Bert, you don't preach your high-school morals at me, and you buy me a drink now because you damn sure owe me one."

He finished as quietly as he'd started, but when he stalked off into the bar she followed him, meekly and pink-cheeked, called the order and paid. Bert took a large swallow of the *strega* and rested comfortably with his long, bony hands propping him on the bar. Katy sipped the *bianco*, glad the wine was chilled and hoping it would cool the blood in her face. She waited for the blow to fall. Home. It was not so appealing now.

After a minute, Bert said amiably, "Katy, do you think we two can get along?"

Katy did not hesitate. "Oh yes, Bert."

He emptied his glass. "O.K. Same again." He grinned at her. "On me."

Their ship was to sail from Brindisi on the evening of the fifteenth of June. The train from Taranto that day was crowded and hot. The Italians were excited and happy about the war; Mussolini had promised them an African empire. There was an ugly moment when one of them suspected Bert and Katy of being English, but they waved their passports and the moment passed in smiles. Just the same, that brief confrontation with hostility left Katy nervous and with a sense of foreboding.

At Brindisi they were glad to get down from the train, to breathe again and drink coffee in a bar before taking a cab to the ship. A radio yammered behind the bar and the Italian conscript soldiers and clerks that filled the place all cheered wildly. Bert glanced at Katy, who sat stunned. They both spoke Italian well enough to understand: the Germans were in Paris.

Katy was glad to be out of the train but the foreboding was still with her. She told herself this had nothing to do with her, this was Europe's war: she would do her job and then go home. She tried to think about Jamie Dunbar but somehow could not bring his face to mind. Other images pressed in on her instead.

Bert said, "They think it's all over, bar the shouting. They're wrong. This war's only starting and it's going to be a long one."

The cab was waiting with its engine running. Katy and Bert went out to it and down to the ship, on their way to war.

BOOK TWO

The Schooling

1

Action off Calabria

He had made an unholy mess of it.

Mark Ward flew Ethel in a wide, anti-clockwise circle with the other eight Swordfish, waiting his turn to land on. *Eagle* was steaming into wind at the centre of that circle. Ten miles ahead of her and tiny on the horizon were the two battleships, *Warspite*, Cunningham's flagship, and *Royal Sovereign*, with their destroyer screens. Eight miles ahead of them, over the horizon and only marked by their smoke, was the British 7th Cruiser Squadron. The coast of Calabria, the toe of Italy, was less than a hundred miles away on this course.

This had been his first torpedo attack, his first testing under fire, and he had failed. He had seen flak before when *Eagle*'s guns had opened up against Italian raiders and he had tried to imagine what it would be like at the receiving end. But the reality was immeasurably worse than any nightmare conjured up inside his head.

This was the ninth of July, just a month after Italy's entry into the war. In the course of that month France had been defeated and forced to seek an armistice. Britain was left to fight alone. The French ships in the Eastern Mediterranean, instead of sailing with Cunningham, now lay at Alexandria. They were neutral, disarmed with fuel oil discharged. Motionless, toothless hulks.

Cunningham's Mediterranean Fleet had sailed from Alexandria on the seventh to cover the passage of two convoys from Malta to Alexandria. The Italian Fleet had sailed also, from Taranto, to cover the passage of a convoy to Libya. Mussolini was building up his army there for an attack on Egypt, there was no doubt of that. On the morning of the eighth the British submarine *Phoenix* reported to Cunningham that an enemy force, including two battleships, was at sea. Now that force was between Cunningham's Fleet and the coast of Calabria.

This could be Cunningham's chance to bring the Italians to action – if they were ready to fight, or could be forced into it. The Italian ships were faster than his and that speed advantage might allow them to escape. So just before noon the Swordfish had flown off to launch a torpedo attack in an attempt to cripple and slow the enemy battleships.

Mark thought now, with bitter after-knowledge: Good idea, but putting it into practice was something else. If you knew the enemy was at point x at a certain time, steaming a certain course and speed, then you could work out an interception. But if the enemy changed his course then the needle had slipped away to a different haystack. Mark and the other Swordfish had found not battleships but cruisers, smaller, leaner, quicker. They attacked them.

The flak! Christ! The memory of that was horribly vivid. And of the ship he was attacking, seeming to wobble towards him because Ethel was skittering all over the place as he swerved her away from the tracers and the bursts of shell. He did not remember the drop although he knew he must have let the torpedo go, and he had no idea where it went. The rest was a jumble of pictures in his mind.

Before they flew off, Tim Rogers, nervous, too cheerful and unable to stop talking, had asked, "D'you suppose it'll be like the practice runs?"

"No," Mark answered. It was a silly question, jerked out from apprehension: they both knew nobody fired at you on a practice attack. But he too wondered what it would be like.

Now he knew.

He banked Ethel to bring her in over the round-down of *Eagle*'s stern, watching the batsman standing on the port quarter. He held the bats, like big table-tennis bats, half out from his side, straight-armed and pointing down at the deck. Mark obeyed the signal "too high", and eased the stick forward, brought Ethel down. He was still in that state of

34

numb unreality which had gripped him in the attack, felt that somebody else was moving his hands and feet, flying Ethel for him.

The bats were lifted above the shoulders now, the arms making a V: "O.K." Ethel slid over the round-down and the bats whipped down to be crossed in front of the batsman: "Cut!" Mark set her down. It was not a *bad* landing, but stiff, wooden. The hook dangling under Ethel caught on the arrester wire and brought her to a halt. He stopped the engine and the deck-handling party ran in, swarmed around the Swordfish and rolled her to the forward lift.

Laurel was there, eyes scanning Ethel for signs of damage then looking up to the forward cockpit. "Did she do all right, sir?" Hardy's fat, round face peered sweating over Laurel's shoulder. Both wore stained overalls in striking contrast to Ward's khaki flying overalls.

He answered, "Fine, thanks." He saw them grin then he unclipped his harness and climbed down Ethel's high side to the deck, edged through the crowd to stand clear of it on *Eagle's* starboard side. He waited there for Tim Rogers, his observer, and looked back along the flight-deck, watching the next Swordfish lining up to land on. All the squadron had got home, anyway.

He had been in *Eagle* for little more than a month but already thought of her as home and a fine, old, happy ship. He and Tim had joined her together as replacements in late May. There were always replacements. Even in peacetime there were crashes, aircraft sliding off the deck into the catwalk alongside – or the sea. In their month they had been coached by the senior pilots and observers, having the rough edges of their inexperience rubbed off patiently but remorse-lessly. And Mark had worked on creating his team. Rogers and Campbell, Laurel and Hardy, they knew more of each other now and of Mark, the man up front. There was mutual respect, cohesion, some trust and a little affection. Though they still had some way to go.

Eagle had been laid down on the Tyne as a battleship, *Almirante Cochrane*, for the Chilean Navy but she was still on the stocks when the First World War broke out and the Admiralty bought her. They eventually completed her as an aircraft-carrier but her origins still showed in the battleship bow; there was no round-down forward and the long rectangle of the flight-deck ended sheer over the bow. At the outbreak of this war she was on the China station and only joined Cunningham in May after a tour of duty in the Indian Ocean.

He needed her. She was the only aircraft-carrier in the Eastern Mediterranean.

Eagle carried eighteen Swordfish in two squadrons, and three Gladiator fighters. Mark could see the latter ranged on the starboard side, aft of the island. Keighley-Peach, the Commander (Flying), had got them out of store in Malta. He was a former fighter pilot and had trained four of the Swordfish pilots to fly the others. They were the only fighter cover the Fleet had once it sailed, as it had now, out of range of the Egyptian bases of the R.A.F. – who were desperately short of fighters, anyway.

Tim Rogers came over now, carrying the bag that held his chartboard and instruments. As observer he was also navigator, and in the last month had proved he was a good one. A year before he had been training as an accountant. He was a slight young man, his head barely reaching Mark's shoulder. He pulled off his leather flying-helmet and the wind snatched at his sandy hair, ruffling it. He was normally cheerful, talkative, but he did not speak now.

Doug Campbell joined them. Ethel was struck down to the hangar deck below, to be refuelled, serviced, brought up to the flight-deck again later, ranged aft and rearmed.

Tim Rogers broke his silence to voice Mark's thought: "We'll have to go again."

Mark turned and started aft along the starboard side, Rogers on one side of him, Campbell on the other and a half pace behind. *Eagle* was still steaming into the wind at twenty knots to land on and fly off Swordfish and the gale sweeping in over the bow thrust at the backs of the three of them.

Campbell looked shorter than Rogers but was not; it was

simply that his broad shoulders gave him a stocky look. He was a regular, as much a seaman as any of those working the ship, had joined the Navy as a boy and was rated able-bodied before he took the course for T.A.G., Telegraphist Air Gunner. When he was ordered to join Ward and Rogers he was wary of flying with officers he regarded as amateurs. He did not say so, of course, but Ward knew. Campbell was a stoical young man, with his share of imagination, but not given to worrying over things he could do nothing about. He knew his job and did it, expected Ward and Rogers to do the same.

This had also been his first real torpedo attack and he had known fear, but now he was ready for his midday meal: a bit of beef and veg with a figgy duff after and this time the cook might ha' put a few more raisins in that flamin' pudding. Rogers was saying nothing for once and that big Ward had a face like thunder. What was the matter wi' the pair o' them? Had they been expecting to sink the whole bloody Eyetie Fleet on their first torpedo attack? The morale of young officers was none of his business. Still – "Went all right, sir, didn't it? Pity we didn't get a hit but there weren't enough of us. Don't think anybody else scored."

He shouted it, but a Swordfish was flying off, engine bellowing, on anti-submarine patrol, and the two officers, sunk in thought, did not hear him. They turned into the island then, headed for debriefing, and Campbell thought, To hell with it. They'll feel better when they've had something to eat.

He went below, dodging around a canvas sack hung in the companion where it took a cooling breeze. The sack was beaded with moisture and held water for drinking. *Eagle* was an old ship and there were no refrigerators or ice-boxes aboard her. And because she was old her condensers could not purify enough sea water and after a few days at sea the supply of water for washing was restricted. These were facts of life and Doug Campbell accepted them, as he did the rats and cockroaches that infested the mess decks. The messes were scrupulously clean, scrubbed out daily, but the rats and roaches waited to come out at night.

Tim Rogers' words echoed in Mark's mind all through debriefing. He felt the little he could remember added nothing to the picture the debriefing officer was trying to put together. Tim seemed to recollect more but he did not know where their torpedo had gone, either. There was no question of claiming a hit.

"We'll have to go again."

They ate lunch in the wardroom and Mark found to his surprise that he was hungry. Afterwards he lounged in an armchair with a cup of coffee. Tim was relaxing, returning to normal as the horror of the morning receded to the back of his mind. He talked idly, steadily, and Mark only had to interject a grunt here and there. His silence was not noticed because he was given to bouts of it. If he had nothing to say he kept quiet. Out of the corner of his eye he could see the piano. He hoped to God they wouldn't ask him to play. He knew his hands would be all over the place, stiff-fingered, jerky, clumsy. But no one suggested it. At his best he was an indifferent pianist and wished he could play like Charlie Kunz. Now there was a man with the touch. Mark had often listened on the radio to Charlie, who had sometimes played one of his compositions. That was always a great feeling.

He wondered: What the *hell* am I doing here? Why was he flying a Swordfish on torpedo strikes?

He supposed because of Danny Soloman.

He had always known he had some musical talent, but not the kind his mother hoped would blossom into a brilliant concert career. Still, to please her and because there was nothing else he wanted to do, he had enrolled as a student at the Royal College of Music in 1935 when he was seventeen. Most of the students, like him, were paying fees of fifty pounds a year and were supported by their families. Mark lived in lodgings in South Kensington near to the College and his father, managing director of a firm producing car components, allowed him two hundred pounds a year. He lived comfortably, worked hard, conscientiously, and unspectacularly for two years. At the end of that time he was no better than an average student of composition, but he had discovered he could write songs, catchy little tunes he would never dare to play inside the august walls of the College.

He was playing and singing some of these in a pub off the Charing Cross Road in the spring of 1937, not professionally, because he was a mediocre pianist by pub standards, and a terrible singer, but to entertain a group of friends, and Danny Soloman had cornered him after he had finished playing. Danny was dark, dapper in a good suit, and wore a regimental tie to which he was entitled; he had served more than a year, from 1916-17, on the Western Front and still had shrapnel in his leg.

He asked Mark, "Where did you get those songs?"

"I knocked them out myself." Mark was defensive because he knew the songs were lightweight affairs, but he could write what he liked and thought it was none of this little man's business. He was wrong.

Danny asked, "Hawked 'em around?"

"What?"

"Have you tried to sell 'em?"

"No, I just play –"

"Written 'em down?"

"No, I haven't –"

"Can you score music?"

Mark resented the barrage of questions and particularly this last. He answered stiffly, "I'm a student at the Royal College of Music."

"That's not an answer." But Danny grinned to take the sting out of that. "So you can score and do arrangements?"

"Yes. But what do you –"

"You write them down. I'm the professional manager of a music publishing house. That means I meet the professional entertainers and find songs that are right for them. I'll get a chap I know to put some lyrics to your tunes and I'll sell them."

"They've got words. Didn't you hear –"

"Rubbish," Danny grimaced. "Mind you, most lyrics are rubbish these days but there's rubbish that sells and rubbish that doesn't. So – are you on?"

Mark was unready, not sure what to make of this offer. "It's awfully kind of you –"

"No, it isn't. It would be if I wasn't taking fifty per cent for the house, but I am, so it's business."

Now Mark suspected exploitation and burst out, "You want fifty per cent?"

Danny chuckled. "Think you're being taken for a mug? Those terms are usual. The house has expenses and we work for you. Ask people in the business if you don't believe me."

Mark looked him in the eye, then nodded. "I believe you. It just seemed a lot."

Danny said patiently, "Now look here, son. How much have you made out of these songs so far?"

"Well – nothing."

"So who wants fifty per cent of nothing? Are you on?" Danny held out his hand.

Mark took it, laughing down at him. "All right, I'm on."

But he had still been doubtful, not of Danny's terms but of his own confidence. Ward wrote down his songs, hoping for a few pounds but expecting nothing. Danny had lyrics written for them, and titles using words like love, June, moon, forever, good-bye, heartbreak, happiness. He sold them, and asked for more. He was scrupulously honest and paid Ward's royalties on the nail. Mark was suddenly wealthy beyond his wildest dreams; he was only nineteen. He did not become rich overnight but he ran a little M.G. sports car on his earnings – and he learned to fly.

One weekend he had motored down to Brooklands to watch the big racing cars hurtle round the banked circuit and he saw the flying training in the aerodrome inside the circuit. He knew at once that this was something he wanted to do, and now he could afford it. In the course of two happy weeks in the summer vacation he took eight hours of dual instruction on a De Havilland Moth and then went solo. It cost him thirty pounds, at a time when five pounds a week was a good wage. By the end of the fortnight he had his "A" licence as a private pilot – and hungered for more.

He continued at the Royal College of Music, worked as

hard as before and only achieved the same standard of passable mediocrity. He did not mind because he always did his best and he was enjoying life. The songs were bringing in three or four hundred a year on top of the two hundred his father allowed him, and he had all the money he needed. There were parties and girls, his M.G. – and flying. It had been a fine life while it lasted.

He looked around the wardroom at the other young officers, wondered what Danny would say if he saw him now, and grinned. His reaction would not be sympathetic. More likely: "There's no percentage in mooning over this morning's balls-up. That's past. This is *now*, when you've got to earn your money. Didn't they teach you anything at that fancy school?"

Yes, they did. One or two things.

He had to do better next time.

He walked out of the debriefing in the island and aft along the flight-deck past the big crane for hoisting seaplanes in and out. His heart was thumping.

In a torpedo attack you flew into the muzzles of the enemy guns like a man walking towards a firing squad. To have any hope of scoring a hit you had to release the torpedo when flying straight and level and at some thirty to sixty feet above the sea. At any greater height it was probable the torpedo would enter the sea at too acute an angle, dive too deep and be lost. But when you flew straight and level like that you set yourself up to be shot at. For the enemy guns it was easy as a clay pigeon shoot. The attack was best made on the beam so the whole length of the ship offered itself as a target. This also meant that all the heavy artillery on the broadside of the ship – a maximum concentration of its armament – could be fired at the attacking aircraft. And Mark knew now what that was like.

Tim came trotting behind him, hurrying to catch up. He fell into step alongside, the bag holding his chartboard tucked under his arm. He panted, "Do you think Cunningham's caught them?" He was talking of the Italian Fleet.

Mark stared out to the westward, where *Warspite* with

Cunningham aboard, and the rest of the Fleet, were out of sight over the horizon – and in action. *Eagle* was steaming independently with only her escorting destroyers, *Vampire* and *Voyager* for company – and the partially disabled cruiser *Gloucester*.

Mark said, "Maybe they're hoping to catch *us*. We're getting close to their airfields." The Fleet had been bombed repeatedly by the Italian air force. *Gloucester* had taken a hit on her bridge that killed her captain and a score of other officers and men. It had also smashed her director control so, with her steering and her guns controlled only from the emergency station aft, she was pulled out of the line and sent to join *Eagle*. Now *Warspite* and the cruisers were engaging the enemy but they were fighting in an area not of their choosing, right in the Italian backyard. Was this an attempt to lure Cunningham into a trap to be sprung by submarines and bombers from the mainland?

But none of this concerned Mark now. He knew an Italian Fleet of two battleships, sixteen cruisers and close on thirty destroyers was less than forty miles away and his squadron was to attack it.

The nine Swordfish were ranged in a herringbone from *Eagle*'s stern, a line of them along each side, noses pointing at an angle across the deck and inclined towards her bow. Their wings were folded so they could be packed more closely together. Chocks were jammed under their wheels and the metal propellers whirled as the fitters ran up the engines.

Mark walked the uneven plates of *Eagle*'s deck to where Ethel waited, third in the starboard line. Campbell was already up in the aftermost cockpit, the upper half of his stocky body jutting up out of it, stubby fingers busy on a final check on the Vickers machine-gun. Mark beckoned and Campbell leaned over, the straps of the as yet unbuckled flying-helmet flapping against his jaw. Ward bellowed up at him: "Torpedo attack on the Eyeties!"

That was all the briefing Doug Campbell would get. He might have heard the shouted words above the din of the engines or more likely read the message on Mark's lips – or simply guessed, because torpedos were slung underneath the Swordfish. He stuck up his thumb and Mark mentally added another possibility: Campbell doesn't give a bugger, anyway.

He was wrong. Campbell did not worry about where he was going but he did wonder bleakly if he would come back. So he took a good look at Mark Ward, thought the big feller was looking calm and confident, and that was the main thing.

Mark climbed up to the cockpit. Hardy eased his bulk out of it and Mark slid into his seat on top of the parachute already resting there like a cushion. Hardy belted him into the Sutton harness, slapped his shoulder and bawled, "Good luck, sir!" Then he manoeuvred his way down to the deck. The sad-faced Laurel was settling Rogers into the observer's cockpit between Mark and Campbell, passing him his chartboard and instruments.

Now it was routine for Mark, going through the checks, looking up at the weather. Two tenths cloud, slight sea and a wind out of the north-west about Force 5. *Eagle* was steaming into it now and he could see the steam jet in her bow trailing a white streamer down the centre of her flight-deck. Up there in the cockpit he was only aware of the slipstream from his engine, flapping Laurel's voluminous overalls like a flag hung round his skinny body.

And all the while Mark was thinking: Better this time. Better this time. Got to do better this time.

A light flashed from the island and the flight-deck officer gestured "come-on" with his two flags. The chocks were whipped away from under the wheels of the first Swordfish and it rolled forward, turning, then halted when the F.D.O. signalled. It stood with its nose pointed into the wind, towards *Eagle*'s bow. The wings were swung out and locked in place, the engine run up until it thundered. Then the two flags snapped down and the Swordfish surged forward, lifted off slowly under the three-quarter-ton weight of the torpedo, dipped out of his sight as it cleared the bow then a second later rose into view again, climbing.

Mark watched the others go at ten second intervals then saw the flags beckon to him. Laurel and Hardy, flat on the

43

deck on either side of Ethel's wheels and gripping the ropes attached to the chocks, whipped them away from under the wheels and Ethel rolled forward. The fitter and rigger scrambled to their feet and stood together close to the side out of the way of the remaining Swordfish. They watched as Ethel lumbered into the air, held their breath as she sagged from sight over the bow, let it out as she rose again. That was always a gut-sinking moment for them.

Mark climbed, joined the circling Swordfish and fell into formation when the rest joined them. They headed for the Italian Fleet beyond the horizon, all the while searching the sky for enemy fighters.

The squadron flew in a formation of three "vics" of three, each "vic" with its leader and a wingman flying on either side of him but a few yards astern so that they made a V. They climbed over a layer of patchy cloud and through a hole Mark caught a glimpse of sea glinting far below like hammered, polished pewter, its many facets reflecting the sunlight like a bank of mirrors. He was reminded, curiously, of the tunnel. Once, when caught by a storm while he was flying, he had seen a passage through the black clouds that narrowed down to a window of clear, blue sky. He had flown through the cloud tunnel with them closing in, and then burst out through the window into sunlight.

He wondered why he had remembered that now . . .

Ships! Lean shapes in line ahead, Italians, each trailing its banner of smoke and cutting a white arrowhead in the sea. And always the words ran through his head: *Got to do better.*

He spoke into the mouthpiece of the Gosport tube, the intercom of the Swordfish, joined to the earpieces of his helmet like a doctor's stethoscope. "Enemy fleet ahead!"

But not the battleships. Away to his left smoke was banked like a monstrous, dirty blanket cast on the surface of the sea. The battleships had done their disappearing act, retreating behind that smoke-screen to evade the fire of *Warspite*, far astern of Mark and hidden by cloud. The ships ahead were cruisers.

"Seen!" That was Tim Rogers answering. He and

Campbell were standing up in their open cockpits now, seat harnesses unclipped and only the "jock-strap", a single long band of webbing running from each man's belt to an anchorage on the cockpit floor, to save them from falling out if Ward was forced into aerobatics.

Mark watched his "vic" leader, eased the stick forward to follow him into the dive. The ships might only be cruisers but they were big, and there were four of them in line ahead with an escorting screen of destroyers. Their wakes left white hatchings scoring the blue surface of the sea. They grew in size from small toys to big ones as the altimeter unreeled and the needle on the airspeed dial crept around to 160 – 170 – 180 knots.

Mark pulled Ethel out of the dive and levelled her off at fifty feet above the sea. He had been aware of flak bursting while in that dive but none of it was near him. Now he was flying into it, the black smoke-balls appearing ahead and above. He worked stick and rudder gently with hand and feet to try to swing Ethel away from the bursts, watched the ship ahead of him grow, all her upperworks sparkling with red flashes as she fired her anti-aircraft armament.

She was in the torpedo-sight, a yard-long, calibrated bar mounted across the engine cowling in front of Mark's windscreen. But she was heeling under helm, turning towards the attacking Swordfish so that they would not get a shot at the full length of her but only at her bow. Mark checked on the airspeed: 130 knots and falling. The ship filled the torpedo-sight but he could barely see her through the bursting flak. His left hand was on the firing button down by the throttle.

Now.

Tim's voice squawked in his ear: "Torpedo's gone!"

The cruiser loomed huge, rushing at him and Mark swung Ethel into a turn, climbing and banking away over the stern. There was briefly no flak around him but instead the looping, glinting arcs of tracer from the cruiser's heavy machine-guns. Then he left her behind and tucked Ethel close down to the sea to run away.

Tim's voice came again. "A hit! I'm sure that was a hit!"

Mark kept Ethel swaying and swerving from side to side to evade the bursting shells that followed her from the escorting screen of destroyers. "Ours?"

"Somebody's. It could have been ours. All the squadron dropped their fish, I think."

That was better, anyway, much much better. This time Mark was not frozen in shock. He had been frightened by the flak but able to deal with it.

Now there were no more shell bursts and he inched the stick back, set Ethel climbing. He peered about the sky, saw the other Swordfish of the squadron gathering and altered course to join them. Ethel settled snugly into her place in the formation and they all headed back to *Eagle*. They had suffered no casualties and Ward marvelled. How could the entire squadron fly through such a curtain of fire without a single one of them coming to harm? Was it perhaps because the Swordfish were so slow and the gunners were trained to fire at faster-moving targets, and thus were leading them by too big a margin?

Tim Rogers spoke but the words were distorted; the Gosport tube did not always work.

Mark said, "Say again?"

More squeaks and rumbles, then, "Can you hear me?"

"I can now."

"I said, back in time for tea."

Mark agreed, "That's right." Provided he didn't make a mess of landing on and ran into the island, or skidded over the side to finish up jammed nose-down in the catwalk, or overshot and dived into the sea.

He did none of those things but made a neat landing on all three wheels. Then after debriefing he sat in the wardroom with Tim and they sipped at cups of tea with the other returned aircrews, while the white-jacketed Chinese stewards moved quietly among them. They were Chinese because *Eagle*'s last commission had been on the China Station and the stewards had stayed with her.

Tim said thoughtfully, "Funny sort of war."

Mark looked around the wardroom at the pilots and ob-servers stretched out in armchairs, listened to the quiet buzz of conversation with an occasional burst of laughter. They were in a battle, two fleets manoeuvring, one seeking a death-grip and the other striving to evade it. Just over the horizon the great guns were hurling their huge shells across fifteen miles of sea and men were dying. You flew an attack before lunch and another before tea.

Mark answered, "Yes."

Tim asked, "Do you think we'll have another go?"

"It's on the cards. They're servicing and re-arming in the hangar now."

Laurel, working on Ethel, saw Campbell passing through the steel box of the hangar and called to him, "Hey, Doug! How did it go?"

Campbell paused for a moment. He was on his way to get his head down for a kip because he could be flying again before this day was over. "It went all right. Hairy, but all right."

Laurel did not pause in his repairs to Ethel's fuselage, rent by shrapnel from the flak, but he asked, "What price your amateurs now?"

Campbell looked from the rigger to Hardy's bulk perched on a staging as he bent over Ethel's engine. Hardy turned his head and winked. Doug Campbell remembered the fitter telling him that Laurel himself had described Ward as a "weekend sailor". Campbell said, "The big feller can fly and Rogers hasn't got us lost. I could do worse than those two." That was the highest praise he could give.

Laurel said, "Ward doesn't say a lot, but he can crack a joke and take one. Right?"

This time Hardy spoke, "Aye. But I wouldn't cross him."

Laurel blinked, then captured the conversation again. "Oh, sure. I reckon he's got a temper. But like I said, it's Rogers does most o' the talking."

Campbell eyed the two R.A.F. men and said solemnly, "I've known oppos like that, one with all the chat and the other not getting a word in."

Laurel nodded agreement, "That's right. I've known some."

Hardy said, "Ah."

Campbell grinned and went on his way.

Warspite had scored a hit with a fifteen-inch shell on one of the Italian battleships but then their fleet had made off behind a smoke-screen, headed for home. Cunningham kept up the pursuit until his ships were only twenty-five miles from the coast of Calabria. Only then did he turn away. His fleet was attacked by bombers of the Italian air force, operating from its bases ashore and *Eagle* was bombed five times inside ninety minutes, but no ship was hit. The Swordfish were not ordered to make another attack because it was now too close to nightfall and the Italian ships were too far away.

The British Fleet joined up and steamed south through the night.

The trouble with the dawn patrol, as always, was that it started the previous night when a midshipman made his way down to the hangar deck. He handed over the orders detailing the aircraft to fly off at first light and how they were to be armed, then went off.

The petty officers and the Air Force sergeants read the orders, blasphemed, then shouted for the fitters and riggers. They squeezed between the tight-packed aircraft and gathered under the glaring lights that made the sunburned, sweating faces an oily yellow, with the blue stubble of the day's growth beneath. They listened to the voice of the P.O., lifted above the throb of the ventilating fans, echoing in the vast steel sounding-box of the hangar, bawling out the numbers of the two Swordfish slated for the dawn patrol, the first ones to go onto the lift in the morning.

Hardy looked at Laurel who pulled a face and said, "Sod their luck." Ethel was on the dawn patrol.

Hardy mumbled, "Sod ours."

Now they all had to turn to. The eighteen Swordfish, wings folded, were parked neatly – and closely – two by two along the narrow length of the hangar. The task now was to shuffle the pack, picking out the two chosen Swordfish and bringing them right aft to stand by the lift. Obviously two other aircraft were already there, so not only had the chosen pair to be worked aft through the others, but all those others had to be moved forward to take up the spaces vacated by those two and to make room for them aft. It was like solving a huge puzzle where the pieces were not finger-slid squares of polished wood in a frame, but ungainly aircraft, each weighing over two tons. They had to be manhandled, shifted around by muscle, craft and sweat to an accompaniment of cursing and yelps of pain as a finger was torn or a knuckle bruised.

Meanwhile the sergeant armourer searched the ship, rats in the shadows skittering away from him, for the members of his party. *Eagle* was crowded, as are all ships in time of war. Men did not sleep below the waterline and there were never enough sleeping berths. So many slept where they could, tucked away in corners, in stores, even curled up inside cupboards. The armourer tracked them down one after another and detailed them to carry out the bombing-up of the Swordfish in the last of the night.

It was all done, was always done.

Laurel and Hardy snatched a few hours' sleep and were out on the flight-deck in the twilight before dawn as Ward and his crew climbed into Ethel and flew her off on patrol. The fitter and rigger stood by the catwalk on *Eagle*'s port side, trailing by the ropes the chocks they had yanked from under Ethel's wheels to let her run, and watched the Swordfish clamber slowly into the dark sky. Some stars still prickled palely, remote, dying with the coming of the day. Ethel's silhouette became shadowy, blurred, but still marked by the blue formation lights on her wings, the glow of her exhaust.

Laurel admitted, "He's a bloody good pilot."

Hardy nodded his bullet head. "Ah."

The deck heeled under them as *Eagle*, after steaming into the wind to fly off the two Swordfish, turned to resume her course. They flew their patrol and returned without sighting the enemy.

The Fleet was now cruising to the south of Malta and *Eagle* flew off anti-submarine and reconnaissance patrols all through that day. But it was a Sunderland flying-boat from Malta, far outranging the Swordfish, that found Italian ships. Its wireless operator reported three cruisers and eight destroyers in the harbour of Augusta on the coast of Sicily.

In the early evening the squadron assigned to the operation flew off from *Eagle* to make a dusk attack. Mark stood with Tim Rogers by the island and watched them go.

Tim muttered, "Good luck."

"Better them than Ethel," said Mark, remembering the attacks of the previous day. But it would be Ethel again, sometime.

After the last Swordfish had flown off he and Tim strode rapidly up and down the flight-deck, stretching their legs after the day's flying, until the night closed in. Then they went down to the wardroom, drank a glass of beer each, slowly, savouring it, then turned in. They were to fly anti-submarine patrols the next day.

But they had already returned from their first patrol and were up in the goofer's platform aft of the bridge in the forenoon when the striking force returned. After carrying out their operation the squadron had gone back to Malta rather than risk unnecessary night-deck landings on *Eagle*. Now they slid down one by one, wings rocking gently, in over the round-down of the stern and settled on the deck. Each ran briefly until its trailing hook caught on the arrester wire and halted it, when the deck-handling party shoved it onto the forward lift and it was struck below to make way for the next.

Mark and Tim counted them and saw with relief that all were present. They raced down from the platform and caught one of the observers as he made his way aft, chartboard under his arm. They asked him, "Any luck?"

He shook his head. "The birds had flown. The harbour was empty. We scouted around, found one destroyer further up the coast and sank her. Better than nothing but not what we had hoped for. That bloody fleet will be back in Taranto by now." He went on to his debriefing in the island.

Tim said despondently, "So now it's back to Alex."

Mark peered at him, amazed. "What's so wrong with Alex? When *Eagle*'s there you're ashore every time you get a chance."

"Oh, sure. But you know what I mean. It's a bit of a let-down. Pity they didn't stand and fight."

Mark grinned at him. "In a bloodthirsty mood?"

Tim said seriously, "Look, I'm no keener on being shot at than the next man –"

Mark put in drily, "And that's me."

Tim said flatly, "Ho, ho!" He went on: "– but as I see it Cunningham has to control this end of the Med. if we're going to hold Egypt. To do that he has to cripple the Italian Fleet and if he can chew it up a piece at a time, so much the better. That's why I wish we could have settled with those two Italian battleships. As it is, their fleet's intact, strong as ever. We've got it all still to do."

Mark shrugged. "The Italians know all that and they won't give Cunningham a chance if they can help it."

"So they won't come out?"

"They will, but only for a definite purpose – like covering a convoy as they did this week. That's the only hope Cunningham has of catching them at sea." Mark glanced at his watch. "We're flying the next patrol and I want to look over Ethel before they bring her up from the hangar. Come on."

They walked aft along *Eagle*'s starboard side and Tim said, "You heard what they were saying last night?"

"About the plan?" Some of the more senior pilots had talked in the wardroom of a plan for an airborne torpedo attack on Taranto. It had been worked out and practised in the years before the war when the Swordfish of H.M.S. *Glorious* had carried out simulated attacks on the Mediterranean Fleet in Alexandria.

"Right," said Tim. "I wouldn't fancy that. There must be guns strung like a fence around Taranto."

Mark thought a night attack on Taranto would be like flying into his tunnel, but with a stone wall at the end of it. Still, sufficient unto the day. He laughed, "That makes two of us. But don't lose any sleep over it. For one thing, *Eagle* doesn't carry enough Swordfish for that job."

2

Skirmish

Bert and Katy had Egyptian visas, due to his foresight and long experience. When their ship docked at Port Said they took the train to Cairo. There they settled into a quiet hotel he had found three years before when on his way to report the fighting in Abyssinia. The next day he presented his credentials, including a letter from his editor, to the Press Bureau. Within a week he and Katy were accredited as war correspondents.

Then they waited. Every morning they went to the Press Bureau for news handouts and for Bert to renew his cajoling, demanding, threatening and pleading to be allowed to visit the front in the Western Desert. Meanwhile Katy stood in the background, looking cool in a flowered cotton dress and smiling at the major behind the desk. Until Bert gave up for that day and stomped bad-temperedly out of the office, muttering savagely, "For Chrissakes! I'm a correspondent! All I want is to see the goddam war! What's wrong with that?"

On the third day Katy said, "I'm going to take a look around. Are you coming along?"

"Are you kidding?" Bert was sweating already from frustration. The heat of the day was still to come. "I'm going to sit in the shade with a cold drink and try to make some sort o' story out of the handouts they give us. You go ahead and do your sight-seeing. I've had it, baby."

Katy rode in a gharry swaying behind a lethargically plodding horse, past the tall minarets, the bars and cafés, through the narrow, crowded alleys. She went to the huge stone pile of the Citadel and to the Pyramids, winced at the raucous braying of donkeys and the cries of hawkers and beggars. She occasionally saw a British army truck or car in drab khaki and brown paint, and once some young women in white and scarlet who were nurses in tropical uniform. There were a lot of Egyptian soldiers but Katy remembered that Egypt was not in the war. The British were preparing to fight here to defend the Suez Canal.

Inside three days she had done some sight-seeing, but more importantly found out all she needed to know about one particular soldier. She made her plans and then cannily waited for the most favourable moment to present them. That came at the end of their second week in Cairo. When they went to the Press Bureau early that morning they were given details of a naval battle fought on the ninth of July – two days before. Bert scribbled notes feverishly. Outside again, Katy said, "I guess you'll be writing it up so I'll see you later."

"Sure." Bert hardly listened, his mind busy. "Cunningham's given them a bloody nose but he needs to do a lot more than that. He's got to neutralise the Italian Fleet."

"Neutralise?"

Bert explained abstractedly, "Hurt it so that it's not a threat any more and he doesn't have to keep looking over his shoulder to see if it's going to jump him. That means he's got to sink maybe half of their capital ships, the battlewagons."

Katy left him to it, but when she returned to their hotel at noon after several protracted long-distance telephone calls she was ready to argue her case, determined to win it. She found Bert in the bar, as usual, with its floor and pillars of marble, palm trees growing in the corners. He lounged in a cane chair with his long legs outstretched in rumpled cotton trousers, shirt sleeves rolled up to show skinny arms. A glass misted with frost stood on the table by his elbow. His pad and pencil lay beside it and for the first time since they had come to Cairo Bert looked content with life and not fuming with impatience. The cane chair creaked as he saw her and stood up.

Katy smiled at him brilliantly. "Hi, Bert! Written your copy?"

He answered lazily, "Written and filed. Sit down and I'll

shout you a drink." He pulled up another chair for her and they sat.

Katy said breathlessly, "We've just had our first stroke of luck."

Bert snapped upright in his chair. "Some new story broken? What is it?"

"No! We've been offered an apartment to rent in Alexandria! One of the staff in our embassy heard of it and told me, so of course I grabbed it. I've got an option on it for three months."

Bert stared at her, bewildered. "*Alexandria!* What in hell do we want there? Cairo is where we get the press briefings every day and where we'll get a movement order – if and when we get one. This isn't the Grand Tour, baby. We stay in Cairo till they let us out to see something."

Katy leaned forward, her explanation prepared. "The Navy is at Alexandria. If there's another battle – you said the British would be trying to catch the Italian Fleet at sea – we'd be on the spot."

Bert flapped a bony hand. "Boloney! If there was a battle we'd hear about it in Cairo as soon as at Alex, like we did today, and Cairo is where we file our stories, when we get 'em."

Katy was ready for that and shifted her ground: "O.K. Suppose you stay here and I go to Alexandria. When something breaks there I'll have it covered, and if ever you need me back here you just pick up the 'phone. That way we cover *both* ends."

Bert watched her out of narrowed eyes. "I gather you want to live in Alex. What's the reason?"

"I've told you." Katy saw his face did not change and she smiled wanly. "But they do say it's cooler there. The heat here is getting to me a little."

Bert remained unconvinced. "Like hell it is."

Katy asked, "What's that for?"

Bert said, "I'm just wondering what you're up to?"

So had the major at the Press Bureau when she'd asked him about Jamie Dunbar. Katy protested innocently, "I told you –"

Bert flapped his hand. "O.K., O.K." Katy was flushed and clearly determined. He knew it was no use arguing when a woman got an idea fixed in her head, but boy! Was he glad he wasn't the father of a daughter. "So it's unprofessional but you're not a professional."

Katy's lips tightened. "I'm trying."

"You're trying me all right," Bert said drily. "Well, there's no action in Cairo for you to take pictures of and I suppose I can sit in on the briefings here, pick up any movement order. So – O.K., you board in Alex. But when I blow the whistle, you come running."

Katy sat back in her chair. She had got what she wanted. Now it was time to change the subject for a while. "Movement order? What's that?"

Bert pulled a Camel from his shirt pocket and explained patiently, "Look, baby, you just don't wander about in a war. If you want to go to the front or some military installation, you get a movement order – that's an order that authorises your movements. It comes with a vehicle, a driver and an escorting officer who goes along with you to make sure you don't get shot by his own side."

Katy nodded, "Got it." She stood up. "Well, guess I'll go and make a start on my packing before lunch."

"Packing?" Bert paused with the cigarette halfway to his open mouth.

"There's a train to Alex at nine in the morning." Katy stooped to kiss his forehead then walked lightly away.

Bert shook his head and called after her, "Yeah, I know. I was thinking of taking a brief run up there myself. We can look at the ships, see if they show any damage from this fight they had." He added morosely, "I don't expect anything much, like a story for instance – the word I'm getting is that the Royal Navy is still the silent service and keeping its mouth shut."

Katy had paused, head turned to him, was about to move on, but then he asked, "Hey! How many soldiers have you seen around the streets while we've been here?"

Katy checked. She answered neutrally. "Lots."

"British?"

"Only a few. All the rest were Egyptian. I suppose the British are all up at the front."

"Yeah?" Was that agreement or doubt? "Maybe you're right. Where else would they be?" Katy waited a moment but Bert left it there, lit the cigarette and sat thoughtful as she went on to her packing.

When *Eagle* was still some miles from Alexandria her Swordfish were brought up from the hangar deck on the after lift and ranged aft for flying off. While the carrier was in port they would operate from the airstrip at Dekheila, five miles west along the coast from Alexandria. The evolution was routine and carried out with slick efficiency – until the accident.

Mark Ward had walked aft along the starboard side towards Ethel, the pulsing roar of the ranked Pegasus engines all around him. There was a brief hiccup in the roar and spray that lashed him. It was not sea water but sprinkled dark red on the khaki of his flying overalls. He saw men running and a body on the deck before one of the Swordfish, beneath the scything circle of its three-bladed metal propeller. The body lay spreadeagled, limp and loose as if there was no man inside the stained overalls. Then for a moment he thought the body was alive because it twitched, but realised that must have been some reflex muscular contraction because no man could live without his head.

Tim Rogers came up to his shoulder and bawled through cupped hands above the bellowing of the engines: "*He walked into the prop!*" When Tim lowered his hands his face showed bloodless, his tan a sick yellow.

It was a bright, clear, blazing hot day. Ward looked down at his blood-spattered flying overalls. There was no time to change. The Swordfish were ready to fly off and *Eagle* was heeling as she turned into wind. He walked on with Tim to Ethel and was seated in the cockpit when Doug Campbell ran up. He halted below Ward before climbing up to his place aft of Tim Rogers, and mouthed: "Dead, sir." Mark knew that. Campbell drew a finger gruesomely across his throat but his set face showed it was no crude attempt to make light of the matter.

Mark thought, Bloody fine start. He had doubtless known the man, probably exchanged a few words or a joke with him. Now he was just an entry in the log, kit to be packed, a letter to be written to a mother or a widow. The deck-handling party would be one short. They had lost a friend, one of the team. Mark put it from his mind. He had to fly and other men's lives depended on him.

But once in the air and gently banking Ethel onto course for the short flight to Dekheila, he could think with a part of his mind while still concentrating on his flying. That there were teams within teams within teams, like one of those intricate ivory balls carved by the Chinese, a ball inside a ball inside a ball . . . There was the little team of three inside the Swordfish now, that was part of the larger team of five when you included Laurel and Hardy, who kept the Stringbag fit to fly. Ethel was one unit of a flight that was part of a squadron which, with the other squadron aboard *Eagle* made up her striking force. The other team aboard *Eagle* comprised the men, from captain down to stoker, who worked the ship as any other warship. And *Eagle* functioned as a unit of the Fleet.

The Swordfish landed one after the other at Dekheila. There were two hangars, some offices and sheds beside the strip. One hut served as the officers' mess but everyone lived in tents. There were flies, sand, heat and cold but a chance to bathe in the sea close by. And there was Alexandria, only five miles away.

When *Eagle* was shackled to her buoy in the harbour the ground crew loaded their kit and stores into lighters that ferried them ashore. There they transferred the whole lot again from the lighters to trucks parked on the quay for the trip to Dekheila. Laurel and Hardy, sweating rivers at the work, saw a platoon of marines falling in on the quay, badges and buckles flashing like jewels.

Laurel started the lower deck gag: "Royal Marines will march past in column of fours . . ."

Hardy, rumbling, took it up: "Royal Navy will shamble past in a bloody great heap . . ."

And Laurel finished: "Taking their time from the dockyard clock, January, February, March."

The marines formed part of the burial party for the man killed that morning. They waited now for the body to be brought ashore.

The loading of the trucks was completed and the men climbed in over the tail-boards to sit on the stores or the floor. The trucks ground off along the coast road to the airstrip.

Bert and Katy had been standing at the window of her apartment, watching the Swordfish fly in from the sea. Bert muttered, "Where the hell are those glasses?" He rummaged in the haversack he had brought with him from Cairo, dug out binoculars and turned quickly back to the window. He focused the glasses, watched the distant aircraft for a moment, then said, "Yeah. Swordfish. Torpedo-bomber-reconnaissance planes, off the carrier out there." He could see the Fleet, hull-up now and the flat-topped *Eagle* among them, closing Alexandria.

He passed the glasses to Katy, who examined the big old-fashioned biplanes incredulously, then said, "They've got open cockpits! Are you sure they're war planes? Are they still making them without canopies?"

Bert nodded, "Yep."

"They're a little ancient, aren't they?"

Bert sniffed. "Nothing wrong with having a few years behind you if you still do the job."

Katy lowered the glasses and smiled. "Nothing personal, Bert. You may be able to, but – can they?"

"They operated in France and Norway. Did all right." He took the glasses then glanced around the cool, high-ceilinged room. Through the doors they had left open during their first inspection he could glimpse the small kitchen, bathroom and the bedroom with its big double-bed. "Well, you got your apartment."

He dragged an armchair over to the window, lowered his

thin frame into it and lifted the glasses again. "Guess I'll sit here and watch the Fleet come in. Maybe later on we can hire a boat for a closer look. Come the cool of the evening we'll go look for a drink and maybe find some sailor ready to talk about the battle, though I doubt if the goddam censors would let me file the story, even if we did." He glanced around at Katy. "You said you could fix us something in the kitchen." She had brought a bagful of groceries. "How about coffee and a sandwich? Then you can unpack your duds and settle in."

Katy replied acidly, "Thanks for your help, going to all that trouble to organise my day."

"Think nothing of it." He settled more comfortably in the chair. "I never shirk my end."

Katy shook her head and made for the kitchen. "Are you staying in Alex?"

Bert thumbed his lighter into flame and lit a Camel. "Yeah. I've booked a room at the Cecil. I'll stick around a couple of days and case the joint." And maybe find out what the hell's going on with this girl.

Bert Keller escorted Katy into the Cecil Hotel that evening. Arab waiters in their long robes like nightshirts moved among the tables and there were several groups of officers scattered the length of the long bar. Katy checked them quickly, then her gaze settled on the young man in civilian clothes who sat alone at a table. She had already learned, back in Cairo, that everyone who was anyone went to the Cecil. He faced the door, lounging in his chair with legs outstretched and crossed at the ankles. His shoes gleamed and his well-tailored English lightweight suit was not new but stylishly, easily worn. He saw Katy and his brows came together as he searched his memory.

Katy had no trouble remembering. She smiled and walked over to him, Bert trailing behind her. The young man rose to his feet and now he snapped his fingers: "Katy Sandford."

She laughed, "That's right. Jamie Dunbar, isn't it? Lieutenant Dunbar?"

The Englishman drawled, "Captain now. Nothing to boast about, it comes with the passage of time."

"Oh, Bert!" Katy made the introductions and explained, "Jamie and I met when he was in the States on a vacation two years ago."

Dunbar held out a hand. "That's so. I was mixing business with pleasure. I met a number of your chaps, Army and Navy, and compared notes."

Bert nodded, "Hi!" He saw a walking-stick hooked on the back of his chair, but the hand gripping his was broad and surprisingly hard. He thought this guy was probably quite something, tall, broad, handsome with curly red hair flattened into waves by the brush. His easy smile showed teeth white against the brown of his face and his eyes were startlingly blue. There was an inch-long scar like a comma over one of them that only added a certain raffish attraction to the face.

Jamie Dunbar ushered them into chairs, swearing to himself at the sudden intrusion, lifted a finger for a waiter and ordered drinks. He sat again in his chair facing the door. "So what are you doing here, Miss Sandford? Not some sort of Cook's tour?"

Katy told him of Bert's assignment and Jamie said, "My word! War correspondents, eh? Not many of you about."

Bert grumbled, "Nor doing any good. I've been trying to get a movement order –"

Katy had heard enough of that these last days and cut in, smiling at Jamie. "Imagine meeting you here! What an extraordinary coincidence."

Jamie's brows lifted. "You didn't know I was in Egypt?" Katy kept her face still and Jamie went on, "I write to your father every two or three months because he's asked me to keep in touch. Can't put my address on the letters now, of course, but I was writing to him from Cairo before the war and the censorship started so he knows where I am. I suppose he forgot to mention it. Pity. If you'd asked in Cairo they'd have told you I'd moved up here. I know most of the johnnies in the Press Bureau."

Bert watched Katy, deadpan, but thinking, Boy! I shoulda known.

Jamie said, "I only came up from Cairo a couple of weeks

ago. I'm on sick leave at the moment. I thought Alex would be cooler and the sea air might bring the roses back to my cheeks." In fact, in Cairo Pamela's husband had returned from Palestine and that had made things a bit awkward. Jamie knew he would have to forget her for a bit, and meanwhile – he kept his eye on the door to the bar.

Bert, his face expressionless but his tone ironic, said, "Still, quite a coincidence. Yes, sir." The drinks arrived and he took a mouthful of his Scotch then eyed Jamie's suit. "Mind if I ask if you're on the Staff?"

Jamie shook his head, "I'm infantry. My truck ran over a mine and blew up. Nobody was hurt, I'm glad to say, except myself. I busted my knee. It's still wonky and the doctors say I have to give it a few weeks before I go back to regimental duty. An infantry officer with only one good leg is a bloody nuisance to everyone." He glanced at Bert, "You're looking for somebody on the Staff?"

Bert grumbled, "Like I tried to say a minute ago –" He cocked an eye at Katy but she was biding her time, letting all the talk of "coincidence" slip into the past. Bert went on: "We need a movement order and an escorting officer to go up to the front and we're still waiting. I thought if I could get alongside some guy on the Staff he might be able to fix me up."

Jamie agreed absently. "You need somebody who can pull a few strings." The Katy of two years ago was a dim memory and even then she had never been more than a big-eyed face in the background. Now he was getting messages, loud and clear. She had blossomed into a pretty little thing but was still a lightweight.

Bert was saying, "That's about the size of it. I need copy and I need it soon."

He paused to take a breath and Katy slipped in, smiling at Jamie: "I've managed to rent an apartment and I'll be staying a while. Alexandria sounds fascinating. Do you know it?"

She waited for his reply but instead Jamie lifted a hand in greeting to a group of three who had just entered. The man was in his thirties, well-dressed. The two women were younger, tall, long-legged and full-bodied in thin dresses. Following Jamie's gaze Katy thought, French, then caught a few words of their conversation that confirmed it. The man nodded at Jamie and the women smiled as they passed, seeking a table.

Jamie thought to himself, Disengage and retire. He prompted Bert: "They didn't help at the Bureau?" Then listened sympathetically to Bert's complaint about bureaucracy in Cairo as his eyes searched the faces at the bar, saw no hope of escape there and anxiously scanned the room. Another group entered then: half a dozen young naval officers in white drill. Jamie blinked in surprise, then grinned. He shoved up out of the chair and said, "Hold on a moment, Mr Keller, I've seen someone who may be able to help you."

He limped quickly across to intercept the officers heading for the bar and stood in the path of Mark Ward. "Hello! What a horribly small world it is. I had a drink the other night with a chap in the Guards who said he'd met you in here."

Mark nodded coldly. "I knew you were somewhere in Egypt. I asked if he knew you."

"Thinking of looking me up?"

"No."

"No," Jamie agreed. Then: "Look, I've been talking to a lady about you and she'd like to meet you. Come on over for a minute, will you?"

He smiled but Mark did not. He looked over Jamie's shoulder and saw the girl watching them. His eyes moved back to Jamie. "What rubbish have you told her?"

Jamie chuckled. "I've told her nothing yet, except that you might be able to help her with a spot of trouble she's in."

"Me? How?"

"Come over and I'll explain." And Jamie added, "We're keeping her waiting."

Mark hesitated, still suspicious. Tim Rogers said from behind him, "She's a popsy."

Mark agreed with that. And besides, he could not flatly refuse such a request. He said, "I'll see you later, Tim."

He walked to the table with Jamie Dunbar, who quickly

introduced him to Bert and Katy then picked up the walking-stick and gestured at his chair. "Sit down, Mark, old chum." And as Ward perched on the edge of the chair: "He flies a Swordfish torpedo-bomber. He's seen bags of action and he'll have plenty of er . . . copy for you, Mr Keller." He smiled around at them, then: "Now, if you'll excuse me, there's a man I have to see. Duty calls, you know."

He limped away and Katy's gaze followed him. She was not smiling now. He stopped at the table where the man and the two women were seated, pulled out a chair and settled down.

Bert asked, "What'll you have, Mr. Ward?"

Mark answered shortly, "Beer, please."

Bert ordered it and turned back to the tall young pilot. He sat erect, politely attentive, silent, and Bert thought, Not much like a sailor on a run ashore, not exactly whooping it up.

Mark knew what Jamie Dunbar had engineered, neatly, efficiently and with smooth charm. He had gone after what he wanted. Jamie was running true to form.

Katy tried not to believe it. She told herself Jamie wouldn't do that kind of thing. He had spoken the truth, gone to discharge some official duty. The man escorting the two Frenchwomen was probably an off-duty officer, or a contractor to the Army.

Bert said, "So Captain Dunbar is a friend of yours?"

Mark answered, "His mother and mine are cousins. He's a distant relative." At the moment, he thought, not distant enough. "Not a friend."

Bert did some quick rethinking and probed cautiously, "You don't see eye to eye?"

"I don't like him."

Katy broke in sharply: "Why not?"

"With respect, that's my business."

"You shouldn't malign him behind his back."

"He knows my opinion already. And one of these days, when I catch him in some quiet place, I'll tell him it again."

Jamie had seduced a girl Mark knew, a friend of a friend,

then walked out on her. Mark had fought Jamie in the secluded area behind the house, at a rare family gathering. They had tried to beat each other unconscious but their mutual cousin, big John Ward, had separated them. Mark found some satisfaction now in recalling that Jamie still bore the scar over his left eye.

Bert tried to steer the conversation: "So you're a flyer and you've seen action. Maybe you were in that battle the other day? It would be a big help to me if you could give me some details."

Mark shook his head, "I'm sorry, but I can't do that. I'd need to get permission from my commanding officer."

Bert grinned ruefully at Katy. "What did I tell you? The Navy is keeping its mouth shut."

Mark asked, "I suppose you want to send reports to newspapers in America?"

Bert said wrily, "I sure hope so, one of these days. People in the States want to know what's going on. A lot of them are worried about this war."

Katy put in quickly, "Worried they might be dragged into it. But they won't be. Not this time."

Mark frowned. "I wouldn't be too sure."

Katy leaned forward. "Why? This is a European war. Why should America get involved?"

Mark shrugged. "We're not in Europe now. This is Africa. Italy wants the Suez Canal. Hitler and Mussolini have occupied most of Europe. Where do they go next?"

"They won't go to America."

"We'll see." Mark did not want to argue with this girl.

Katy threw herself back in the chair and shot a bitter glance at Bert. Unsure of Jamie, she took it out on Mark. "Great. The British are playing the same old song. For years now they've been watching Hitler and Mussolini rant and rave, build up their forces, threaten and demand. Hitler grabbed Austria and Czechoslovakia and Mussolini took over Abyssinia. The Allies did nothing except appeal to the League of Nations and that couldn't solve anything. Now the dictators have cut loose, trampled all over them and they're yelling for help from us again."

Bert said, "Easy, baby, easy. The guy only came over here because —"

"Because Jamie thought he might help. Well, he didn't. Instead he started making sniffy remarks about an officer who was a guest in my father's house back in the States."

Mark stood up, looked from Katy to Bert and told him, "Well good luck, Mr Keller. It seems to me you need it."

Bert started, "Now, hold on, son —"

But Katy took the point and snapped back at Mark, "Go play with your toy airplane!"

Ward saw again the man stepping back into the whirling scythe of the Swordfish's propeller, the spurting blood. "You can go to hell for all I care."

He turned and walked away, looked for Jamie Dunbar but he, and one of the glamorous young women, had already gone. Mark had a drink with Tim Rogers and then they drove back to Dekheila.

The Swordfish were there at the request of the R.A.F. but Mark was not called on to fly the next day. He had time for his anger to cool and to think over the row. He decided he had been partly to blame, had been bloody-minded from the outset. Jamie's smart-alec trick had riled him. And then there was the dead seaman. The girl had provoked him but she obviously thought Jamie was the cat's whiskers and she wasn't the first woman to feel like that. Mind, she wasn't the type Jamie usually stalked: the tall ones with a lot of top hamper.

She was a pretty girl and Ward realised suddenly that he fancied her.

All right. Next time, try a little harder.

That evening he walked into the Cecil and immediately saw Katy sitting at a table with Bert Keller. To Bert he said, "Excuse me." Then to Katy: "I want to apologise for last night. I'm sorry."

Katy was silent, taken aback, but Bert said mildly, "Seemed

to me it wasn't all your fault, and maybe you had something on your mind."

"It wasn't, and I had."

Bert nodded to a chair. "Grab a seat and I'll buy you a beer."

But Mark waited for Katy. She smiled at him, "O.K. You've taken back your half, I'll take back mine. One war at a time is enough."

Bert heaved an inward sigh of relief, then as Mark sat down, said, "So you're off that carrier in the harbour, *Eagle*."

Mark nodded. "That's right, Mr. Keller."

"Call me Bert – and this is Katy."

Ward said, "Mark."

Bert went on: "But at the moment you're all flying from the field at Dekheila." Mark shot him a sharp glance and Bert chuckled, held up a hand. "Take it easy. I'm not fishing, I got that from a bartender."

Mark shrugged, "It's impossible to keep a thing like that secret. They see us fly out."

Katy said, "We saw you fly in yesterday. Those airplanes are a little old, aren't they?"

Mark said defensively, "Not really. Stringbags like Ethel look a bit pre-historic, but they work."

Bert detected Mark's affection for the Swordfish. He had known this before in flyers for aircraft, seamen for ships.

"Ethel?" Katy laughed. "You call her Ethel? Why? After a girl?"

Mark smiled slowly. "No, an old aunt of mine. As I said, she looks old-fashioned, and she's never one to hurry but very easy to handle."

Bert said, "Well, you sure as hell couldn't call her Katy."

They all laughed at that.

Later Bert took them out to dinner at Pastroudi's restaurant and they spent a pleasant evening. Mark had relaxed and talked easily, made dry remarks that made them laugh and never mentioned the war. He saw there was friendliness and mutual respect underlying the sparring between the two

66

Americans. Once he asked, "Are there many American women working as war photographers?"

Bert shrugged. "Are there any other women war photographers? I only know of this one."

Mark was impressed, but thought that, of course, the girl would not be risked anywhere near the fighting. Towards the end of the meal Jamie Dunbar came in with the previous evening's tall, busty beauty. They sat in a far corner of the room and Katy's eyes shifted there from time to time. Mark did not appear to notice.

Outside, Bert held out his hand. "Hope I'll see you next time I'm in Alex, Mark, but tomorrow I go back to Cairo." And with a glance at Katy, "Somebody has to look after the shop."

Mark shook the hand, noted Bert's use of "I" and asked Katy, "Not you?"

She shook her head, "I'm staying."

Bert asked, "Will you be in town tomorrow night?"

"I don't know." Mark looked at the girl. "Are you on the phone? If I get in maybe we could eat?"

Katy hedged, "Maybe." But she told him the number. He did not telephone.

3

Tobruk

The night was clear and there was a big, yellow moon. Mark, in Ethel's cockpit, could see the other eight Swordfish of the squadron to port and starboard, dark silhouettes marked by the dim blue formation lights on their wings. They rose and fell gently as they flew, like ships riding a moderate sea. The coast lay somewhere to port and about twenty miles away, where the dappled silver sheet of the sea ended in blackness. There was the droning clamour of the Pegasus engine and the tearing roar that was part propeller slipstream and part the windrush of ninety knots.

Ward was no stranger to night-flying. When he won his "A" licence as a private pilot in 1937 the flying bug had set its teeth in him. In the summer of 1938 he asked his parents to let him take leave of absence from the College of Music for a year. They took little persuading, were already philosophically accepting that he showed no promise as a classical musician and they privately believed he would never return to the College.

They were right. He knew now what he wanted to do. His songs were being sung by artists like Gracie Fields and Sam Browne, played by the bands of Geraldo, Jack Payne and Henry Hall. But the money he made from the songs he wrote for Danny Soloman he regarded as a stroke of luck, product of a talent that had come out of the blue and could as easily vanish again. But as a commercial pilot he could make a reliable living, even a career. So he went to Brooklands again and trained for his "B" licence. It took him seven months. There was a tough medical, examinations, and flying tests that included cross-country and blind flying – and a night-flying test from Croydon to Lympne. He got his "B" licence as a commercial pilot in February 1939.

It had cost him over £300 and the second-hand De Havilland Puss Moth he wanted then would set him back another £350. He did not have that much money and would not ask his parents for their help. He was almost twenty-one, a professional man making his own way.

He visited Aunt Ethel in Bedford, as she demanded he should every month. He found her in the garden dressed in an old overcoat and wellingtons, fiercely wielding a fork to uproot a bush. She stopped when she saw him, rubbed a grimy hand over her face red from her labour and grumbled, "Never did like the damn thing here. It has to come out."

He shifted it for her and afterwards she took him into the house for tea: "Wipe your feet before you come in!" And he told her about the Puss Moth. She sniffed. "So you're a commercial pilot now. You've learnt about discipline. Well, I smacked your behind often enough. Glad it seems to have done some good. How much do you want?"

"Three hundred quid."

"Good God!" Aunt Ethel eyed him severely. "And what do I get out of this, apart from the blame if you break your silly neck in the thing?"

Mark had one answer ready: "The going rate of interest." Then he thought of others. "My undying gratitude, though you've got that already. And, tell you what, I'll call her after you."

He earned the money to repay her by flying the Puss Moth on Army co-operation flying. The Army was practising its anti-aircraft gunners to meet air-raids in Britain and needed aircraft to act as raiders. Mark had to fly at night along prescribed courses, navigating himself, for two hours or more in a night and they paid him three pounds an hour. He had put in nearly two hundred hours of night-flying by August 1939. Then he painted over the name "Ethel" on the nose of the Puss Moth, sold her and joined the Navy.

Tim Rogers' voice came through the Gosport tube from where he sat in the observer's cockpit with the chartboard on his knee, lit by the orange glow of the little cockpit light: "Tobruk should be ten miles ahead and to port. Anything seen?"

Mark leaned to his left to peer ahead and with his goggled and masked face outside the protection of the windscreen he felt the full blast of the slipstream. He stayed like that for a few seconds then pulled his head in and told Tim, "No. Think we should stop and ask a policeman?"

A snort came through the tube. "You play with your aeroplane and don't worry. I'll get you there."

"And back?"

"One thing at a time."

"Play with your airplane." Katy had said that. Mark grinned inside the mouthpiece of the Gosport tube strapped up against his face. He waited, but Tim did not speak again. He guessed the observer was nervous. He was nervous himself.

The squadron had flown from Dekheila westwards along the coast to Sidi Barrani during the day. They were briefed to attack enemy shipping lying in the harbour of Tobruk, and it included two destroyers. The Swordfish were refuelled at Sidi Barrani and the flying crews snatched a few hours' sleep before it was time to take off again.

Because this was to be a torpedo attack again, Mark had recalled the strikes of the ninth of July off Calabria, and so the tunnel. The two memories were linked in his mind. Probably it was not surprising that when he slept he dreamt of the tunnel. He flew again between the black walls of the clouds but this time there was no window of light at the end. The walls ran away, narrowing in perspective, to end in distant darkness. He did not reach the darkness but woke to Tim Rogers calling him: "Tea in the mess!"

He was not thinking about the tunnel now.

They would turn soon. It was two in the morning and cold; he felt it on the exposed parts of his face. He wore an Irvine leather and sheepskin-lined flying jacket, serge trousers tucked into zipped-up flying boots. The heat of the day was long gone.

A blue torch blinked a signal from the leader and the squadron wheeled to head towards the coast. Ethel's port wing dipped as Mark took her around with the others in a banking turn that straightened into a shallow dive. He said, "Tim." There was no answer and he reasoned that the observer had probably disconnected the Gosport tube to stand up in his cockpit and take a look.

Mark waggled Ethel's wings gently and Tim, responding to that signal, plugged into the tube, "Yes?"

"Give Campbell a nudge, just in case." The airgunner would be keeping a listening watch on the wireless but he needed to be warned that they would be attacking soon.

Tim said, "Done that. He's ready."

The after cockpits were really one long cockpit divided laterally by a low bulkhead. Doug Campbell stood at the rear now, manning the Vickers machine-gun. The gun was housed in the fuselage above the wireless. He looked out over its breech and barrel, past the rudder that was offset at a slight angle – Campbell tersely described it as "soddin' cock-eyed" – to offset the effect of the slipstream that tended to pull the Swordfish off course. His eyes searched the night sky that was clear and moonlit. He could remember a girl he'd taken out on a night just like this . . . But it was bloody cold now as the ninety-knot wind roared around him. Things would warm up soon, though.

He glanced quickly over his shoulder and saw Rogers moving bulkily, awkwardly in the dim orange glow of the observer's cockpit. Campbell could have guessed what Rogers was doing now without looking; all three had learned the quirks and habits of the others. The observer was carefully stowing away his chartboard, navigational instruments and any other loose gear. What did Mark call it? "Doing his housework." Campbell grinned and returned to his lookout.

Time was running down now and the Swordfish were still descending. The final approach would be low and going in over the sea. Mark, peering past the blur of the propeller, thought he saw – Tim beat him to it: "Enemy coast ahead!"

There was something more substantial than just darkness

where the silver sea ended, a blacker irregular line running between sea and sky. The Swordfish were still in their shallow dive and the needle of Mark's altimeter was ticking back around the face of the instrument. It read 500 feet when Tim said, "Ships! Six to a dozen."

Mark saw only the thicker shadows on the sea, did not separate one from another or count them. He concentrated on his flying, eased Ethel out of the dive and held her steady and straight, forty to fifty feet above the waves. The moon lit the sea and cast the flitting shadows of the nine Swordfish in distorted crosses on the wrinkled surface.

Now he could see and pick out one ship from another inside the harbour opening ahead. There was one biggish freighter, three – no, four smaller vessels – and *that* was a destroyer. He saw the searchlights glow aboard her as the arcs heated, and then become two beams of white light that jerked about the sky above him. They meandered nervously for a few seconds, then one of them snapped down and lit a Swordfish away to Mark's right, slipped off it then returned and held it in the beam.

A rash of little prickling flames spread around and across the harbour as if someone had set light to a chain of fireworks. The guns had opened up. Light glared in Ward's eyes as the second searchlight beam jerked down towards the sea and found him. He turned Ethel to the right, curling away out of the beam, then immediately back to the left so he passed from light to dark then through the light again and finally into darkness.

He had slipped the beam. It had tried to follow his first turn and was hunting again away to his right. He could see only one other Swordfish, ahead and to port and affording him plenty of room. The rest of the sky was a mad pattern of yellow bursts of shells, balls of smoke and strings of slow, curving tracer from machine-guns.

He was forty feet up, airspeed 125 knots, holding her straight and steady. He saw the bursts of the flak before him, felt Ethel shudder as she ran through the turbulence and he threw her sideways again to get her out of it.

The destroyer lay off to port. Height was now only about thirty feet. 120 knots. Ease to port a touch to bring her into the torpedo sight – there. Hold her with the right hand, the left hand on the firing button down by the throttle. Now.

Tim: "– gone!"

Mark banked Ethel tightly to starboard, his head turning as he looked for other Swordfish, but he saw none. Then the flak found them again with flashes, bursts, smoke, the shuddering – and this time a jarring as if someone was kicking Ethel's tender, canvas sides. He jerked her about, weaving, but holding her low over the sea and heading out into the night.

They were clear of the flak. He could still see some of it in his mirror but the yellow splashes and the red tracer beads were falling astern.

Tim's voice cracked in his ears: "A hit! And there's another!"

Mark asked thickly, still shaking in the aftermath of the flak, "Ours?"

"Our destroyer. It might have been our torpedo but there were two or three of us having a go at her."

"Were there?"

"Didn't you *see* them?" Tim sounded incredulous.

."No." Mark's eyes had been focused on the destroyer in the sight.

"Good God! And you're supposed to be driving this thing."

Silence for a moment, then Mark said, "Stringbag to starboard." He eased Ethel over to close the other Swordfish.

Tim said, "The others are coming out now. I can see four – five." That was seven all right. Tim went on, "The flak was nasty. The second lot – I thought they'd got us. I can see a few holes but nothing seems to have fallen off."

"Everything's working." Then Mark asked, "How's Campbell?"

"Fine. He got in some shooting."

Doug Campbell had emptied a magazine on the ships and the guns, was loading another now.

The squadron, all nine of them, met out at sea, settled into formation and flew home. They landed at Sidi Barrani an hour before the dawn. As Mark cut the engine and the propeller gave its last kick then was still, he thought it could well have been a sort of rehearsal for an attack on Taranto. That also, when it came, if it ever came, would be a night torpedo strike. But there the resemblance ended. Tobruk was not one of the most heavily defended ports in the world. Taranto was.

His legs felt stiff and cramped, colder than was usual, even after a night-flight, as he climbed out of the cockpit and down to the sand of the airstrip. There he found out why. There were several holes in Ethel big enough to shove his fist into and two were on either side of his cockpit. Unofficial ventilation. He could see straight through from one side to the other. Something hard, lethal and the size of a cricket ball had smashed through the cockpit within inches of his legs, little more than a foot from his stomach and groin. He remembered the jarring, when it felt as though someone was beating Ethel with a hammer.

Tim said, "We had a close one, then."

Mark shrugged it off: "Close ones don't count."

As they walked over to the mess the thought came to him that the attack had not been at all like the tunnel. There were flak and glaring searchlights blinding him, then the destroyer stretching wide and black, clean-cut against the night. But no narrowing walls. And no dark ending.

It was cold on the Sidi Barrani strip in this last hour before dawn and a wind drove the sand to scour his face. He took comfort in the thought of Katy. She'd given him her phone number. And she'd said, "Maybe."

When the squadron returned to Dekheila he telephoned the girl and that night took her to dinner at Pastroudi's. During the next week, whenever he could get leave and a lift or a taxi into Alex, he saw Katy. It might be for an afternoon or an evening or just an hour or so. They played golf, badly, at the Sporting Club, swam in the Mediterranean or lay on the beach, played tennis, danced.

Mark flew several operations but said nothing of them. He

talked a great deal of Ethel, Tim Rogers and the rest of his little team. Katy recognised that they were important to him. He drew her out to talk of her home and her life in America, her hopes and ambition as a photographer. And he told her about the songs he wrote for Danny Soloman, his flying in the days of peace and the first Ethel.

Once they almost literally ran into a sailor and two airmen piling riotously out of a bar. Doug Campbell, Laurel and Hardy side-stepped to avoid a collision with the girl, threw up salutes at Ward and made off. But they'd taken a good look at Katy and she'd seen it, now asked, "Anyone you know?" Mark told her and she said, "They seemed a bunch of nice guys."

Mark grinned, "They are, but it's a good job you can't hear what they're saying about you." He'd heard them talking of women before.

Katy laughed because she thought she could guess. And if she couldn't it didn't matter. She found she was laughing a lot, enjoying herself.

At the end of that week Mark telephoned to say he could get into Alexandria for an hour and so, in the evening, they sat in the bar of the Cecil. Jamie Dunbar was also there, escorting the same rangy beauty. Katy studied him pensively. He was not as she remembered him. After a while Jamie rose and murmured to the woman with his head close to hers, his hand around her waist. Then he crossed the floor, heading for their table.

Katy said quickly, "No trouble, *please*!"

Mark shrugged. "I won't start it."

Jamie now walked without the stick and with only a suggestion of a limp. He smiled down at Katy. "Thought I'd pop over and say 'Cheerio'. I'm off to Cairo tomorrow to be passed fit for duty."

Katy asked, "You have to see the doctors there?"

"That's right." Though not for some days. But Pamela's husband had gone back to Palestine and Jamie thought it was about time, too. He asked, "Have you any messages for your friend Keller?"

Katy shook her head, smiling. "No. When I talk to him on the phone he comes through hopping mad because he can't get up-country. Soothing words from me only make him worse."

Jamie said thoughtfully, "I remember now; he did mention that. I might be able to see a chap or two, pull some strings . . . Well, see you again." He walked away.

Katy turned her head and found Mark watching her. He left early.

She slept badly that night, restless. In the morning she looked down to the harbour and saw that the Fleet, and *Eagle*, had sailed in the night.

It was a long week later that she woke in the dawn to the drone of aircraft engines. That sound, familiar to her now, sent her running to the window, barefoot in her nightdress. She lifted a hand against the low morning sun that hurt her eyes and watched the squadrons of Swordfish winging in from the sea. After breakfast she waited for the telephone to ring.

In the evening they sat in the Cecil again but it was not the same. They had reached an awkward stage and there was an uncertainty between them, a tension. Tim Rogers had just taken his leave, too tactful, after chatting for a half-hour.

Katy made conversation: "I feel a fraud."

Mark asked, "Why?"

"Drawing my money as a war photographer when all I do is laze around here."

"Is Bert Keller complaining?"

"No. I confessed my guilt feelings to him on the phone the other day. He said," and she made her voice gravelly: "'Listen, baby, in this game you earn your money when the action breaks. You're sittin' around in Alex? So what am I doin'? Sittin' around in Cairo. Just take it easy, baby, and keep your camera dry.'"

Mark laughed. "That sounds like Keller. So how do you spend your days – reading good books?"

"I take some pictures, local colour, just to keep my hand in. One or two are pretty good, though I do say it myself."

"How do you get them developed?"

"I can fix up a darkroom."

"Clever girl."

"I'm a professional." But she wondered, was she a professional like Bert? She had yet to learn and was not eager to find out.

Mark asked, "Got any pictures of yourself?"

Katy eyed him warily, "Why?"

"I'd like one." Mark grinned. "Did you ever see a painting called *September Morn*?"

Katy said drily, "Yes, and no."

"What do you mean, 'yes and no'?"

"Yes, I've seen it, and no, you aren't getting one. As I recall, the lady in that picture ran a risk of catching pneumonia."

Mark walked her back to her apartment and left her at the door. Katy did not invite him in and he did not ask. He had the feeling that would still be a bad mistake.

Katy thought how she could have gone back to Cairo. Jamie Dunbar was there now. But she had not gone, and did not want to.

Mark shared a taxi with Tim and two other aircrew, bouncing along the coast road to Dekheila. In the tent they shared, Tim said, "That's a cracking girl you've got there."

Had he got her? Mark sat on his camp bed and pulled off his shoes. No, he hadn't. He said, "I thought you were promised to another." Tim wrote to his fiancée in England at least once a week.

"Can still judge form, old boy."

They turned in. The wind fluttered the sides of the tent, blew in sand and the smell of the sea.

Tim said yawning, "There's rumour of a move."

"Where?"

"Up the road. Nearer the sharp end."

Mark said ironically, "Thanks very much. Good night." How much time did he have? How much did they all have?

★   ★   ★

Jamie woke to the shaking of his shoulder and saw Pamela's startled face pale above his in the gloom, her hair falling around him. She whispered, "Someone's come in!"

Jamie said huskily, "What?"

"Someone just came in the front door! I heard it open and close! It must be Harry!"

"Blast!" Jamie slid out of the bed, grabbed his clothes from a chair and padded naked to the French windows. He could hear footsteps on the stairs. Pamela was stooping, breasts swinging, to pick up her nightdress from the floor. He paused for a second to watch appreciatively, then stepped out through the curtains to the balcony.

He shivered in the cold, put down his clothes then began to dress quickly. There was no moon and this side of the house stood in shadow but there was enough light for him to see. He heard an opening door and then voices in the room behind him. Pamela's sleepily: "Darling! I wasn't expecting you!"

Jamie thought, Too bloody true. You're supposed to be with your regiment in Palestine. Dammit, you only went back to it two weeks ago. Couldn't you stay put and do some work for a bit? You're a waste of the taxpayer's money.

He heard shoes thump one at a time to the carpet and Harry saying in that bray of his: "The colonel sent me back to attend a conference. He didn't want to come himself. Bit of luck, what? I say, I can't find my hanger."

Jamie muttered to himself, "Stick your clothes on the chair, old man, as I did." Then as he found his socks were missing: "No, don't!" They would be on the chair. He dragged his shoes onto his bare feet and heard Harry say, "Hah! Found it."

Jamie was ready. He peered at the garden below. There was no way to climb down but it wasn't much of a drop. He swung his legs over the rail of the balcony and thought, Harry's won a pair of socks, anyway. He heard the creak of the bed, And that's not all. Busy night for Pamela. There would be questions asked in the house about those socks but Pamela would think of an answer. She always did.

Now he hung by his hands, legs dangling. Well, it had been good while it lasted but now it was time to go. He let himself fall. There was soft earth below and only one rock but his right foot landed on that and pain lanced up his leg from his recently healed knee. He climbed to his feet and limped away through the garden, swearing softly, "Of all the bloody luck."

Katy did not see Mark for some days but that had happened before and she told herself there was no need to worry. Then he telephoned her apartment one evening. "I'm in Alex for a couple of hours. Would you like dinner at Pastroudi's?"

"O.K. Thank you. Where have you been?"

"Oh, flying or on stand-by." He always dismissed his absences thus.

Katy chuckled into the telephone: "That sounds like: Sorry, dear, I've been working late at the office."

"Something like that."

"You're sure you haven't another woman out there?"

"Half a dozen, but all brunettes. A change is as good as a rest, you know."

And they exchanged repartee like that over dinner while he thought that they were playing a game, and he might not have much time. There would be another convoy to escort to Malta soon, or the threatened move nearer the front, many more operations if – when – the Italians invaded Egypt. And if their Fleet came out at the same time? He could not wait much longer.

Katy's thoughts and feelings were not clear. She had come to Egypt looking and hoping for Jamie. She had not found the Jamie she remembered, but her memory of him from two years ago was vague and unreal. Now she sensed Mark's mood and as they got up from the table she wondered what she should do. Couldn't that decision wait? Because she was not ready to make it and there was always tomorrow, the next day and the next. She would wait.

The war would not. She checked. Mark took her arm then and she changed her mind. But at the door they met Bert

79

with – amazingly, wasn't he supposed to be in Cairo? – Jamie Dunbar.

Katy whispered, "Mark, please!"

"Yes, I know, no trouble." Mark growled it, then under his breath: "You picked a hell of a time to visit, Bert." But he said aloud, to Katy, "I'll be seeing you." He took one last look at her, then walked away.

Katy called after him, "Take care!" She had never said that before and now it came so softly that he did not hear. He passed the two men with a smile and a word of greeting for Bert, a curt nod at Jamie, then was gone.

Katy said, eyes on the door, but speaking to Jamie, "You're limping again. Didn't they return you to duty?"

Jamie grimaced. "They did. Mounting was all right but I fell getting off."

Katy said, puzzled, "I thought you were infantry?"

Bert burst in, impatiently, "Listen! It's an ill wind – Jamie's got us a movement order. We're going to the desert."

4

The Desert

The four Swordfish, Ethel among them, lifted off from Dekheila in the early morning. The rumoured move had come to pass. Air Commodore Collishaw, commanding the Royal Air Force in the western desert, had asked the Navy for the assistance of its Swordfish in attacks on ships supplying the Italian army in Libya. He was desperately short of aircraft.

The Swordfish headed westward over the sea as far as El Daba then followed the line of the railway that ran along the coast through Fuka to Ma'aten Bagush. The railway continued for another twenty miles to Mersa Matruh, and the metalled coast road for a still further eighty miles to Sidi Barrani, but the four Swordfish landed before noon at the R.A.F. field at Ma'aten Bagush.

Ward and Tim walked over to the mess, were made welcome and settled in. Later that afternoon Ward looked at his watch and said, "The ground crews will be in any time now. Think I'll stroll over and meet them."

"Hang on a second and I'll come with you." Tim Rogers was sharpening one of his pencils, paring the shavings into an ashtray. He used a big claspknife with a wooden handle that fitted comfortably into his palm. The blade was six inches long, slim and wickedly sharp.

Mark stared at it, "Where did you get that?"

"Bought it in Alex."

"Bit big, isn't it?"

Tim explained, "I kept losing the small ones."

"It looks like something the doc would use for an amputation."

Tim stood up and closed the knife, put it in his pocket.

"You wouldn't want an observer without a decent pencil, to do his navigation."

"All I want is an observer who can navigate, and one of these days I might get one."

Tim sniffed. "All *I* want is a pilot who doesn't get nasty great holes in our nice aeroplane."

They walked out to the field and Tim said, "Here she comes now."

The ancient Victoria transport lumbered in and bumped down creakily on the strip. It was loaded with tools, spares for the four Swordfish, and the ground crew of fitters, riggers and armourers. Laurel and Hardy climbed out with the others, all of them grousing and swearing, sweating in the heat.

Mark asked, "Everything all right?"

Laurel grumbled, "Lovely trip, sir, thanks. Regular joy ride with my arse on a tool-box."

Hardy stretched thick arms, "Ethel go O.K., sir?"

"Fine, thanks. She handles very sweet."

Hardy nodded and edged past, looking around and muttering, "Join the Navy and see the world."

"I'm not in the Navy," Laurel peered at the desert shimmering beyond the strip. "And the world around here is always the bloody same."

Mark grinned. Their morale was high. "Well, a change is as good as a rest." He remembered he had said that to Katy.

Each day they flew anti-submarine patrols while they waited for an Italian convoy, but without a sighting. In the evening they would sit in the mess, making one glass of beer last till lights out because they were flying the next day. Tim argued with the others about cricket and Mark let his thoughts drift back to Katy Sandford in Alexandria. Until someone said, "It looks as though Cunningham will have to do a Nelson." Mark frowned. The man's meaning was as clear to him as to the others: if the Italian Fleet would not come out of Taranto then Cunningham would have to attack it in harbour, as Nelson had attacked the Danish Fleet at Copenhagen. Except that instead of ships he would use torpedo-bombers: Swordfish.

But in the following dawn as he sat in Ethel's cockpit and her engine thundered before take-off, his thoughts were not of Taranto. He stared past the spinning propeller, feeling the slipstream beat morning-cold on his face as the first trace of red on the eastern horizon lit the desert, and thought of Katy. She would still be asleep in the cool, quiet apartment in Alexandria, to wake to peace and a day without fear. It was a warming thought.

"Stand to! C'mon, baby! Stand to!"

Katy woke to Bert's whisper, his long arm hooking over the tail-board of the eight-hundredweight truck to shake her. The driver had made a space just big enough for her on the truck's floor, with rations and stores piled around. She could not see them now, saw only the black cut-out that was Bert's head standing above the tail-board against the night sky. "O.K." She whispered back at him, "Cut it out." His hand stopped its tugging and was withdrawn, his head disappeared.

Katy wriggled out of her sleeping-bag. She had slept in her clothes, matching khaki shirt, trousers and socks, had only to pull on her boots and drag a thick sweater over her head. She picked up her hat and the heavy overcoat that had been wrapped around her sleeping-bag, clambered over the tail-board and dropped to the ground.

The desert was dark, quiet and bitterly cold. She shivered as Bert helped her into the overcoat. The hat, wide-brimmed and with a chin-strap to hold it in place against the wind, she clapped on over her blonde hair. She had got Bert to hack her hair off short the first night they were in the desert. She could still feel sand in it now, gritty.

The black humps of vehicles loomed all around her. There was a company of infantry, 120 men carried in fifteen-hundredweight trucks, a troop of four twenty-five-pounder field guns and six Rolls-Royce armoured cars. She and Bert had come with them through a hole in the wire two nights before. This was a fence, ten feet wide, of thickly meshed, staked barbed wire, erected by Mussolini's army along the border between Libya and Egypt, intended to stop Libyan

Arabs getting out. It had never stopped the Arabs and now British infantry and engineers had cut a hole through which the vehicles passed into Libya.

They had spent two days in patrolling, seeking out the enemy, trying to find his positions, strengths and weaknesses, his convoys. Their orders were to harass the enemy and so they sought a target. They had found one the previous evening; a fort, seemingly lightly defended.

The vehicles were close-ranked now, in laager. In the day they had been widely dispersed as they moved, with gaps of four or five hundred yards between them. That way they were less likely to suffer casualties if attacked from the air, and it saved them from driving in the sand cloud thrown up by the next vehicle ahead. Each driver still got a fair amount of sand.

A cautious reconnaissance had located and assessed the fort, then at nightfall the vehicles had closed in warily behind the leader in six columns, only a few yards separating the columns from one another, each vehicle from that ahead. They were out of sight and sound of the Italians in the fort. The tight-packed phalanx turned off the route they had followed through the day and drove into the desert for nearly a mile, then halted as darkness closed in, and formed a laager. This attack would be mounted at dawn. The field guns and soft-skinned trucks stood in the interior columns, with armoured cars and infantry on each side and closing front and rear. That was a laager.

And this now was "stand to", in the last cold minutes before first light. Men moved quietly, low-voiced, to take up defensive positions with rifles and Brens around the outside of the laager where sentries had patrolled all night. Katy watched the preparations, what she could see of them, shivered and huddled inside her overcoat. What the hell was she doing here? She had never realised the desert could be so cold. The sky was dark but clear and frosted with stars that looked like a million specks of glinting ice.

She waited through the first light and the false dawn and then suddenly on the eastern horizon a band of red shafted sunlight. Starters churned, then engines burst into life and she climbed into the front of the eight-hundredweight beside Bert and the driver. The columns moved forward behind the lead vehicle of the commander with its flag on the wireless aerial, then fanned out. The laager broke up as each vehicle returned to its daylight, dispersed position.

This was a dangerous time, when the low, level sunlight shone into a man's eyes and you did not know what enemy awaited you. But this morning was quiet. An armoured car patrol had gone out before first light and found no sign of enemy tracks.

The eight-hundredweight halted beside another. They were stubby vehicles, smaller versions of the fifteen-hundredweights used by the infantry sections. The driver sat in front under a canvas tilt with room beside him for another man, or one thin man and a slim girl. There were no doors; a canvas curtain at each side, waist-high, kept some of the sand out when they were on the move. The canvas-covered rear of this one held rations, kit and water. The other eight-hundredweight, Jamie Dunbar's, carried the wireless and its operator.

They all got down, except the wireless operator. Jamie walked over, his greatcoat flapping open and showing the corduroy slacks, khaki shirt and sweater beneath. On his feet were old suede shoes. He had told a staring Bert: "Most comfortable footwear in the desert, old boy. Most of the chaps wear them." That meant officers; the other ranks wore ammunition boots.

Jamie said now, "Morning all. We're just having a quick brew while the old man takes a look from the ridge. Then I expect we'll be off."

The ridge was half a mile away and extended across their front for maybe a mile. It was a rocky outcrop rising gradually to some fifty feet. Jamie said, "They won't see us from the fort." Katy knew the fort was a mile or more beyond the ridge but she had not seen it. A truck was stopped at the foot of the ridge and two tiny figures lay at the top of it. One of them was the "old man", a major of twenty-eight.

The two drivers, still in greatcoats, huddled around a stove made from half a petrol tin, punctured like a brazier around its sides and half-filled with sand doused with petrol that now burned under a kettle. The petrol tins were flimsy affairs that leaked much too easily, but they made good stoves.

Katy turned her back on the vehicles and the men. She was well aware that most of them had been out in the desert for months and she – hat, overcoat, trousers and boots notwithstanding – was the first woman they'd seen in all that time. She stared out at the desert, not dunes of sand here but a plain of rubble and powdered rock, scattered here and there with clumps of low, dry scrub.

"Cup o' char, miss." Powell, the driver of her truck, was offering the enamel mug, steam rising from it like smoke, and she cupped it in her hands. As he turned away he apologised, "Well, only half a cup, really. Got to watch the water, you know."

She did know. After three days in the desert, rationed to a gallon of water a day, she knew only too well. That gallon was not hers to do with as she liked. The driver, Bert and herself had first to meet the needs of the eight-hundredweight out of their rations, and in the daytime heat of the desert its thirst was demanding. What was left must serve for washing *and* drinking. Her daily wash had to be carried out with no more water than was now held in the mug. Yesterday she had seen Jamie shaving in the last half inch of his tea. Shaving daily was King's Regulations.

Bert said, "I suppose we correspondents aren't too welcome – the water we use."

Jamie chuckled, "More welcome than the padre when he comes up. At least you brought some whisky."

Jamie. Katy had watched him since leaving Alexandria. Bert had muttered, "One thing: he's a natural soldier, that's for sure." Jamie might seem casual but in reality he was quick, efficient, tireless, a far cry from the elegant client of Pastroudi's and the Cecil. But whether there, or here in the desert, he was not the irresistible male she remembered from two years before and had come eagerly seeking. Now she wondered if that person had only been fashioned from her own desires and imagination.

"Here we go!" Jamie had been watching the ridge and had seen some signal there. He limped across to his truck. The stove had been doused with sand and loaded on board. Katy and Bert crowded in beside Powell and he started the eight-hundredweight, put it in gear.

Bert asked her, "Got your camera handy? You'll need it today."

Katy nodded, opened her overcoat to let him see the Rolleiflex camera on its strap around her neck but still wrapped in one of her spare shirts to keep out the all-pervading dust. She had found it necessary to spend an hour or more each day crouched in the back of the truck, after it was at rest and the dust had settled, cleaning dust from the camera with a little artist's paintbrush, brought along with blessed foresight. Now she steadied herself with one hand on the dash as the truck rolled forward over the rocky and uneven surface. All the vehicles were on the move, and the guns were being brought into action, unhooked from their towing trucks and hauled up onto their round steel platforms from which they fired. The armoured cars were nearer the ridge and heading to pass around one end of it, the fifteen-hundredweight trucks of the infantry bouncing after them.

Jamie led his little party straight to the ridge and halted the two trucks at the foot of it. He jumped down and waved a beckoning hand at Bert and Katy. They followed him as he climbed the ridge with quick strides, still limping a little but keeping ahead. They joined him, panting, where he stood just below the crest. Higher up the ridge and twenty yards to their left was the major. The artillery observation officer lay beside him, binoculars at his eyes and compass by his side. His truck with the wireless link to the guns stood just below where he lay. Katy stared back to where the guns were lined out a mile away, waiting for fire orders.

Jamie said, "Have a *shufti*."

"What?" Katy blinked. He was offering his binoculars.

Bert explained, "The British Army's been stationed all over

the empire for the last two-hundred years and a lot of their slang comes from local languages. I think *shufti* is Arabic. It means 'look'."

"Oh." Katy faced forward, accepted the glasses. There was the fort, as far away as the guns, but in front of her. It reminded her of Beau Geste, square, white, with a tower at each corner. There was a cluster of buildings like sheds, outside it and about a hundred yards to its right.

The observation officer called an order down to his signaller at the wireless. Jamie said in a conversational tone, "The idea is for the armoured cars to go in first and shoot the place up with their machine-guns. The infantry will chase along behind them and when they're close under the walls they'll be out of the enemy's sight. Then they blow the gate and go in. The gate is in the right-hand wall, facing those sheds."

Bert grunted and peered through his old binoculars. Katy felt warm now because the sun was well up. She peeled off the overcoat as she watched, let it fall and started working with her camera. With the sun had come flies and she flapped them from her face with one hand between taking pictures. The Rolls-Royce armoured cars were rocking around the end of the ridge now and heading towards the fort. They looked to have been left over from an earlier war, standard limousines converted by having armour-plate riveted around them and a round turret clapped on top. Each carried a single machine-gun in the turret.

One of the twenty-five-pounders fired from the rear and seconds later Katy saw the puff of dust and smoke as the shell burst short of the fort. The observation officer called down a correction. When the gun fired again she did not see where the shell went but Jamie said, "Over." The observation officer called another correction.

The infantry trucks were swerving and lurching over the rock-strewn ground as they followed the armoured cars. Every vehicle trailed its plume of brown and grey dust that merged with the brown and khaki camouflage paint so vehicle and dust became one.

Bert asked, "What about mines?"

"Remembering the one that bust my knee?" Jamie grinned. "Our engineers were out last night. They marked a route and it connects with the one the Italians marked for themselves. Doubt if you'll pick out the markers in all that dust but the trucks are following them."

The guns of the twenty-five-pounder troop *slam-banged!* as one, and Katy saw flame and smoke erupt from the walls of the fort. Jamie murmured, "Won't do much damage but it should keep a few heads down."

Katy thought the scene was unreal: the flat banging of the guns; the cars and trucks like toys swerving across the desert; the white fort. A flame glowed and died on one of the fort's towers and Jamie said, "Hello! They've got a gun into action." One of the infantry trucks had turned onto its side and was smoking. Small figures spilled from it but became indistinct as the gathering clouds of dust and smoke hid them, the vehicles, and eventually everything but the towers of the fort.

The twenty-five-pounders stopped firing and the observation-post officer stood up, brushed dust from his corduroy trousers and lit a cigarette. Machine-gun fire rattled in the distance. There was a sudden *thump!* and Jamie said, "Sounds like they've blown the gate."

Bert muttered, "Is that a white flag? Looks like it."

There was a flagstaff on one of the towers and the flag flapped from it on the same wind that swirled the dust and smoke around it. Jamie said laconically, "Probably a damask table-cloth. The Italians like their comforts."

There was no more firing.

Katy thought, Was that it? Finished? It seemed it was and she heaved a sigh of relief.

Bert asked, "Did you get any pictures?"

"Sure. Tele-photo."

He grinned at her, "Thought you might have forgotten."

"I'm not an amateur."

Jamie circled his hand in a "wind-up" signal and his driver started the engine of his truck. Bert said, "Guess I'll go down with Jamie and take a look. Why don't you hang around here with Powell and I'll see you later."

Katy shook her head, "I want to go along."

Bert tried to override her: "What for? You've seen it. So take it easy now and –"

Katy broke in determinedly, "I want to take pictures. That's my job. Isn't it?"

Bert looked at her thoughtfully, "Well – O.K. But they might not let you use them."

"Why not?"

"Could be they'd upset some people."

"Why?" She guessed at what he hinted, that there were things he did not want her to see. But this *was* her job for now, and while it was, she would do it.

Bert saw the stubborn set of her face under the wide-brimmed hat and he lifted a hand to wave at Powell in their truck, "O.K., O.K. Let's go."

They walked down the ridge, leaning back against the slope, and climbed into the cab, squeezed close together. Katy held her camera carefully on her knee. The truck ground along below the ridge after Jamie's, then they turned together to climb it where there was a saddle and the crossing was easier. On the far side of the ridge and down on the plain they made better going. Ahead of them the dust had settled and the smoke blown away. Vehicles were grouped to the right of the fort where the sheds stood.

In the middle distance lay the truck that had been hit and thrown onto its side. They meandered down to it, Powell steering between the bigger lumps of rock and deeper holes that might wreck the suspension, and following the taped path through the mines. They passed close by the truck – and a body.

It was one of the infantrymen and someone had driven the point of his bayoneted rifle into the earth so it stood as a marker. The eight-hundredweight trundled past only feet away and Katy looked down at it. She thought of the body too as "it", could not connect this with a living man. It lay face-down, the limbs splayed out awkwardly, unnaturally, as in some of the pictures she had seen. The steel helmet had fallen forward so she could see the hair, close-cropped like

Powell's. The khaki shirt and shorts were darkly stained.

Powell said tersely, "Bought it."

Bert asked, "Did you know him?"

"Dunno. Couldn't tell. Maybe."

They drove on and when they were close to the fort they saw that the walls and towers were pocked with shell-holes. It was still unreal to Katy. She still half-expected Foreign Legionnaires to show on the ramparts, and a band to strike up something from *The Desert Song*. The gate was in the side wall of the fort and an armoured car stood there, its commander leaning out of the top of the turret, smoking a cigarette. The other armoured cars were scattered about the area.

Infantry with rifles, bayonets fixed and glinting wickedly in the sun, moved among the sheds and buildings outside the fort, herding prisoners with their hands held high. The Italians wore bluish-grey shirts and baggy trousers that were wrapped around with puttees below the knee.

The truck stopped close by the wall where there was shade from the rising sun. Bert and Katy got down and walked to the gate. The two leaves of it hung, sagging, where they had been blasted open by an engineer's charge. Katy cried out, "Bert! What's all the paper?"

He answered, "There's always paper."

Scraps and sheets of it were blowing out past the splintered gates and Bert trapped a sample under his boot, picked it up and glanced at it before throwing it again to the wind. "It looked like a page of somebody's letter home."

They walked through the gateway. Inside the fort was a square and more prisoners were collected in a group at one side of it. All of them clutched some belongings: a bundle of clothes or a pack or a blanket. They looked untidy and vacant and sad. Some of the infantry stood around the prisoners, on guard, their rifles slung over their shoulders. Other soldiers moved purposefully in and out of the low buldings built against the walls of the fort. Bert said, "They're looking for intelligence, maps and orders."

Shells had fallen inside the walls, smashing the roofs of

some of the buildings and making small craters in the square. There were dead lying in the square. They were horribly dead. Headless. Faceless. One with the intestines spilled out. Katy held down the contents of her stomach and took her pictures.

They went to look into the towers and found there was a gun in each tower. Katy did not know what kind they were but they looked smaller than the twenty-five-pounders. Three were intact but one had taken a direct hit before the surrender and its crew were scattered around it. Horror again.

Bert glanced sideways at Katy then led the way back across the square, walking quickly with his familiar long, disjointed, shambling gait. Paper was blowing about the square, letters, documents, old news-sheets, pages from books.

Outside the fort again, they returned to the truck where Powell had his stove burning once more and a kettle on top of it. He said cheerfully, "Breakfast in a minute. Nothing to shout about, just bully beef, biscuits, jam and a wet, but –"

Katy said, "No, thank you." She walked around to the back of the truck where nobody could see her, leaned against the tail-board and closed her eyes. It made no difference; she could still see them.

Some time later, Bert said, "Here."

Katy opened her eyes and saw he carried a mess-tin and a mug in one hand while with the other he flapped at the swarming flies. She protested, "I told you I didn't –"

"I know you don't want to but you've got to. You need the food and the liquid. Anyway, it's only biscuits and jam."

She could not have faced the warm and greasy corned beef, but she sipped at the tea and forced down the biscuits that were dry and hard, like the kind you fed to a dog, and smeared with jam. She felt a little better afterwards, took off the hat and shook her short hair, seeing the dust fall from it. She wiped the sweat from her brow with a grimy handkerchief and replaced the hat.

Bert was writing in his notebook. When he'd finished, Katy said, "Well, I saw it. Finally."

"Uh?" Bert glanced at her.

"The war."

"Oh, that." He dismissed it with a shrug, then asked, "Did you get plenty of pictures?"

"Yes. And I see what you meant. They won't let me use most of them. I've never seen pictures like that anywhere."

"Your first time."

First. There would be others. She wondered how many times Bert had witnessed such scenes – and worse. She asked, "Do you – get used to it?"

Bert looked at her, stone-faced. "No."

The column headed slowly back to the gap in the wire, herding their prisoners along with them. They passed through the wire into Egypt that night and next morning Jamie broke away from the column with his two trucks and set out across the desert to the long coast road to Alexandria. Once on the road they made better time. They passed through Sidi Barrani, then Mersa Matruh and shortly afterwards Powell, hunched over the wheel, said the airfield in the distance was the Royal Air Force base at Ma'aten Bagush. That held no significance for Katy; she did not know Mark Ward was there.

Then the khamsin blew, a wind like the breath of a furnace, driving the fine dust of the desert in suffocating clouds. In the trucks they could not see ten yards ahead. It was mercifully short-lived – the khamsin sometimes blew for several days – but through all that interminable day and in to the night they huddled inside the closed trucks where the heat was that of an oven. They wore cloths over mouth and nose but the dust still got through.

The khamsin blew itself out in the night and they brewed tea at first light, ate corned beef, biscuits – and sand, then went on. Powell's eyes were red and weeping from the dust; he could hardly see.

Katy offered, "I can drive that thing."

Jamie shook his head, "Not on, I'm afraid. Army vehicle, so only the Army is allowed to drive it. I'll do it."

"What about your leg?"

"The leg is all right. I'm due to go to Cairo as soon as this jaunt is over, anyway, and they'll pass me fit for duty."

Jamie drove them into Alexandria at mid-morning, threading the eight-hundredweight through the traffic. He dropped Bert at his hotel and Katy got down to bid him goodbye. Bert was going to clean up then catch a train to Cairo to file his story. Katy's films were in his pocket.

She said, "I'll be hearing from you."

Bert nodded and squinted at her, the sun in his eyes. He asked, "Form any conclusions?"

Katy remembered the action at the fort only forty-eight hours before the dead. She said flatly, "Only that I was right and America should stay out of this bloody business."

Bert did not answer her but glanced at the truck to make sure Jamie was out of earshot. "Nothing more . . . specific?"

Katy said, "What did I make of the war in the desert? It seems you send a few armoured cars, guns and soldiers through the wire, patrol and maybe shoot up a convoy or capture a fort, then back through the wire again. Men die, but for no apparent purpose. Does that sum it up?"

"The Italians don't patrol through the wire."

"So are the British preparing to attack?"

Bert did not answer that either, but asked instead, "Remember I asked you in Cairo how many British troops you'd seen? Well, how many have you seen now?"

Katy thought, Plenty. Then thought again. A troop of the elderly armoured cars here and there. Four tanks. Two batteries of twenty-five-pounder field guns – or was that the same battery, seen twice? Several platoons of infantry, a platoon being twenty to thirty men. "Not a hell of a lot, I guess."

Bert nodded, "That's right. And I've been checking around, talking to some of the British newsmen, putting two and two together. I don't think they've got much of anything: planes, tanks, guns or men, not a tenth of the force the Italians are building up in Libya behind Sollum. They've got five *divisions*!" He paused. "You ever watch the fights?"

Katy was lost by this sudden shift in the conversation, "The fights?"

94

"In Madison Square Garden. The boxing." And when Katy shook her head, Bert went on: "Sometimes you see a guy jabbing to keep the other feller off balance and you know he doesn't want to punch it out because he don't have a punch."

Katy said blankly, "So?"

"So the British are jabbing. I think Wavell is trying one hell of a bluff." Wavell was commander-in-chief, Middle-East. "He's making these raids and pinprick attacks to keep the Italians unsettled and thinking he's stronger than he is. He's aiming to win time to build up his strength but damn near everything he needs has to come the long route around the Cape, and it's a slow business. So far the bluff has worked. But when that big Italian army starts rolling there's precious little between Sollum and Cairo to stop them."

Katy paled, thinking, And we'll be in the way. They were neutrals but a shell could not discriminate. She had gone to the war and been sickened by it. Now it was coming to her.

"Hey!" Bert gripped her by the shoulders. "You look like hell. Snap out of it. That's the way I figure it but I could be wrong. I don't know much, I just have this gut feeling."

Katy smiled at him lopsidedly, "O.K."

He studied her. "Do you want out?"

"No." She shook her head, definite. "I'll see it through." She was not a quitter.

Bert nodded, "Right. You did pretty good out there. See you, kid." He shambled away into his hotel.

Katy returned to the truck and Jamie drove her on to her apartment, carried her kit up himself and set it down by her door. He smiled at her, "Everything all right?"

Katy pushed at a damp tendril of hair, felt the sand in it, "Yes. Fine. All I need is a shower, and sleep."

Jamie lifted one hand to his cap in a casual salute. "I'll be seeing you."

Inside the apartment weariness flooded over her. She had to force herself to go through to the bathroom and run hot water. She stripped and stood in it, eyes closed, letting the ache soak out of her. Finally she aroused herself enough to get out of the shower and towel her body.

She crawled into the bed, lay in a daze and thought that she was overtired. She wondered if Mark had telephoned while she was away, whether he would call her tonight. Suddenly she was wide awake and uneasy, for a moment certain that something bad had happened to him. Was that a premonition? Then her common sense reasserted itself. She told herself she was just exhausted and had seen too much of death and destruction. She was letting her nerves take charge. Mark was all right.

But she did not sleep for some time.

5

Bomba

Mark knew neither apprehension nor premonition that morning. He thought of Katy as he often did, because she fascinated him, and of Taranto because it forced itself on him.

He sat in the cockpit of Ethel on the Royal Air Force field at Ma'aten Bagush. Hardy, the fitter, stood on the port wing, meaty hands curled around the long starting-handle protruding from the engine cowling, shoulders lumpy with muscle bowing and lifting as he wound the handle slowly.

The night before, when the *khamsin* blew, the pilots and observers of the four Swordfish were called to the operations room. All save the flight leader, who had been carried off to hospital with bronchitis, left the mess and groped their way over to the ops room. They were muffled against the hot rasp of the wind and the scouring dust, only their eyes showing and their hands lifted to shield them. Conversation was impossible and their swearing at being dragged from the mess was drowned by the wind.

They sat or stood about in the ops room, trying to wipe sand from their sweating faces as the briefing officer's voice, straining above the roar of the wind outside, told them: "The Blenheim flying reconnaissance today spotted a sub heading into Bomba Bay, and a ship – probably a depot-ship for the sub – already in there." Bomba was in Libya, beyond Tobruk, some three hundred miles from Ma'aten Bagush. "The Met people tell us this *khamsin* will have blown out before morning. The scheme is that you take off at seven in the morning, fly up to Sidi Barrani, refuel there and wait for the dawn reconnaissance flight to report. If the ship and the sub are still there, they're yours. Questions?"

Mark asked, "What about the flight leader, sir? He's in hospital."

"We've sent a signal to Dekheila asking for a replacement." The briefing officer went on to give what information was known of enemy defences at Bomba, then paused and looked around at the thoughtful young faces in the yellow light. "Any more questions? No? Then I suggest an early night."

Mark offered, "I'll tell the ground crew." He fought his way, head down against the wind, to their quarters and found some of them in bed, the others about to turn in. Sand swirled across the floor of the tent and lay over everything.

Hardy stood in cotton undershorts and vest; Laurel peered out sadly from his blankets and said gloomily, "It's got to be bad news, sir."

Mark told them. The bed opposite those of Laurel and Hardy was occupied by the Leading Torpedo-man, whose job it would be to arm the four Swordfish with bombs or torpedos. He grumbled, "Roll on my bloody twelve."

Laurel sniffed, "Won't do you any good. The war'll still be on when your twelve years are up, so you'll still be in."

"Cheerful bastard." The Torpedo-man turned over.

Mark left then, grinning, knowing the Swordfish would be ready in the morning and on the top line.

They were. Six 250-pound bombs were slung under Ethel's wings while a torpedo hung below the belly of each of the other three Swordfish. It was a fine, bright morning, the sky a clear, empty blue. Hardy heaved on the starting-handle. Mark was settled inside his harness, a khaki overall covering his white shirt and shorts, comfortable old shoes on his feet.

Tim's voice came through the Gosport tube: "Is this miracle of communications working?"

Mark answered him: "I can hear you."

"Can't ask for more, I suppose."

Hardy had wound the starting-handle up to a good speed now. Laurel climbed onto a step on the undercarriage, set his own hands on next to Hardy's and kept up the momentum while Hardy swung more easily, resting his hands on the handle.

Mark glanced along the line of Swordfish again and saw Ollie Patch's head sticking out of his cockpit. Ollie was a short, wiry captain, Royal Marines, who had first learned to fly with a Royal Air Force commission. He had been flown up from Dekheila at first light to lead the operation.

Hardy was now winding in earnest again, he and Laurel together, the handle whirling round. The full heat of the day had not yet come but Mark could see the sweat drip from Hardy's chin.

Fast enough. Mark reached out his left hand to the ring on the bottom of the control panel, pulled it to let in the clutch and the engine fired, the propeller kicked and spun. He warmed up the engine, checking temperatures and pressures, while Hardy pulled the starting-handle from its socket and passed it up to Tim Rogers to be stowed in his cockpit.

All four Swordfish were running up their engines now, sending sand swirling and billowing across the field. Mark felt no excitement, no expectation of action, and thought, Early yet; might all be for nothing if the sub and the ship have flown the coop in the night. He carried on with his pre-flight checks and at seven o'clock the Swordfish trundled off one by one and followed Ollie Patch into the sky.

Ninety minutes later they landed, cautiously and warily, at Sidi Barrani. Mark peered over the side of the cockpit as he came in: this rough desert strip was close to the sharp end of the war and had suffered several air raids since the Swordfish squadron had staged there on the way to attack Tobruk. The surface was a moonscape of bomb craters filled with sand and rock and roughly levelled. He had to pick a way through them. The landing was bumpy, and thoughts of the bombs under the wings lurked at the back of his mind, but Ethel rolled safely to a halt and he cut the engine.

Tim Rogers said into the silence, "Not exactly Imperial Airways, are we?"

Mark told him, "Stop wingeing about the ride. There is a war on, you know."

"Go on. Is that a fact?"

"Know where we are?"

"Place looks familiar. I was going to ask someone." Tim nodded at the R.A.F. ground crew, in ancient, oil-stained khaki shirts and shorts, closing in to refuel the four Swordfish.

Mark said, "Find out at breakfast. Maybe there'll be somebody there to tell you the way home as well."

They climbed down and a fitter pointed Campbell towards the cookhouse, where he could eat, then said to Mark, "That's your mess, sir – and the ops room as well – over there." But they knew it from their previous visit.

Mark and Tim walked over to where it lay, set back from the strip. The mess-cum-ops-room was built out of petrol tins filled with sand, roofed by a tarpaulin and draped with camouflage netting. Tim muttered, "Not exactly the Dorchester, either."

Mark grinned and ducked his head to pass in through the doorway. There were two long tables inside and after he and Tim had dragged off their overalls they sat on camp-stools. The atmosphere was thick with dust and tobacco smoke, buzzing with flies. The air crews crowded in around the tables. Patch with his observer, young Midshipman Woodley, husky with tonsilitis but determined to make the flight, the other pilots, Wellham and Cheesman with their respective observers, Marsh and Stovin-Bradford. They breakfasted on tinned sausages, gritty with sand, and stewed tea, brown and strong.

Mark dug a knife into a four-pound tin of marmalade and smeared a generous helping on a slice of bread. He nudged Tim and asked, "Better now?"

Tim flapped his hand at the flies, "Much. Give my compliments to the chef."

A Royal Air Force officer entered with the report from the Blenheim's dawn patrol over Bomba. "They're still there: one submarine, one steamer that looks like a depot-ship, and a destroyer –" He looked down at the flimsy torn from a signal-pad and sucked at his pipe, sending a cloud of smoke to clear the flies from his face and further thicken the atmosphere. "Inshore there's another steamer and a few sailing craft."

Ollie Patch gave his orders, "We could fly straight there,

the shortest route, but that's over enemy country so they'd know we were coming long before we got there and they'd be ready. Besides, it's a near-certainty we'd run into fighters on the way. So instead we'll go out over the sea and come back likewise. That means flying at nearly extreme range and there won't be much fuel to spare, but we should avoid the fighters both ways and have a good chance of making a surprise attack."

They left the oven of the mess for the baking heat of the desert strip and walked back out to the Swordfish, a straggle of young men in white shirts and shorts. Mark knew this operation would not be like the raid on Tobruk. "Daylight job," he said, "so we'll be able to see what we're doing."

Tim nodded, but pointed out, "And they'll be able to see *us*."

"You heard Ollie. He's trying to surprise them by flying in low from the sea."

"Stands a chance of working. We might get in before the guns know we're there." He glanced at the bombs hanging fat under Ethel's wings. "Let's hope we get rid of those bloody things before the shooting starts."

A direct hit on one of those bombs would blast Ethel into splinters of scrap metal and shreds of canvas, but Mark was still in cheerful mood.

Tim said thoughtfully, "We cruise around eighty knots. You have one machine-gun at the front and Campbell has another at the back. I have a pencil. Suppose we're jumped by fighters. We can't run and we can't fight. What do we do?"

"Duck." Mark grinned at Tim then called out to Doug Campbell, waiting by Ethel, "Had breakfast?"

Campbell shrugged thick shoulders, "Just about, sir. Sandy bangers again. Not too bad, though, more bangers than sand."

"We're going after those ships in Bomba Bay."

"Aye, aye, sir."

They clambered up into the cockpits and at ten thirty the four Swordfish rolled away along the most rubble-free part of the strip and lifted off. Mark slotted Ethel neatly into position astern of Ollie Patch. Cheesman and Wellham, piloting the other two Swordfish, were out on either flank so the four were in a diamond formation with Mark Ward at the tail. They flew low over the sea until they were fifteen miles out, then turned to port to fly parallel to the coast. At only thirty feet above the sea they were hidden below the horizon from any Italian fighters patrolling along the coast.

Or should be. Mark kept a sharp lookout for fighters, just the same, and reminded Tim and Campbell. Then he was silent, busy with his flying and searching the sky. But still a part of his mind returned to the fragment of conversation from a few days ago: "Cunningham will have to do a Nelson." Cunningham could not take his ships into Taranto harbour, as Nelson had at Copenhagen, could not even sail within gun range. Leaving aside the threat from the Italian shore batteries, submarines and minefields, he would be in easy striking distance of bombers flying from bases ashore. Closing the harbour would inevitably end in disaster.

No. The attack would have to be made by torpedo-bombers, but even so there was still the problem of range, shown up by the operation Ward was flying now. The four Swordfish had had to stage at Sidi Barrani to refuel because they could not fly directly from Ma'aten Bagush to Bomba. So *Eagle* would have to steam close to Taranto, again within easy striking distance of Italian airfields, in order to fly off her Swordfish and land them on afterwards, and that would be suicidal.

The attack on Taranto might be moving from being desirable to necessary – but it was still impossible.

At noon, as Katy in Alexandria lay weary but uneasily awake, Ollie Patch altered course and led the flight in towards the coast. They still flew low, at a wave-hopping thirty feet above the sea. The blazing sun cast the shadows of the Swordfish sharp and black, racing along on the rippled surface right under them.

Mark said into the Gosport tube, "Here we go!" He was intent. There on either hand were the the two headlands enclosing the Bay of Bomba that lay ahead. There were the ships, tiny as yet, so that he could not make out which was depot-ship and which destroyer – and Ollie's Swordfish kept obstructing his line of sight. But he could see that one ship was distant, tucked well inside the bay, the other nearer.

The Swordfish rapidly closed the gap. Soon Mark could see that the nearer vessel was in fact a submarine, and beyond it lay not one ship but two, moored side by side. The submarine was under way, running on the surface, but she was only moving slowly, with little white water at her bow. The gun forward of her conning-tower was not manned so clearly the Italians had indeed been taken unawares by the torpedo-bombers' approach low over the sea. They would wake up soon, but as yet there was no flak.

Now the commander of the submarine had seen the danger and was turning her towards the Swordfish to make her a smaller target. But Ollie Patch had dropped his torpedo with barely three-hundred yards to run and climbed away, swinging to the right. Mark climbed as well but banked to the left, copying Wellham's turn but steadily lifting above and astern of him. He heard the yell of Tim Rogers: "Hit her!" He knew Tim meant that Ollie had got the submarine but he took his word for it and concentrated on his flying.

The depot-ship and destroyer were ahead and to the right. Wellham was still moving out to the left, obviously planning to turn soon to run in on the two ships when they were broadside to him and offered the biggest target. Cheesman was far to the right so he was going to attack the ships from the other side. So –

There was another ship, a small coaster, deeply laden, ahead and close inshore. Mark decided: that one. He levelled the Swordfish out of the climb and flew straight for the coaster. She lay at anchor, motionless and broadside to him. Good. She seemed to be sliding across the sea towards him and still there was no flak bursting near him or anywhere that he could see. It was easy, almost like shooting a sitting bird. Except that Ethel was running at seventy knots and a split-second error in timing could mean a wash-out, not one hit out of the six bombs. And this sitting bird could be loaded with supplies for the Italian army, or petrol to drive them on their way to Cairo.

Coming up. Steady . . . Steady . . . Now! He pressed the button and the bombs fell away one by one. The ship flashed beneath him and there was the shore ahead. He eased back on the stick to climb again and started to turn to the left.

Tim's voice came, jubilant. "Two near-misses and one direct hit! Right slap bang into her!"

So that was that: three out of six had told. Mark answered, "Home, James". He held Ethel in the turn, the brown earth slowly wheeling beneath the port wing, then eased her out of it to point towards the sea again.

Tim said, "She's on fire!"

Mark could see it for himself: a climbing tower of smoke rising from aft of the coaster's amidships superstructure – and was that the yellow of flame at the base of the tower, pale in the bright sunlight?

Flak! He saw it bursting away to the right and put Ethel's nose down in a dive, to leave the bay as they had entered it, flying low above the sea. The flak was high now but swinging round onto him; there were bursts above and ahead. He lurched to the left, away from it, and levelled out of the dive. The bursts were off to the right again now. Good enough.

There was the ship they had bombed, right ahead. As it slid towards him he saw that they would just miss the edge of the smoke tower on this course, and so he held it. For a second his focus widened and he looked for the submarine but did not find it. He thought: Sunk! Wellham was turning away towards the sea – and his torpedo hit: the depot-ship exploded in smoke and flame and a fountain of soaring wreckage.

Here was the smoke from the coaster, the black column flicking past the starboard wingtip, the ship herself glimpsed below him –

It felt like a kick from a huge boot as Ethel jumped under him. His vision blurred and he gasped for breath. He never afterwards remembered coherently what happened then. He had blinks of memory, of Ethel nose-down and starboard wing down, sliding. Of fighting her. Of the sea rushing close beneath.

The sea! Christ! He eased back on the stick and felt Ethel respond and the nose lifted. *Gently!* His eyes went to his instruments, running over them, checking. They looked all right. He was flying level and low now, some fifty feet above the sea and heading for the mouth of the bay.

He remembered the others and asked, "Are you two all right?" There was no answer so he repeated his question but with the same result. He gently waggled Ethel's wings and this caught the attention of Tim Rogers.

His voice came, sounding breathless: "Sorry. We'd got unplugged and hadn't noticed. We've been tossed about a bit." Which had pulled their Gosport tubes from the pipe which connected all three cockpits.

Mark asked again, "Are you two O.K.?"

"Campbell's got a bloody nose and my ribs are sore, but that's all."

Mark said, "I think our ship blew up underneath us."

Tim's voice climbed: "*Think?* I'm bloody sure it did. It isn't there any more. I'll swear I was hanging outside by my strap for a second. How about you? And Ethel? I can see a few holes."

Mark did not answer for himself. He was sure he was uninjured but he still felt numb, moving like an automaton. He checked his instruments again, ducked his head to peer under the cockpit cowling at the fuel gauge sited some two feet ahead of him. That looked steady: at least they didn't seem to be losing any petrol. He straightened up and said, "Everything's working."

"Thank the Lord for that." Then Tim asked, "Does my voice sound funny?"

"Yes."

"So does yours."

Mark thought, For the same reason: we've both had a hell of a fright.

They did not talk much after that. Outside the bay they

found the other three Swordfish, fell into formation astern of Ollie Patch again and he led them home.

They landed on the strip at Sidi Barrani to refuel, picking their way between the patched craters. When Ethel was at rest and the engine still they clambered down from the high cockpits in the silence and shimmering heat and stood in a little group well away from the fuelling. Even in just shirts and shorts they sweated in the glare of the sun now that the slipstream was not blasting at them.

Campbell lit a cigarette and sucked in smoke hungrily. "That was bloody close, sir." His nose was swollen and there was dried blood on his face and forehead from when he'd been slammed onto the breech of the Vickers machine-gun. He muttered, "I've got a hell of a headache."

Tim Rogers said quietly, "I thought for a moment we'd had it." He glanced at Ward. "It beats me how you kept her out of the drink. We've never been that close before."

Mark shrugged carelessly, "Well, we're here." He lifted his wrist as if to look at his watch but really to be sure his hands were not shaking. They were steady. He said, "It was a good show though."

Tim nodded. He pulled off his helmet and ran his fingers through his short, sandy hair so that it stuck up in spikes. "A submarine and its depot-ship sunk. And our coaster was full of ammunition, no doubt about that. It wasn't tins of Italian army issue spaghetti that sent Ethel up like a rocket."

Mark remembered the huge kick but then nothing until he had hauled Ethel up from the reaching sea. Had he been unconscious or in shock? Tim and Campbell obviously thought he had pulled off a miraculous piece of flying. He didn't know about that but it had been a closer shave even than at Tobruk. Disaster was creeping closer all the time. Was there a progression you could plot on a graph, up to some point of oblivion? He told himself that didn't follow. Some of the operations were routine, like the anti-submarine patrols earlier in the week, uneventful to the point of boredom. He supposed you remembered more clearly the ones that almost killed you.

This one had.

They flew on to Ma'aten Bagush and there Mark ordered Doug Campbell to the sickbay, where the doctor diagnosed concussion and sent the gunner to bed. Mark ate in the mess with the other air crew, hungrily. He did not have to talk because Tim Rogers was unwinding volubly. Ward did not want to talk. Back in Alex he'd thought he might not have much time left. Now he'd had the thought confirmed.

A flight-lieutenant of the Air Force stopped beside them. "Heard the news? You chaps have been recalled to Dekheila, flying back tomorrow. Stores to be crated during the morning and the Victoria flies in around noon to pick them up."

Mark heard himself say, "How about going now?"

Tim blinked at him, startled, then caught on and looked quickly away. Dekheila was only a truck ride away from Alex, and Mark's girl was in Alex.

The flight-lieutenant said, "Well, as it happens, there's a major in the Engineers over at the office trying to cadge a lift to Alex. He's been ordered there in a hurry and doesn't fancy a drive through the night."

Mark took off with the major sitting in Tim's cockpit and Tim taking the place of Campbell as gunner and wireless operator. Night fell before they reached Dekheila but Mark had only to follow the line of the railway and the coast road. They put on the landing lights for him at Dekheila and he landed neatly and on time.

He and Tim had brought their kit with them, stowed in the rear cockpits. Mark washed and changed, his face without feeling, like perished rubber under his hands. As he pulled on his shirt Tim ducked into the tent they shared and said, "Ops say, no flying before noon tomorrow at earliest. And there's a truck going into Alex in a few minutes."

"Thanks."

Tim sat down on his bed, dug the villainous-looking knife out of his pocket and began to sharpen a pencil. "Heard about the smash?"

"Yes." One of the Swordfish at Dekheila had crashed that day. "Bad luck."

Tim squinted at the pencil. "Funny. We flew through all

that stuff this morning and got away with it, while another poor blighter on a routine flight –" He did not finish but shook his head over the vagaries of chance. The pilot was dead. He would be an entry in *Eagle*'s log: "Killed in flying accident." He had been the same age as Mark. Tim said, "Nice chap."

"Yes." Mark thought, For Christ's sake, Tim, leave it alone. He asked, "Are you coming into Alex?"

Tim shook his head. "I've had enough for one day. I'll have a drink in the mess because I need it, then turn in."

Mark was parched but did not wait. He got a lift in the truck, sitting beside the driver as it rocked along the bumpy road. When the driver set him down Mark made for the nearest bar. He ordered a cold beer, drank it thirstily then called for another. He was about to telephone Katy, then decided against it. He had done with talking.

She woke from her afternoon nap in the last of the light, rested and alive, saw the sky outside the window red with the sunset and stretched like a cat, sensuous. She pulled on a light robe, chilled a bottle of wine, made herself a meal, and drank a glass of the wine while she ate. Afterwards she fixed her darkroom – the bathroom, its window covered with a thick black cloth. She had kept back one roll of film when she gave the others to Bert and now she developed and printed it.

This was the first roll of film she had taken in the desert, to get her hand in: pictures of a sunset, an arab, the empty, desolate landscape. There was nothing newsworthy in any of them but she was professionally curious to see how they came out. The sunset was an expected disappointment because the film was black and white. She was pleased with the others. In one she had caught Bert, his long lean face turned wrily humorous to the camera. That was Bert to the life. Even the picture he'd insisted on taking of her, was good. Truthful. No fashionplate this, but alive.

Was that herself? She felt a lot older than the laughing girl in the photograph, but that girl had not been to the fort, had not seen the war up close.

She left the prints spread in a neat line and went out to the sitting-room. The night was cool now but with the curtains drawn across the windows she was warm enough in her thin cotton robe.

She was restless, wondering how to spend her evening, shying away from her desert kit that stood by the door, still to be unpacked. It could wait until morning.

When the knock came at the door she went to it quickly, thinking: Mark?

Jamie Dunbar stood on the landing, handsome brown face carefully shaved, casually elegant in a lightweight suit. He held up a bottle of wine as he walked in. "Therapeutic. A little of this always helps after an action – if you can get it. A lot of it helps quite a bit more."

He closed the door behind him and slid an arm around her waist. "Time to relax. We've earned it and there's a war on. We mustn't waste these opportunities." He smiled down at her. "You – look – gorgeous."

She was caught off balance, startled, tried to pull away but his arm only tightened around her. She gasped, "Look, Jamie –"

He bent his head to kiss her and she slapped him. She had little experience in slapping faces and judging the force needed. Her right arm was free and her hand came up in a round-arm swing that rocked Jamie's head on his shoulders.

He gasped, "For Christ's sake –!" But he still held her.

She drew back her arm. "Let me go! Damn you! Let me go!" She hit him again.

He shoved her away from him so she banged against the wall and she stayed there, glaring at him. He rubbed at the flame-coloured weals on his face, his mouth tight. Then he said quietly, "Now what the hell is all this?"

"Get out. I didn't invite you here."

"You didn't –?" Jamie laughed at her. "You've been giving me the come-on ever since you got to Alex!"

There was truth in that – or there had been, in the beginning – and she flushed.

When she didn't answer he said, "And these last few days."

"No." That was different. She had just watched him and wondered at how changed he was from the man she remembered – or had imagined?

"No? You were eager enough. I heard you run to the door."

Had she? Yes, but only in the hope that Mark – "Will you go? Please." But – it was a demand, not a request. "I don't have to explain anything to you."

Jamie watched her shrewdly, "No, you don't. You were expecting somebody else."

"I told you, I don't have to –"

"You had that look about you when you opened the door. I thought it was for me." He took a step towards her, set one hand on the wall by her head and leaned over her. He said, "Mark."

Katy demanded, "What about him?"

He grinned now and did not answer her directly. "You've probably gathered that we're not exactly the best of friends. There's something about me he doesn't like and I think he's a – well, we've never got on. Not that we ever saw much of each other, just the occasional family get-togethers, and he's a silent type as a rule. But a couple of years ago he got riled over something – never mind what it was – and he called me a flash, skirt-chasing bastard. I didn't mind the skirt-chasing bit – I've always believed there was no sense in wasting time – but the 'flash' riled me. I may be many things, but *flash* I am not. Anyway we had a fight and now he goes his way and I go mine." Now he answered her original question: "You want to go his way."

She shook her head. "No."

"So? What does Mark want? Because now, remembering odd remarks made by Bert, and one or two others, it seems to me you've been seeing quite a bit of each other lately."

Katy flushed again, "It's none of your damned business *who* I see! Now – get – *out!*"

Jamie nodded as if he had his answer, but still leaned over her. "I will." And with mocking solemnity, "Out of your life forever." He laughed and went on, "As I said, I don't believe in wasting time and you've made it clear I'd be wasting it around here. Getting the brush-off – as I think you'd put it – doesn't bother me. But Mark might be different." Jamie was still smiling, but he was very serious now. "So you should be sure how you feel about him. Don't keep him on a string; play things straight with him." He paused, thoughtfully. "You've seen those Swordfish, the things Mark flies?"

Katy nodded. She had seen them often, taken note because she knew they were what he flew.

Jamie said, "Big biplanes, like something left over from the last war. They fly some pretty lethal operations. He doesn't need to be screwed up on the ground as well."

Now he pushed away from the wall and opened the door. He stood there a moment. "I told you Mark and I don't get on. Neither one of us would like to see the other come to a sticky end though, so think about it." The door closed behind him.

Katy felt drained by anger and shock, confused. The horrors of the desert returned, stark pictures, and Jamie's words tumbled in her head: You were eager . . . had that look . . . play straight. She stayed slumped against the wall, face buried in her hands, for long minutes. She was alone among strangers, thousands of miles from home, and needed time to sort out her thoughts and emotions.

She was not granted that time. The door shook to a double knock. She thought Jamie Dunbar had returned to taunt her and steeled herself to open it. She would not hide; if he wanted a fight she was ready –

Mark stood outside. His face looked gaunt and his eyes stared but that did not matter. He walked in as of right and she clung to him.

He talked in the night, when their passion was spent and they lay close in the quiet. He told her about the raid on Bomba, was able to tell her because the danger was blunted now, here. He could talk quietly and she listened, remembered Jamie Dunbar's words: "They fly some pretty lethal operations." Bomba had been one of those.

She did not tell him about the desert. Once he asked,

leaning over her, "What have you done to your hair?" He ran his fingers through the soft, short waves, that were jagged-ended as Bert had cut them.

She answered, "It was too hot. I'll have it done properly tomorrow."

In the morning she cooked him breakfast. They had an intimacy now and yet were self-conscious. He was hurrying at the meal's end because he had to get back to Dekheila. He picked up his cap and said, "Cheerio!" No promises, but he stooped to kiss her.

She held him tight then pushed him away, said breathlessly, "Better not start that again." At the door she suddenly remembered: "I'll have to go away again for a few days and it may be soon. I'll let you know beforehand, if I can"

He paused, "Again? You've been away?"

"Bert and I finally got a movement order. We went into the desert."

He stared at her, incredulous, "You mean, among the fighting?"

"I saw some."

"Good God! Why?"

"It's my job." She wouldn't talk about it, wouldn't remember.

Ward said impatiently, "You're not a war correspondent. You just came along with Bert on this one tour. You told me yourself that as soon as your contract runs out you'll be going home."

Maybe she was here with him now, had spent the night with him, because of her time in the desert. She did not voice this thought, but she had argued the other issue before: "It's something I said I'd do and I keep my word, right down the line."

He knew the destruction wrought by the bombs he dropped. An Italian shell could do that to her. "Taking risks up there and all for a few bloody photographs! You're not going again. You don't have to."

"Of course I have to! Just the way you have to fly on – on missions."

112

"It's not the same at all. Can't you see that?"

They were nearly shouting now. "No, I can't! And anyway, it's my decision, has nothing to do with you! Don't give me orders! You don't own me!"

"Oh, for God's sake!"

The door slammed behind him. She stood poised, her anger draining away as quickly as it had come, and heard the clatter of his feet on the stairs, going away, gone. She went to the window and watched him walk off along the street with long, fast strides. Then she sat on the edge of the bed with her hands in her lap and after a while she cried.

Much later she saw there was a space in the neat line of prints. The photograph of herself had been taken.

6

"Fighters!"

Mark found the airfield at Dekheila boiling with activity. Trucks, tail-boards lowered, were backed up to the hangars and stores sheds. Men hurried back and forth, loading the trucks. He found Tim Rogers, who greeted him with: "Where the hell have you been?" But he was grinning, relieved because he could see Mark was not the same man who had walked out last night, stiff-faced and eyes distant.

Mark answered amiably, "Alex. You know damn well. What's going on?"

"I know you went to Alex and I know I told you there was no flying before noon, but you should have shown up on morning parade. Your absence was commented on."

Mark knew that, too, "Well, I suppose I'll be logged." He knew he'd be, but he thought it was worth it.

Tim, nodding towards the loading, told him, "The Fleet has sailing orders."

Two men of the ground crew staggered past, carrying a crate of Swordfish spares between them and cursing its weight.

Mark said, "Morning. Nice day for it."

They laughed, "Morning, sir." They swung the crate in rhythm at the back of a truck and hurled it up and inside.

Mark asked Tim: "We're to escort another convoy to Malta?"

"Suppose so." Tim shrugged, "I only know we're sailing."

Mark went to their tent and packed his kit. That took only minutes. While he was in the taxi rolling out along the coast road from Alexandria he had thought he would go in again this night and see Katy – if his duties permitted. His anger had cooled but he still thought she was taking unnecessary risks in going out into the desert. He was a pilot, the risks he took were not unnecessary. But she'd been right – he could not give her orders.

Now he wondered if she'd also been right when she'd said that going to the desert was her job, as flying was his. Looked at coldly, that was logical. But he could not look at it coldly, because he cared. And now he did not know when he would see her again – if ever.

That thought stopped him dead, staring out of the tent at the airfield. It had often occurred to him before that he might not return from an operation. But now the possibility existed that he might return and she might not . . .

The Victoria transport aircraft wobbled in from Ma'aten Bagush in the afternoon bringing Doug Campbell, rested and clear-headed, Laurel, Hardy and the other fitters, riggers and armourers back from the R.A.F. field. They went on to Alexandria with their stores and kit, to be ferried out to the ship by lighter. *Eagle* and the Fleet sailed in the night, weighing anchor at three forty in the morning of the thirtieth of August. Mark took off in Ethel with the other Swordfish from Dekheila at first light and they flew out to join *Eagle* at sea, on course for Malta.

Katy woke at the distant drone of the engines, ran to the window and watched the big biplanes until they became tiny, then were lost over the rim of the world.

The Fleet had not in fact sailed only to escort a convoy – though convoy there was and they saw it safely to Malta – but also to make a rendezvous south of Sicily.

On the morning of the second of September Mark stood with Tim Rogers on the goofer's platform abaft *Eagle*'s bridge. Their hands were lifted to shade their eyes as they peered out over a sea that glinted in the glare of the low morning sun.

Tim said, "She's big."

Mark nodded, "New."

They were talking of another aircraft-carrier, H.M.S. *Illustrious*. She had come, with the battleship *Valiant* and two

A.A. cruisers, *Calcutta* and *Coventry*, to join Cunningham's Fleet. This rendezvous was the main reason for the Fleet's sailing.

Tim said, "She's tough, from what I hear." *Eagle*'s flight-deck was steel plating clapped on to her World War I battleship hull, but that of *Illustrious* was the top of an armoured box built throughout of steel three inches thick.

"And fast," added Mark. "She can make thirty knots." *Eagle*'s shuddering, flat-out top speed was a bare twenty knots.

A sleek monoplane raced along the flight-deck of *Illustrious*, lifted off and climbed swiftly, steeply. "One of her Fulmars," commented Tim. *Illustrious* carried a squadron of the fighters besides her two squadrons of Swordfish. "They'll take some of the weight off our poor bloody Gladiators." Until now *Eagle*'s three ageing Gloster Gladiators had provided the only fighter cover for the Fleet when out of range of the R.A.F. bases in Egypt or Malta.

Mark summed it up: "She's going to make a difference. And A.B.C. will find work for the two of us."

Admiral A. B. Cunningham did. Two days later Mark made his way up to the gale-swept flight-deck of *Eagle* two hours before dawn. Thirteen Swordfish, Ethel among them, were ranged aft with their engines blatting. Doug Campbell was already aboard, Tim Rogers climbing up. Hardy, the fitter, had swung out of the cockpit and stood on the wing, waiting while Mark put his foot in the first step set in the fuselage and started up.

Six bombs, 250 pounds each, again hung fat and deadly under Ethel's wings. All the Swordfish were similarly bombed-up. They were taking off now in order to raid the Italian airfield of Maritsa on the island of Rhodes at dawn. It was not the only dawn raid to be made on Rhodes that morning. Swordfish from *Illustrious* were to strike the island's other field at Callato.

Mark settled in the cockpit as the twin lines of the deck lights came on, stretching away to *Eagle*'s bow. A green light flashed from the bridge and the first Swordfish rolled forward as the flight-deck officer gestured with his pair of green torches. Mark thought: Thirteen Stringbags? Unlucky? Rubbish. He counted them as they lumbered away along the flight-deck to lift off into the night. One . . . two . . . three . . . four . . . five –

"Hell!" As he said it he heard Tim's anguished cry over the Gosport Tube: "Oh, my God!"

The fifth Swordfish had skidded, smashed one wing and crashed on its nose on the deck. Its load had broken loose under the impact and the six bombs were sliding and skittering about on the rocking flight-deck.

Not long before *Eagle* came to the Mediterranean, a bomb like one of these had exploded in the arming room, killing fifteen men. Such disasters were not forgotten. But now men swarmed unhesitatingly across the deck, hunting down the rolling, lunging monsters, trapping them, wedging them. Armourers carefully removed the detonators and then the bombs were cleared away below.

Meanwhile another party worked feverishly to lift the crew out of the wrecked aircraft. Then it was shoved by hand yard by yard towards the bow. Laurel and Hardy were there, Laurel already inside the cockpit of the wrecked Swordfish with a screwdriver, removing whatever instruments and parts he could. An armourer in the airgunner's cockpit handed out the Vickers and its ammunition, the observer's chartboard, instruments and compass. All of these were precious. They worked in darkness as the wreckage bumped, rocked and slithered along the deck and a howling gale swept in over *Eagle*'s bow as she steamed into wind at close on twenty knots.

When they came to the bow the armourer rolled over the side of the cockpit and dropped to the deck. Hardy climbed onto the crumpled wing and grabbed Laurel under the arms. "Come out, you daft bastard! She's goin' over!"

He yanked Laurel out of the cockpit like a cork from a bottle and the pair of them fell to the deck then crawled clear of the legs of the men shoving and straining at the tangled mass of spars and fuselage.

Laurel stared at it, silhouetted against the night sky. "It looks more like a bloody great bundle of old umbrellas than anything made to fly!" The wreckage disappeared over the edge and the party scattered, running to get clear of the flight-deck.

The green light flashed again from the bridge and the sixth Swordfish rocked forward, the flight-deck ahead of it now clear for the take-off. Ward looked at his watch: they had lost half an hour through the accident. The blue torches of the flightdeck officer beckoned to Ethel and Ward lined her up then took her charging along the deck between the lines of lights and lifted her off into the darkness.

Laurel leaned into the wind, back at his station on the after flight-deck, and sucked gashed knuckles, bleeding from his furious work in the smashed dark cockpit with its score of unseen projections to tear the flesh. He and Hardy watched the small blue glow on Ethel's wings – her formation lights – climb until they were only pinpricks in the night and then they were gone. Another Swordfish flew off and as the thunder of its engine faded Laurel said worriedly, "We lost some time over that crash. Think they'll be all right?"

Both men knew the operation was timed for the Swordfish to strike their target at dawn and no later, catching the Italian fighters still on the ground.

Hardy muttered doubtfully, "Should be . . . well, maybe – if they don't lose any more time."

They did lose more time. The wind had veered around and the Swordfish were flying into it. Dawn came well before they sighted Rhodes and it was broad day when they dived on the airfield at Maritsa and dropped their bombs. As Mark circled away he saw two hangars burning, other buildings in flames and belching smoke from one huge blaze that looked like a fuel dump.

Tim Rogers said, "So far, so good."

Mark did not answer. His eyes behind the goggles searched the sky, narrowed against the low sun, looking for enemy aircraft – but seeing none. As the minutes ticked by he began to hope, even believe, that they might have got away with it.

They were out over the sea when Doug Campbell's voice cracked harshly: "*Fighters!*"

Mark concluded later that the attack from *Illustrious* had gone in on time, at dawn, and stirred up a hornet's nest, so that the Fiat C.R.42s were already in the air and hunting as the twelve Swordfish from *Eagle* turned for home. But such speculations came later. Now there flashed through his mind Tim's wry question before the raid on Bomba: "Suppose we're jumped . . . What do we do?"

And his own answer: "Duck." Then he was trying to suit action to the word. He threw Ethel about desperately to try to avoid the streams of tracer that lashed at him from the swooping Fiats. They were biplanes, like the Swordfish, but smaller and stubbier, and nearly twice as fast. Mark saw the Swordfish on his right go down in flames, then a second. The smoke they trailed drew scars across the white-hatched blue of the sea below. It was a beautiful, golden morning.

Campbell's Vickers hammered again and again. He stood with legs braced wide, feet on the firing steps set on either side of the cockpit. The extra height gave him a better view and field of fire, but it also exposed most of his upper body. Logically he would have been no safer down in the unarmoured cockpit but he felt horribly naked as the C.R.42s came tearing in, their gun muzzles red with flame. He had seen airgunners who had lost this kind of duel, had helped to lift them out of the cockpit and cleaned it afterwards.

He yanked the empty drum from the Vickers and dropped it to the cockpit floor, snatched the spare drum from where it was clipped below the cockpit coaming and fitted it on the Vickers. He was sweating and swearing, tossed around like a spoon shaken in a cup as Ward threw Ethel about the sky, but his fingers were quick and did not fumble, carrying out a drill practised to the point of automation. He cocked the gun and fired as a C.R.42 floated into the ring sight and saw it haul away. Then there was another –

Tim Rogers could do nothing but hold tight as the

Swordfish sideslipped, dived, banked, climbed, hung on the prop near to stalling then fell away so that the streams of enemy tracer lashed the empty air. He could not even take his parachute from its stowage at the front of the cockpit and clip it to his harness.

He knew he was going to die, that the overstretched luck of Ethel's crew was at last running out – the Swordfish could never escape the C.R.42s that were flying rings around it. Ward's aerobatics had saved him more times in the last few minutes than Tim could count but sooner or later, inevitably, they would be hit, hosed with raking bursts, shot to pieces.

So he clung on and waited for the finish as Campbell's Vickers rattled behind him and Ethel swooped and soared. A frozen witness of the fight, suddenly he saw there were no C.R.42s near them. The Vickers stopped firing and then Ethel was flying straight and level. There were two enemy planes in the distance, attacking another Swordfish but then one of them, too, turned away. The second fired another burst, climbed and circled once, then followed the first. Tim peered round in the cockpit, past Campbell, and saw specks far behind them that were the other Italian fighters, heading for home. He realised they must have run out of ammunition.

The crew's luck was still holding – just.

Mark flew on with the other Swordfish that had survived. He circled with them over *Eagle* as she steamed into wind inside her screen of escorting destroyers. He banked to port when it came to his turn and took Ethel in over the round-down, flying carefully, watching the batsman. He made a good landing.

After debriefing he went down to the hangar-deck and found Ethel, her wings folded, Laurel and Hardy working around her, examining her from end to end. Laurel turned as Ward approached and shook his head incredulously. "She's clean as a whistle, sir. Not a mark on her. Most of the others have holes all over them, but not her."

Mark shrugged. "All due to clean-living; or the devil looking after his own."

Laurel laughed. "Not for me to say which, sir." Then sympathetically: "Bad do, sir?"

There were spaces on the hangar-deck now. Mark took a deep breath. The air of the hangar was tinged with the smell of oil and the dope the riggers used on the fabric of the Swordfish. "Yes. We plastered the airfield all right, but coming back wasn't so good." He thought, Oh, very cool, very casual. Their voices echoed in the steel cave. Suddenly he was reminded that the stairwells of the Royal College of Music had echoed just like that. But the College was a long way off now, and not just in distance. So were the song publishers in Denmark Street. He had not written a phrase of music in months.

And almost as if reading Ward's mind, Laurel said, "We've heard they've bombed London again. They're raiding it every day and night, now."

"Yes." Hitler was trying to blast London into ruins and surrender. Mark had friends and relatives there, as had these men. What comfort could he offer them? He watched them working, steadily, carefully, and thought: None. It was they who comforted him.

He went to the wardroom for breakfast and told Tim, "Laurel and Hardy have been all over the old girl. They can't find a scratch on her."

Tim stared at him, "I don't believe it."

"Fact." Mark helped himself to coffee.

"Some bits must have fallen off from the way you tossed her about up there."

"Don't be bloody rude. That was evasive action."

They ate in silence for a time, then Tim said, "We don't want too many mornings like that."

"No."

They had lost four Swordfish, shot down, and the men who flew in them. Friends: men they knew, had laughed and joked with. Mark remembered them as good men, the pilots among them better than himself, more experienced.

He was getting deeper into the tunnel with its narrowing walls. *Eagle* was no longer the only carrier in the Eastern

Mediterranean. Previously an attack mounted by *Eagle* alone would have meant her sailing dangerously close to the Italian mainland and the bombers based there. Now *Illustrious* had brought out overload tanks that nearly doubled the range of all the Swordfish. An attack on Taranto could now be mounted by the carriers while still two-hundred miles away.

Not only was such an attack theoretically possible now; it was also daily growing more desirable. Cunningham could not go on indefinitely looking back over his shoulder for the Italian Fleet. He had to neutralise the threat they posed and if they would not come out of harbour, then . . .

7

Invasion

Eagle returned with the Fleet to Alexandria and while she lay
in the harbour Mark was at Dekheila with the other air crew.
He flew every day and it was a week before he managed to
get a lift into Alexandria and then only for an hour in the
middle of the day. He went to Katy's apartment and stood
outside for a full minute but there was no answer to his
knocking, only silence behind the closed face of the door. He
decided with a sense of relief that she was out; he had not
been sure how to say what must be said.

He ran quickly down the stairs but slowed in the noonday
heat of the street. The truck that brought him in had dropped
him at the Cecil Hotel and would pick him up there. He
looked at his watch and then went into the cool dimness of
the bar. He had time for a drink.

He was halfway through the beer when there was a step
behind him and Jamie Dunbar stood at his side.

Mark said, "Are you still here?"

"I might say the same only I know you've been busy."
Jamie lifted a finger, signalling for a beer. "As it happens I'm
just passing through on my way to the sharp end."

Ward looked at him, noted the neat but faded khaki drill
shirt and corduroy trousers. "You mean you're actually going
to earn your money? Hard luck."

"Oh, I don't know. You meet some nice people up there."
Mark thought of Tim, Campbell, Laurel and Hardy.
"True."

Jamie sipped at his beer. "Seems they're going to need us
all."

Mark said, "That I can believe." He knew that the Italian

Fleet lay in wait at Taranto and Mussolini's army was massing in Libya.

Jamie asked, "Visiting your American poppet?" Then he held up a hand as Mark stiffened. "All right! I think she's a fine girl and you're a lucky man."

Mark eyed Jamie, who met his glare, then: "You've got the wrong end of the stick. I came in to call the whole thing off. But she's out. Or away."

"Well, well. I thought –" Jamie hastily lifted the hand again. "Never mind. It's none of my business."

"That's right."

"Still, I think you're making a mistake. But I suppose you have your reasons."

They lifted their glasses and drank together. They were alone at the bar. They were kin. They might not meet again for months, or years, or – Mark said, "I've had one or two narrow squeaks and it looks as though my luck may be running out."

"Ah. Luck has that habit. I won't insult you by suggesting that you're getting windy."

Mark shook his head. "No more than anybody else. I've had my nasty moments, but the rest of the time I believe it'll happen to the other feller." He paused, then amended: "Well, most of the time."

Jamie nodded agreement, "I've made my will."

"Go on." Mark stared at him, then grinned, "The female beneficiaries should make quite a list."

"Ha!" Jamie gave a snort. "Very funny. But remember that activity takes two. And besides, maybe I've made some mistakes, but I've heard more than one whisper about you. They travel around the family."

"Such as?"

"When you turned all noble over that girl and tried to knock my head off." Jamie fingered the scar over his eye.

"Ah!" Mark's lips twitched, "Well, that wasn't quite the way it looked. In fact it was her boyfriend I knew, and he was out of the country working for his firm, so I just stood in for him. But the truth is, the whole thing was probably just an excuse. I've not seen you very often, but when I have you've always been so bloody sure of yourself. Superior. So just for once I thought I'd belt you – take the smirk off your face."

Jamie chuckled. "Robbie Burns had something to say about seeing ourselves as others see us. Now me, I always thought you were bad-tempered, bloody-minded, sullen – and that you had it in for me."

"I did. Because –"

Jamie said drily, "Yes, I know. We're back where we started."

Mark said tentatively, voicing a strange thought, one he was unsure of: "Maybe – we're too much alike."

Jamie pulled a face. "That's not very nice for either of us, but there could be something in it. However, harking back and just to tidy things up, you might as well know that the girl didn't exactly need all that much seducing. She gave me the biggest come-on this side of Picadilly Circus." He broke off, then: "You don't seem surprised?"

Mark was grinning. "No. A bit after that, she married the boyfriend's boss. Did very well for herself. Now she has a town house *and* a whacking big mansion in the depths of Surrey."

Jamie said ruefully, "And she's not sitting on the edge of the desert waiting for a truck to take her up the line."

They roared with laughter.

Jamie wiped his eyes and looked at his watch, "Mine should be along in a minute."

"And mine."

They lifted their glasses and Jamie said, "We might do this again, sometime." Mark did not answer and Jamie looked at him, saw him lost in thought, face set. Jamie said quietly, "You're a hard man."

"Me!" Mark was jerked out of his thoughts of other men he had thought to meet again, who had not returned from Rhodes.

Jamie nodded, "I've seen it in some men. They didn't kill by pushing a button or ordering a barrage. They did it with the butt, or the bayonet – or their bare hands. They didn't enjoy it but they didn't hate it either. Killing just didn't bother them, was just something they did, like walking or breathing. I can see that in you."

Mark laughed. Jamie didn't really know him.

"All right," said Jamie, and grinned. "Forget it." But Mark would see, he thought, when the time came.

Mark said, "But as for doing this again – good idea. Next time we're both in Alex. Cheerio."

"Cheerio."

They drained their glasses and walked out together to the trucks.

Katy slept that night at Mersa Matruh, a white-walled village by the sea, with a railway station and scattered palms rooted in parched earth. Bert had cajoled another movement order out of Headquarters in Cairo and they were bound for the front at Sollum. Jamie was not with them: Bert had been told that Captain Dunbar was back with his battalion. Instead they had as escorting officer a youth of nineteen, a very new second-lieutenant with an engaging, white-toothed smile. He said his name was Hartington-Smythe: "But the chaps call me Harry."

Bert said, "O.K. Lootenant. Harry it is."

Katy felt ten years older than the fresh-faced Harry, who was smitten and could not take his eyes off her.

On the second day out of Alexandria they drove on from Mersa to Buq-Buq in the two eight-hundredweight trucks. Harry, his driver and wireless operator were in the first. Bert and Katy followed, driven by Powell as before. The road was a good, metalled surface as far as Sidi Barrani but after that was no better than a track through the desert. Powell drove off to the right of the lead truck, so avoiding the dust cloud it threw up but they still collected their own layer of sand and Powell muttered under his breath, cursing it.

Bert and Katy, squeezed together in the front of the truck beside Powell, bounced and swayed in rhythm with its motion. Bert shouted above the engine's grinding and the creaking of the suspension: "The Nazis are bombing the hell out of London!"

Katy, clinging on, answered automatically, "I know! I guess it must be pretty awful!"

Her indifference must have shown. Bert glanced at her quizzically, "Yeah? Try to imagine them bombing Manhattan."

That was different. She knew Manhattan and could picture it under attack. Katy shivered, even in the heat of the day.

Buq-Buq was just a map reference. There was no building, only a depression in the flat emptiness of the desert in which a few trucks were scattered, camouflaged, with slit trenches dug alongside each truck in case of attack from the air. This was a battalion headquarters and Bert went with Hartington-Smythe to seek information. Meanwhile the drivers brewed tea over their petrol can stoves.

Bert returned and told Katy, "They say there's been a lot more air activity, Italian bombing raids and fighter sweeps, but otherwise the front is quiet." He thrashed a hand at the flies whirling above his mug of tea, then worked a cigarette from the pack in his shirt pocket and stuck it in his mouth, thumbing his lighter into flame pale in the glare of the sun. "Up to now it's been a phony war out here –" He paused. Katy thought there had been nothing phony about the dead at the fort. Bert blew smoke at the flies then finished sombrely, "– But a war like that blew wide open in France not so long ago."

And now Hitler's soldiers lounged on the boulevards of Paris.

In the evening they came to a village and Bert murmured, "I've seen some one-horse dumps in my time –" He surveyed the prospect sardonically.

There was a customs post, a group of small, white stone houses and a short jetty poking out into the blue water of the bay. That was all. Then Bert checked, whistled softly, impressed, and went on: "– but, boy! That is some table-top!" Beyond the houses a cliff rose steeply to a high plateau that ran southwards, away into the desert to be lost in distance.

Katy leaned over Bert to peer out through the dusty wind-screen at the cliff. It was as if the coastal plain along which they had driven had fractured along a sharp edge and dropped to leave the plateau high above them. Katy's eyes came slowly down again to the houses. "We were aiming for Sollum. This is it?"

Bert shook his head. "This has to be the bottom half of Sollum. I guess we want the top half." He pointed to the cliff-top and Katy saw that the road ran on past the little houses then wound up the cliff right over the sea.

"Wow!" She sat back as Powell drove through lower Sollum. Men of the Royal Engineers worked among the houses and along the road.

Bert said, "They're laying mines."

Powell changed down then drove the eight-hundredweight cautiously up the steep and winding road in the gathering dusk. Katy muttered, looking out and down the drop outside the offside wheels, "If it's dark when we come down, I'll walk."

Bert chuckled, "I'll go along with that."

Then the road ran level again and the plateau opened before them. Here was upper Sollum and Katy said drily, "This isn't exactly a boom town, either." In the twilight they could see the loom of a barracks, white and without a light – empty. Nearby was an airstrip, the desert cleared of rocks, straight and flat with a wind-sock flapping from a mast. There were no aircraft.

Bert muttered, "Home, sweet home."

The trucks halted in the rear of the barracks and a hundred yards or more away. The young officer climbed down, came back to the second truck and told Bert: "I'm going forward to tell the chaps holding the line in front that we're here. You may as well bed down. We might have to move at first light."

Bert asked, "Who are the guys out front of us?"

Harry was smiling admiringly at Katy and turned reluc-tantly back to Bert, "We've a platoon of Coldstreams up here, dug in just forward of the barracks."

"The map shows a place called Musaid –" Bert pointed

inland along the plateau, now clothed in darkness, "– over there, right?"

Hartington-Smythe nodded, "Just a few miles south. It's only another old Egyptian barracks, empty, like this one. We pulled our chaps out of there days ago. You'll see it in the morning." He smiled again at Katy then walked away into the gloom.

The two drivers shook out the camouflage nets and draped them over the trucks. When that was done Katy crept in under the net beside their truck and unrolled her sleeping-bag. She spread her overcoat on top of it, both for the extra warmth and to be handy in the morning. Her sweater she rolled around her camera to use as a pillow, then wriggled into the bag. Bert worked into his own bag beside her but sat with his back propped against the rear wheel of the truck, staring through the net at the dark sky. He was silent for a time. They could hear the murmur of voices as the two drivers and the wireless-operator drew lots for the order in which each should patrol as sentry, two hours at a time throughout the night. Then the voices died and there was only the faint scuff of the sentry's boots in the dust, the whisper of the wind and the slap of the truck canopies as the wind beat the canvas against the steel frames.

Bert said thoughtfully, "There's just one platoon, thirty men at most, out there in front of us." His head turned to Katy and she saw the pale blur of his face. He went on: "Remember what I told you after our last trip into the desert? Well, between you and me, it looks like I was right. From what I'm told, what I've seen, the British are in real trouble. Wavell's army is outgunned and outnumbered five to one. He's bluffing. There's precious little between the Italians and the Suez Canal."

Bert shifted restlessly. "Then there's the sea. The Italian Fleet is still as big a threat as ever. Cunningham hasn't been able to touch it." He wriggled down into his bag, turned over to sleep but muttered worriedly, "It doesn't look good. No, sir."

Katy stared up at the stars, heard the young officer return

from the line and exchange a few words with the sentry, then bed down by his truck. She listened to the silence, a brooding quiet, thinking over what Bert had said. This day that was ending was the twelfth of September. There were only two months of her contract left to run.

The quiet . . .

"Stand to!"

Katy woke at the call of the sentry, quickly sloughed off her sleeping-bag and dressed. She sat on the bag beside Bert under the net, huddled inside her overcoat and with the camera slung around her neck. She watched the sky lighten in the east and now there was that eerie red line along the horizon and the first brilliant shaft of sunlight. A white building stood in the distance: the barracks at Musaid.

A shudder ran through the earth beneath her but she did not realise what it was and wondered for a second if she had imagined it. Then she caught her breath as the thunder of the barrage rolled across the plateau and the flashes stood like a long fence of flames where the shells burst around Musaid.

Bert threw at her: "It's started!" He clawed his way out from under the net.

What had started? The Italian invasion? Of course. Katy followed him, shivering in the early chill, as he hurried with long, gangling strides to the corner of the barracks and paused there. Katy peeped cautiously around his shoulder. Together they watched as the barrage went on, finally ceased.

Katy was aware of voices behind her, turned her head and saw the young officer and the soldiers rolling the camouflage net from his truck. Powell was with them; they had cleared away the net from his eight-hundredweight first. Her sleeping-bag and Bert's had gone: Powell had thrown them into the truck.

A runner came doubling back from the direction of the Coldstreams' forward position, running along the side of the barracks towards them. He carried his rifle at the trail, his boots kicked up little spurts of dust and his steel helmet wobbled. He halted when he came up to them. His face, burned reddish-brown by the sun, glistened with sweat that poured down from under the helmet.

He panted, "Officer's compliments, but he says the Eyeties are moving in on Musaid and he reckons this place will be next, so would you please be so good as to get down the road off the escarpment quick as you can?"

Bert grumbled, "I've waited one hell of a long time to get up here and report this war. I don't see any reason to pull out because –"

The whistling shriek cut him off and the soldier bawled, "Get down!" He pulled the pair of them down with him. Then the shells burst. Katy felt each one as a blow on the ears, an upward kick of the ground under her. Dust lifted and hung in a thickening cloud that blinded her and set her coughing. The barrage went on interminably but finally slowed, faltered into silence.

The soldier stood up, coughing and spitting, cursing under his breath. Bert and Katy shakily followed suit. The dust was settling or drifting away on the wind. There were holes punched in the roof and walls of the barracks and craters stippled the desert.

Bert looked back at the truck the soldiers had been working on and said huskily, "Oh, sweet Jesus!"

It had taken a direct hit and was a smoking, crumpled mass of scrap. Bodies were tossed around it. The runner strode over to them, looked at each in turn then across at Powell's truck, only ten yards away but apparently unharmed. He turned and trotted back to Bert and told him flatly, "Nobody can do a thing for them, poor sods." Then he peered past Bert and Katy disbelievingly, and said, "Here! Look at that!"

They turned and saw the invading army drawn up in the middle distance, ready to advance but as if on parade. Motor-cyclists stood in the van, followed by light cars and their columns of trucks that stretched away until lost to sight. The runner said, "There's millions o' the bastards!" Then: "I've got to get back." He looked sternly at Bert and Katy. "Remember them orders. Get down that road *jilty*." Then he straightened his helmet and doubled away along the side of the barracks, back to the twenty-odd guardsmen who waited to take on the advancing army.

Jilty. Katy knew now that it was another Indian word and meant "quick". She did her best, trying not to shake as she took her photographs, thinking: Oh God! Bert's gone too far this time. He's really landed us in it.

His voice came, mildly irascible: "When you're all through here? The truck looks O.K. so maybe we'd better get the hell out."

Katy ran with him to the truck, trying not to look at the dead. But she had to pass close among them, saw more than she wanted, saw Powell, friendly Powell, with half his chest blown away. She gagged, sobbed, sick to her stomach.

Bert panted. He was no longer young, and the run of a hundred yards had left him breathless, leaning on the wing of the truck. "You claimed once before – that you could drive this thing. Now looks a good time – to try."

Holes were ripped in the canvas tilt and there looked to be new dents in the brown and grey bodywork but Katy slid in behind the wheel and the engine fired at her third attempt. Bert had dragged himself in. Katy jammed the truck into first gear, swung it around in a circle and drove down the narrow, winding road from the plateau, the sea glinting blue on her left and below. Engineers were busy along the road and Bert said still panting, "They're getting ready to activate the mines, I guess."

The flat *crack*! and rapping of rifle and machine-gun fire followed them as they wound around the bends. At the bottom Katy changed up and drove along the road back through Sollum and on, until they passed a battery of twenty-five-pounder guns in a staggered line under their camouflage nets. They were not sunk in pits, because the desert made for hard digging, but poked their barrels over low walls of piled rocks.

Bert was improving. He said, "Pull in here," pointing to a shallow depression that ran down to the road, possibly once a river-bed, now lined with straggling scrub. Katy swung the truck into it and stopped the engine. In the silence they could hear the now distant crackle and *thump*! of the fighting up on the plateau.

They got out and draped the camouflage net over the

stubby eight-hundredweight then walked slowly back along the depression towards the guns. Bert's fieldglasses swung from the strap around his neck and Katy cradled her camera in one hand. She thought, March to the sound of the guns. She'd heard or read that phrase. It had an ugly, frightening meaning now.

The depression widened and the guns lay ahead of them, squatting behind their rough parapets. A camouflaged truck was parked in the rear and Bert headed for it. As they came up to it a sergeant ducked out from under the draped nets and confronted them, "Stone me!" He stared at Katy. In spite of the overcoat, slacks and boots, wide-brimmed hat crammed on her head, she was a woman, no doubt of it, and on his gun position. Then, as he turned to Bert, he noted the war correspondent flashes on both their shoulders. "Shouldn't you have a conducting officer, sir – miss?"

Bert said, "We did. He was killed up by the barracks at Sollum. So were the drivers and the wireless-operator."

"Ah!" The sergeant nodded. "Well, the captain's on a shoot at the moment. Maybe when things are quieter he'll be able to see you."

"That's O.K.," Bert said seriously. "We didn't have an appointment."

The sergeant grinned and asked, "Is that a Canadian accent, sir?"

Bert shook his head. "American, U.S. of A."

"Go on. You're a long way from home."

Bert said drily, "Aren't we all? What's going on, anyway?"

The sergeant pointed. "The Coldstreams have pulled out from up on the plateau where you were. Now the Eyeties are coming down the road from the barracks to the village at the bottom."

Bert used his binoculars then passed them to Katy. She adjusted the focus and saw the cliff, the snaking road. Light sparked and she winced, then realised it was the sun's rays reflecting from the windscreen of a truck. It rounded a shoulder in the steep descent and passed out of her sight.

The sergeant said, " See the truck, miss?"

Katy shuddered as the guns fired a salvo, the shock catching her breath. She gulped. "Yes."

"We've noticed that if we fire when one disappears round that bend it'll just show around the next bend when the shells come down there."

She waited and watched with the glasses at her eyes, saw the truck appear again, then it was hidden by smoke and clouds of dust as the shells burst. When the wind blew the clouds away the truck lay on its side. But she saw Italian infantry spilling down past the litter of wrecked vehicles to the plain, like a grey stream washing around rocks. The stream became a river when it reached the foot of the track, flowing slowly through the now shattered buildings of Sollum.

The twenty-five-pounders and the battalion of British infantry who defended the coast road gave before the steadily moving enemy tide. They fought until a position became untenable then moved back to another. Katy and Bert went with the guns on each move and the tide only halted when night fell. It seemed the Italians did not want to risk an action in the dark. Katy positioned the truck in rear of the guns. She and Bert draped the camouflage net over it, ate cold corned beef and biscuits then dozed fitfully, woken again and again by sporadic fire as Italian sentries saw, or thought they saw British patrols.

By the afternoon of the next day, the fourteenth of September, they had withdrawn past Buq-Buq. Red-eyed from lack of sleep, Bert and Katy were still with the artillery. She overheard one sweating gunner mutter, "They can keep the bloody place. There's Buq-Buq bugger all there anyway." That was true enough but the Italians were still advancing.

During the fifteenth the withdrawal went on to Alam Hamid. The twenty-five pounders were firing faster than ammunition could be brought up for them, so when their current supply of shells was exhausted the guns would be hooked on to the trucks and filtered back through the infantry now dug in behind them. The entire operation, apparently, was being described as an "Orderly withdrawal".

Bert growled, "Withdrawal? To me it looks like a retreat.

But I'm damned if I can see what else they can do." He glanced sideways at Katy where she sat at the wheel of the eight-hundredweight intent on her driving, eyes squinted against the clouds of dust thrown up by the bouncing, swayings guns ahead. He asked her, "Have you figured out the forces involved around here?"

Katy said, "I think so. There's something like one battalion of infantry. Under a Colonel Moubray."

Bert nodded, "Coldstream Guards."

"And this battery of guns and the armoured cars."

"That's about the size of it. This Moubray, he's got another couple of companies of foot soldiers and a few medium guns as well, but that's the lot – maybe 2000 men." He jabbed his thumb over his shoulder. "And back there are five Italian *divisions*, 50,000 men! This bout is strictly no contest, a mismatch."

Katy was unamused, "You're not reporting the fights from Madison Square Garden now."

Bert grinned irrepressibly through the sweat. "Boy, do I know it!"

On the sixteenth they had retreated to Alam El Dab and Sidi Barrani was at their backs. Katy waited by the truck, sitting under the spread camouflage netting in the illusion it gave of dappled shade. The sun was overhead, her body ran with sweat and she seemed to have lived through an eternity in the desert. But her main worry was about film. She had taken many pictures and was down to her last three rolls.

Bert had gone to the gunners' command truck to seek what information there was. Suddenly she noticed him hastening back to her, his shambling walk now a shambling gallop. She scrambled to her feet and began heaving off the camouflage net as she saw the gunners hurriedly striking theirs. She had come to know these warning signs, watched for them.

Bert panted up and wheezed, "Let's get the hell outa here! There's fifty Italian tanks working around inland to outflank us. The guns just got the order to pull out." The towing trucks were rolling up now for the guns to be hooked on to.

Bert helped Katy to lash the rolled camouflage net on top of the truck. She slid in behind the wheel, pressed the starter and the engine whirred but did not fire. She tried again without success. Bert muttered, "Oh, Jesus." But then the engine started and Katy gunned it, slotted in the gear and the truck jerked away over the dusty earth. Behind them came the guns.

By nightfall the Italians were in Sidi Barrani regrouping, and the twenty-five pounders had withdrawn to the east. Thankful for the respite, Katy dozed in her sleeping-bag beside the truck but she woke when Bert spread his own bag alongside her. He said quietly, "I hear the British have an armoured division, the 7th, up on the plateau. It's below strength but the plan is, when the Italians reach Mersa Matruh, – and that's only another sixty miles along the coast – the British will hit them with that division. It's supposed to cut off the head of the Italian advance, isolate it and then destroy it."

Katy, watching his face, said, "You don't like that idea."

"It's a great idea – if it works. If it doesn't, then the road to Cairo and the Suez Canal is wide open."

Katy slept badly that night despite the accumulated weariness of long days spent on the battlefield. She stared out through the net at the stars and the flares that drifted and burned occasionally over Sidi Barrani where the Italians were nervously searching for British patrols. Would this be France all over again? Not a terrifyingly quick *Blitzkrieg* like that launched by the German Panzers but a slow inexorable flood of Italian divisions in overwhelming numbers rolling down over Alexandria and on to Cairo.

And she thought about Mark Ward. She'd had to leave Alex without telling him. Many days had passed then. She still needed to make a decision.

It was a quiet dawn, and as the day wore on the Italians made no move. At noon a score of aircraft milled in a dog fight far down the coast towards Sollum. Bert said, "Looks like the British are bombing the roads, trying to cut their supply lines."

Katy remembered Jamie Dunbar's talk of the dangerous missions flown by *Eagle*'s pilots. Those aircraft over Sollum – were they Swordfish? They were too far away to be identified. A man had to have skill, single-minded concentration and luck up there if he was to survive. She watched one of the distant planes spiral down, trailing a thin feather of smoke that puffed into a ball as it crashed on the dust and rock of the coastal plain.

Bert asked, "What's the matter?"

Katy took her hands from her face, "Nothing." She turned and walked away. He started to follow her, puzzled and concerned, but she said, "Just leave me alone, Bert. Please."

The Italians were reported to be digging in and next day Bert said, "We're going to Alex. We'll turn over this buggy to the Army there and I'll leave you and catch the train to Cairo, file my story and be back in a day or two. Give me your films and I'll get 'em developed."

"Do you think they'll let us use them?"

"Some, maybe."

"What about the others?"

"They'll keep them and give them back to you after the war."

"You're kidding."

But he wasn't. Such censorship routines were well established.

Katy spent most of her time in Alexandria either bathing or sleeping. *Eagle* was in port but she did not see Ward and concluded, rightly, that he was flying missions. She was disappointed – or relieved, could not make up her mind which was true.

When Bert returned and they went out to some nameless place in the desert again, in another truck and with another escorting officer, they found nothing had changed. Bert walked back from Headquarters – a widely dispersed group of camouflaged vehicles – to where Katy waited by their eight-hundredweight. He said, "The Intelligence guys report the Italians are building fortifications at Sidi Barrani and they're working on the road up from Sollum. They're not going anywhere for a long while, I guess."

He took off his hat and wiped sweat from his brow with the back of his hand. "I reckon Wavell's bluff is still working. This fighting retreat has got the Italians thinking they're

137

up against tough opposition so they're playing it slow and cautious. They're going to build a good road to bring up their supplies from Bardia and they won't move till that's done and those supplies are stockpiled."

The crew of an armoured car were working around their vehicle nearby. All of them eyed Katy in her khaki drill shirt and trousers and one called across, "How long did you sign on for, miss? Or are you in for the duration, like us?"

Katy laughed with them, but she could go home soon. Less than two months of her contract remained.

Bert said, "Too late to start back today. We'll stay the night and go to Alex tomorrow."

"O.K." Then Katy asked, curious: "You said 'the Intelligence guys report'. How do they find out?"

Bert shrugged. "They take all sorts of scraps of information, put them together like clues, try to make a single picture. Photographs and sightings from aircraft, patrols sent out on foot in the night. Add 'em all up. That kinda thing."

Katy said, "I see."

But she did not, really. It couldn't be as easy as he was making out.

Jamie whispered, "Wait here."

Corporal Timms nodded. "Watch out for yourself, sir."

The rest of Jamie's patrol, six men, were spread out to the rear, prostrate on the sand and rock of the desert, hidden amongst its scrub, invisible.

The Italian line was close. Usually on these patrols you couldn't see a damn thing and found out where the enemy was mostly by listening, but tonight Jamie could see the irregular humps of the emplacements, the strung webs of barbed-wire. He moved forwards, snaking along on his belly. He wore a sweater over his khaki shirt, corduroy trousers and suede shoes. A Balaclava helmet was pulled on over his head. His face blackened, he held his pistol in his right hand. There was no moon but the sky was clear and sprinkled with stars so he needed cover. He had to work from one patch of stunted vegetation or dry scrub to the next.

He was there to assess enemy strengths, to gain some idea of how many men held this section of the line, how many machine-guns, how they were deployed. This was his third and last close reconnaissance of the night. After this they would start the long trek back to their own lines. Jamie had been detailed to lead the patrol because he was good at this, probably the best.

He was near to the wire now, moving very slowly, one hand questing cautiously on the ground ahead for mines. Now he could touch the wire, but he was at pains not to. There might be tins hung on it, or some other form of alarm. The wire spread away into the distance on either side – except for a place to his right, maybe a dozen yards away, where there looked to be a gap. To his left front was a sand-bagged pit under sagging camouflage and *that*, he knew, was a machine-gun emplacement; there was the dull gleam of a barrel in the black hole between the sand-bags.

He edged along to his right, slowly, carefully, and – there *was* a gap. And beyond it, another ten yards on and ten yards behind the wire, was another machine-gun pit, similar to the emplacement on this side of the missing section of wire. He lay still, staring at the gap, and thought: Invitation? "Come into my parlour said the spider to the fly." Balls to that. No point. So, what then? Was this just a place they'd missed out of carelessness? No. He could see double shadows to the wire on either side of the gap, suggesting it had been cut and rolled back on itself. So –

He grinned, squirmed around and worked back the way he had come until he heard a soft challenging hiss in front of him, to which he whispered in reply: "Dunbar."

"Come in."

He moved on and came face to face with Corporal Timms, lying behind his rifle. Jamie said softly, "Wire. Two m-g posts. Good defensive position. Got that?"

"Wire. Two m-g posts."

Jamie nodded. "Right, now I think they've come through, so let's set up a party."

Crawling on hands and knees, he skirted Timms and saw

the men moving, turning to follow him, shifting dark shapes. He knew where he was going and led them, seeking his way, the terrain laid out in his mind's eye. He was soon on his feet, far enough now from the eyes behind the machine-guns for that to be safe, and moving in a crouching walk. Now he was intent not only on the ground in front of him but the shadows and darkness ahead.

This was the place; he'd noticed it on the way over. There was a winding depression between two ridges. It had seemed to offer good cover on the way to or from the Italian wire but he had distrusted it and given it a wide berth.

He waved Timms and the patrol down into cover and went forward alone. Cautiously he worked around to the rear of the lower of the two ridges, scouted its slopes and found them empty. He returned to the patrol and led them around to the rear of the high ridge. Again he left them deployed about fifty yards from the foot of the ridge and went on alone.

He did not have to go far. There was cover and shadow at the foot of the ridge, enough to hide him as he worked in on his belly, but no cover at the top of it. He lay still for some minutes at the foot and was able to see, one after the other, the slight movements of men on the crest of the ridge, easing themselves in cramped positions on the cold earth.

He counted four, but from the way they were spaced along the crest he guessed there were others between them that he could not see. He thought there would be a dozen to twenty. They had come out through the gap in the wire early in the night and laid here in ambush ever since. They had been waiting when he led his patrol over. If he had taken that inviting route through the depression –

He made his way back to his men, moving slowly and carefully. He went to each one in turn and gave his orders, then watched them deploy in a line along the route leading from the ridge to the more distant Italian wire. He took his own place in the line, nearest the Italian wire and farthest from the ridge. He lay down, looked at his watch and thought, Not long now. There was little of the night left. He waited.

He could have done with a drink: a large Scotch. It was

140

bloody cold. He wondered if he might wangle a few days in Cairo while things were quiet? There was a nurse in the Army hospital there who –

The enemy were moving, had given up their ambush for the night. They stood up raggedly and trailed down off the ridge in a straggling file. Although they were still just shadows, as the file headed towards Jamie he was better able to count them, and was certain there were more than a dozen. They would pass within about twenty yards of him and that was close enough for a grenade, so he eased one from his pocket. He waited until the leading shadow was almost abreast of him. The Italians had shape now: square helmets, rifles carried two-handed, slow-trudging legs and boots.

He pulled the pin from the grenade, heard the *twang*! as the clip sprang free, shoved himself up on one keee and lobbed the grenade overhand then sprawled on his face again. He heard a yell, a shot, and reached down, gripped the butt of his pistol and drew it from its holster. Then his grenade exploded, and three more, one – two – three – four, from other members of his patrol. His remaining riflemen opened up a rapid fire.

Jamie raised himself again and squinted to see, his night vision temporarily destroyed by the flashes. He saw enough and yelled, "Cease fire!" He heard the order passed down the line. The men had been expecting it because he had told them, "We want a prisoner or two." That would round off the patrol's success: a prisoner to take back for interrogation.

The firing stopped and Jamie trotted forward, pistol in hand. One enemy soldier was on his knees, his hands in the air. The others lay in a ragged line, as they had trudged. The ambush had been murderous; there was only that one survivor, and he was shaking, in a state of shock.

Jamie thought his condition was little wonder. The Italians had been stiff, cold, hungry and weary, looking forward to breakfast and hot coffee. Then the grenades and rifle-fire had come at them out of the darkness of the desert, at point-blank range. Jamie felt no remorse, however: they had been waiting to do very much the same to him.

He got his patrol moving at the double with two of them hustling the prisoner along between them. As they passed the ridge a machine-gun hammered from beyond the wire and a line of tracer swept slowly across the desert floor like a scythe, but short of the patrol.

Jamie called, "Corporal Timms!"

"Sir?"

"Give me your rifle. Got any tracer?" Jamie took the Lee-Enfield and the handful of clips from the corporal, handed him the pistol. "That's no damn good. You keep going with these ridges at your back. I'll keep 'em occupied for a few minutes."

"Sir!"

Timms loped away and Jamie dropped down into cover at the foot of the ridge. He ejected the cartridges from the rifle, reloaded with tracer, set the sights and settled down. He fired at the machine-guns – two of them were winking now, looking to be the ones he had last located. He aimed carefully and fired steadily, although he knew he had little chance of putting a bullet through the slit in the machine-gun emplacement. But they would know they were under fire and the tracer would show them where it was coming from.

Soon they were firing at him, the little red fire-flies curving in to smack and whicker around the ridge. He worked back until the ridge lay between him and the guns, giving him cover, then got to his feet and trotted after the patrol, somewhere ahead in the darkness.

The machine-guns still rattled away but he took no notice. There was a saying among his men: the Eyeties couldn't hit a barndoor with a shovel. It had been a good patrol he thought: information gathered, a prisoner taken, a nasty, demoralising defeat inflicted on the enemy and no casualties suffered. He felt strong, fit and happy. He thought again of Cairo. There was that nurse – he'd talked to her when last in the hospital to see the doctors and be passed fit – he'd sized her up, unerringly. Damn! What was her name? But he remembered her slender legs, the thrust of her breasts, and her haunches moving seductively under the cotton dress as she walked away, knowing he was watching her. That was something to look forward to –

Katy shivered through the familiar pre-dawn vigil of "stand-to" and then watched the glorious sunrise light the desert. It would be her last for a while. She and Bert were returning to Alexandria that morning.

She stooped out from under the camouflage net, wrapped in her overcoat against the cold of the morning. Bert returned from a restless scouting around the area, talking to soldiers, seeking copy and the human touches to colour his dispatches. His shambling gait was more disjointed than usual because of early morning stiffness. He called to her, "Hey! Let's get over to H.Q. They tell me there's a patrol come back. We might hear something good."

Katy followed Bert across to the camouflaged tent that was the headquarters of the brigade. A soldier squatted on his heels by the side of the tent and in front of the usual tin of petrol-soaked sand that flamed palely in the sunlight. A kettle was starting to hiss on top of it.

A small table covered with a blanket stood at the front of the tent and a staff major sat behind it. A soldier stood at ease before him. The major was immaculate; the soldier less so, streaked with dust and sweat, wearing a Balaclava helmet rolled up on his head like a close-fitting woollen cap. He leaned forward to put a notebook and a bundle of stained khaki rags on the table and said, "He copped it, sir."

Bert stepped in impetuously. "Who copped it? Enlisted man? Officer? What branch?"

The major's face was brick-red from the sun and bisected horizontally by an implacable, bristling moustache. Bert was old enough to be his father but the major glared at him and said frigidly, "Do you mind? I am taking this man's report."

Bert muttered, "Sorry." Katy expected the Englishman to tell him to get the hell out of it.

Surprisingly, the major did not. He seemed to have completely lost interest in the two civilians as he turned the notebook over almost tenderly in his hands. Like the scraps of rag, the book too was badly stained. He said, quietly, "Go on, Corporal."

The corporal said, "It was mortars, sir. He wouldn't have known a thing about it. We heard them stonking the area, and when it quietened down again but he didn't show up, I went back with a couple of men. The place was like it had been dug over. You couldn't put a foot between the craters. That was all that was left of him, that bit of his shirt and the book in the pocket."

The major said, "A great pity."

"Bloody shame, sir. Mister Dunbar was a good soldier, good officer."

"Jamie Dunbar?" The name was jerked out of Katy, like a cry of pain.

The corporal's head snapped around, startled by the girl's voice. The major said, "Yes, Captain Jamie Dunbar." Then watching her, he said carefully, "You – er – knew him?"

Katy guessed what that hesitation meant – a woman who "knew" Jamie Dunbar. But she didn't care; shock kept her face pale under its sunburn. "I met him. I know a relative of his."

Bert was silent on the drive back and they were in the outskirts of Alexandria before he said, "You know, I've been thinking. And it's like this, Katy honey – Mussolini has been threatening Greece for some while. I guess it's late in the year, so he probably won't march till the spring, but – aw, the hell with it!" He flapped a hand, discarding cold logic. "There's no action here and I have this hunch. Sometimes I'm right and sometimes I'm wrong, but how about us taking a look at Greece? What do you say?"

After a moment Katy said, "That's fine by me." She had made her plans and would tell Bert about them soon, but not now.

Bert added, "We'll only be gone three, maybe four weeks, so keep your apartment on."

She made no reply to that.

Bert glanced at her and said, "Too bad about Jamie."

"Yes."

"He was a nice guy –"

Katy cut in harshly, "Let's not make a big production out of it, Bert."

"O.K. I'm sorry."

The truck dropped Katy at her apartment. She did not know the name of this driver. Powell was dead, and young Hartington – "Call me Harry" – Smythe. And Jamie Dunbar. And –

Bert said, "I'll wash up and call around at six. We'll go some place and eat."

Katy promised, "I'll be ready."

She took a shower, luxuriating in it, then put on a white cotton dress, simple and cool. By then it was close to six and she went down to the street to meet Bert because she had promised she would be ready.

Ward was walking towards the apartment building and had almost reached it when she stepped out onto the pavement. They halted a yard apart. Neither cared to move closer. He said, "Hello."

"Hi!"

"I was coming to see you." He saw that in spite of shadows of fatigue around her eyes she looked very pretty. He took a breath; time it was said, time it was over and done with.

Katy knew that his black glower did not signify anger, but rather that there was something on his mind. She got in first: "I wanted to see you, Mark." Get this over with! "I'm going away, crossing to Greece with Bert. Soon. And then on to the U.S. I wanted to say good-bye. I won't be coming back."

"I see."

Did he? There was no change in the expression on his face. She asked, "Have you heard about Jamie?"

Mark had come to make his own speech, was trying to take her words in, scowling. "What's he got to do with it? I saw him a week ago. He was going up the line."

"He was killed in the desert."

"Jamie?" Ward did not want to believe it.

Katy said, "Blown to pieces . . . I'm just not doing any good here, Mark. And I know it's silly, but everybody I get to know seems to die. Except you . . . Anyway, I've made up my mind – I'm going home."

"I think you're doing the right thing." Ward thought she would be well out of this. He was thinking now not only of Jamie but of many others, especially of the pilot killed in training and his young widow in borrowed black at the grave-side, streaming tears, ungainly, so big-bellied with child that she leaned back on her heels. He said, "A clean break. No letters."

Katy nodded, "That's what I want, too. And no hard feelings?"

"No."

"I'm sorry."

One corner of Mark's mouth went up. "So am I. But maybe we'd have been sorrier any other way. So – all the best."

"Take care."

They were still that yard apart. He grinned, turned away and in that awful moment she thought he had a look of Jamie Dunbar – a look of death. But as he strode off she told herself that was only because he and Jamie were cousins.

Bert had seen them together as he wound through the crowds on the pavement. He thought they made a brave, good-looking couple. When he reached Katy he said, "I saw you talking to your Navy flyer. Are we still eating?"

"Sure." She smiled brightly. "He had to go."

Bert studied her. "Is that all?"

"Yes." She would tell him later if she had to, if he pressed her, and she guessed he would. She chattered cheerfully all evening but ate little and blamed the heat.

Mark walked around for a long time, avoiding the bar at the Cecil, then went back to his tent on the airfield at Dekheila.

They were both sure they had made the right, sensible decision.

Ward had been told that morning that the attack on Taranto was a certainty now, and soon, in at most a month. The operation even had a code-name. JUDGMENT.

Intermission

It was quiet in the room but for the slow chunking of the long-case clock standing against the wall. Sunlight streamed in through the window but Sarah shivered. A door banged above them in the house, then again, like a distant gun. Mark Ward got up stiffly from his chair. "The wind has shifted around. I'd better fasten that door."

He walked out to the hall, the labrador slouching at his heels and Sarah was left in the quiet room but not alone – the girl and the young man were still with her.

Ward's story, measured and matter-of-fact, had not been a monologue. Sarah had asked questions, but only when there was some point or technical comment she had not understood. He had not told the full story but she could fill in the gaps he had tactfully skated around. The way of a man with a maid . . .

He returned and stood at the door. "I think we're due for some lunch." He held the door for her and as she reached it she saw a photograph, as dated as the other two, yellowing. It hung on the wall by the clock, where a man looking up to find the time would see it. Some thirty-odd young men in white shirts and shorts were ranked facing the camera. A line sat on chairs with another line standing behind them, while a few sat cross-legged on the deck. They were on a ship with a glimpse of a guard-rail and another vessel, blurred and out of focus, cleaving through the sea in the background. They grinned at the camera, confident, cheerful, their lives ahead of them, and this photograph was a lark.

Sarah asked, "Your friends in *Eagle*?"

Ward shook his head, "Aircrews aboard *Illustrious*." He smiled and growled with affection, "Scoundrels."

"But – friends?"

"Sure. I still see some of them, now and again. But most were killed before the end of the war."

He moved on, leaving Sarah staring at the young faces. Most of them dead . . .

She followed him slowly along the hall to the kitchen: modern equipment under a dark-beamed ceiling. He took salad and cold meats from a refrigerator, poured her white wine from a bottle in a cooler. He drank beer from a keg standing in a dark, cool cupboard. They ate at the big kitchen table, Sarah sitting across from him as she had faced Rob that morning in her flat.

They talked of small things: the weather, of course, and wine. Sarah relaxed and after the meal insisted on washing up. Then, as she dried her hands on a towel: "So it had all gone wrong."

The old man laughed softly and led the way back to their chairs, the labrador flopping beside him. "No. That's only when it started to go wrong."

BOOK THREE

Judgment

1

"You're a Hard Man."

The dawn raid on Maltezana started badly. Mark and Tim came out onto the flight-deck after the briefing in the carrier's island. The darkness was lit by the blue flames of exhausts and filled with the thunder of engines. They paused in the lee of the island to zip up the leather Irvine flying-jackets with their sheepskin linings. Their trousers were tucked into flying-boots. It was deep into October now and the nights were colder.

They both staggered as the flight-deck lifted and plunged beneath them, *Eagle* banging through the swell at nearly twenty knots for flying off the Swordfish. Spray flicked their faces like rain.. While his mind worked on courses and wind speeds, Tim Rogers, chartboard under arm, shouted at random above the noise: "How is that girl, Katy? Did you manage to see her while we were at Dekheila?"

Mark did not want to talk about her, tried to shrug it off: "I packed that in. It was getting to be too serious."

Tim peered at him, suddenly attentive. "Is that the truth?"

Mark could not make out the expression on his face, and answered lightly, "'Course it is."

Tim shouted at him, separating his words to make them clear, "Sometimes you can be a right bastard!" He walked aft along the deck to where Ethel was ranged with the other Swordfish of the strike.

From then on they spoke only through the Gosport tube, just exchanging details like airspeed and changes of course. They flew off in the darkness. Tim sat in the airgunner's cockpit right aft. They were leaving Campbell aboard *Eagle* because the Swordfish for this operation had been fitted with

151

overload tanks to extend their range, and each tank squatted in and on top of the middle cockpit, a huge steel cylinder like a dustbin, holding sixty gallons of aviation fuel.

Maltezana was the Italian seaplane base on the island of Stampalia to the north of Crete. In the minutes before the sun showed its first edge above the eastern horizon Mark thought, Not like the raid on Rhodes. This time we're going in with the first light and we'll be out again before the sun is up. And: I hope to God things work out as well at Taranto.

JUDGMENT was scheduled for this next week, all the air crew were certain of that.

A blue light winked from the leading Swordfish and its nose went down as it dived towards the island ahead. One by one the others followed, Mark among them. As he eased the stick forward he said into the Gosport tube, "Here we go."

Tim answered shortly, "Right." Mark knew he would be standing now, manning the Vickers machine-gun and ready to fire at any target that appeared.

There below was the half-circle of the bay and a seaplane already in the water at the edge, with men working on it. Mark thought: The dawn patrol running a bit late. And the hangars loomed behind, camouflaged, but clear when you knew where to look. He pulled out of the dive, reached his left hand down to the trigger, released his bombs, and hauled back on the stick. Climbing, he leaned over the side of the cockpit and looked out past the tailplane. He saw the flashes of the bursting bombs, one of them at least in a hangar, he was sure –

He felt the kick again, as he had felt at Bomba, but not with the same enormous blast. Although Ethel was tossed sideways, he did not lose consciousness even for a second. He lost control as the plane fell away but worked on stick and rudder and pulled her out. The engine had stopped, was smoking and clearly, had been hit. He saw he was over the island – no more than two hills with a saddle between and all surrounded by the sea. The saddle was away to his left and he was heading to pass over the northern hill. Or *was* he going to clear it?

"Tim!" He called again, "Tim?"

There was no answer. Desperately he hoped it was simply that the Gosport tube between them had been damaged. He wondered why he had seen no flak. Maybe the Italian gunners had been shooting at someone else to start with, as he'd concentrated totally on his target. Or they'd hit him with the first rounds fired. And obviously, not only the engine had been hit. The starboard lower wingtip was completely shot away – but just outside the strut. Which was some sort of luck. The ailerons, on upper and lower wings, were connected through the strut. If that had gone then, he'd have totally lost control and Ethel would have spun to earth like a falling leaf but a hell of a lot faster. As it was, he had the stick hard over and still the starboard wings drooped and the port ones were high.

He could try to turn her around but God only knew what she'd do then. And he thought it likely there would be more Italians on this side of the island where the seaplane base lay. He wasn't going to smash her down in their front garden.

He was achieving some sort of steep, waddling glide, and they weren't actually falling out of the sky, but the summit of the hill was racing up at him with terrifying speed. He'd thought they would clear it and they did, just, by feet or only inches. There was thorn scrub scattered over the crest and he thought the undercarriage caught in some of that. He felt a jolt and heard a crackling – it was eerie to be able to hear outside noises like that, with the engine dead. But Ethel wallowed over and dropped down the other side, still precariously airborne.

He glimpsed a few houses on the shore of an inlet almost dead ahead, and beyond lay the sea. For an instant he wondered if it would be better to ditch in the sea? Would he be able to get Tim out? Was Tim alive? He was saved that decision because Ethel lurched into a still steeper dive. He tried to hold the nose up but she was sliding away to the right and he knew she was going to stall.

He saw the shelf then, a sort of meadow, a level clearing in the scrub halfway down the hill, like a step cut in the side of it. The shelf looked to be fairly smooth and a little bigger than a tennis court. The hill dropped away beyond it to a rocky shore. He lost sight of the shore as Ethel dropped again and knew he had to put her down in the clearing – or else. There was no question of a proper landing because if she ran at all – and he didn't know the state of the undercarriage – it would be over the meadow's edge to fall nose first down the hill. He just had to bang her down onto the shelf.

Nearly there now, the scrub rushing past below and very close.

He prayed that Tim would be all right, and stalled the plane. She hung, nose up, for a long second, then slammed down. The undercarriage held up and she even ran forwards a few feet but then the wheels hit some obstruction and she toppled forward onto her propeller.

He was winded, shaken and shaking, sagging half out of the cockpit and held in only by his harness. The fuselage reared up behind him, almost perpendicular. He hung there for some moments, dazed, then felt liquid dripping on his shoulder and running cold down his face, smelt it. He realised it was petrol from the overload tank looming over him; the fat drum had been holed. It only needed the tiniest spark now, and – he shuddered and struggled frantically, loosened the harness and slithered head first down the side of the fuselage to the ground. Then he had to climb up again to release Tim, who hung from the single long jock strap, secured to the cockpit floor. Mark fumbled with it, gasping in the reek of petrol. Christ! He hoped she wouldn't burn. Not yet, anyway.

He unclipped the strap from Tim's belt and the man's limp weight sagged against him. He tried to climb down carrying the observer but lost his footing and fell back with Tim on top of him. He pushed the dead-weight away – not dead, surely not dead? – stood up and gripped the observer under the arms, dragged him away from the Swordfish for fifteen or twenty yards to the edge of the clearing and the start of the scrub.

He sat down then, and panted. Now he had to burn Ethel. There was an incendiary bomb aboard, carried for that purpose, or he could use the Verey pistol in the cockpit. But first he would take off his leather jacket with its dangerous stink of petrol . . . Just as soon as he got his breath back and his hands steadied.

But he did not have to burn Ethel. There was a quiet *pop*! like the lighting of a gas stove, and a tongue of flame licked up, then in seconds the fire ran the length of the fuselage. Mark felt the heat searing his face and he grabbed Tim again and hauled him away through the scrub until he could no longer feel that hot breath. He sat down then, stared at the pyre and thought, She just went up, could as easily have done while we were still on board.

And: Well, it's odds on they'll get me one day, but I'd rather not go like that.

And then: They haven't got me yet.

He was alive and free – so far.

He examined Tim Rogers as well as he could and quickly. Tim was breathing; that was something. Mark could find nothing wrong except a wound on the side of Tim's head. The bleeding had stopped and already showed signs of caking into a scab. There was an ominous lump.

Mark sat back on his heels, already facing the next problem. The Italians would come looking for them. When they saw the burnt-out Swordfish they might conclude there had been no survivors. Either way, he and Tim dared not stay here.

He stood up and looked about him with the wrecked and burning Swordfish at his back. Before him was the crest of the hill. He reckoned he stood within a mile or so of one end of the island, away to his left. Not much room to manoeuvre there. Most of the island lay to his right. He turned and looked past the Swordfish to the sea. That was the way he had to go eventually, to the sea – but now? No. The Italians would expect any survivors to head that way, seeking escape. So which was the *least* likely direction such survivors would take? He reached down with his left hand and got one of Tim's arms around his shoulders, lifted him with his free right hand around Tim's waist and started up through the scrub towards the crest. He was heading back towards the distant seaplane base. He would probably be able to see it from the crest but he didn't intend to climb so high.

In fact he barely staggered twenty yards before he halted and set down his burden. For one thing, there was a track ahead of him, running along the side of the hill. For another, he could not carry Tim that way. He took out his handkerchief and lashed the unconscious man's wrists together, then heaved him up again and went on, now with the body on his back, legs dangling, arms around his neck, held crossed on his chest. The observer was a slightly built man, several inches shorter and two stones lighter than he. Even so the effort already had him running with sweat, and the sun still not clear of the horizon.

When he reached the track he paused. He would not follow it because he would be too exposed. As for crossing it, although the track itself was only a few feet wide, the bare ground between it and the scrub on either side was ten or fifteen yards in width. And while the scrub might be only waist-high, so that he stuck up out of it, for as long as he was in it, he could sink down into its cover at a moment's notice. So he squinted up and down the track, made sure it was empty, and then left the scrub and crossed to the other side of the open ground as quickly as possible. He almost achieved a wavering trot, carrying Tim that way. When he was a good fifty yards up the slope and into the scrub he took a rest, laid the observer down and sat beside him.

Tim showed no sign of recovering consciousness. Mark wondered, briefly, if he should have left him on the track to be found. He might have been taken to a doctor – but Mark felt he could not abandon his friend like that. Or should he just surrender the pair of them to the first soldiers he could find? He rejected that idea, too. It was a serviceman's duty to attempt to escape and anyway, he *wanted* to. The alternative was, at best, long years behind the wire as a prisoner. He would dare anything to escape that, and so would Tim.

That settled, after a minute or two he lifted the observer again and climbed on up the hill, angling across it to his right to make an easier climb and because that was the way he wanted to go. It was hard work, his load dragged and the scrub caught and tore his trousers. But he laboured at it, first quietly, doggedly, and then fiercely, with hatred of the hill and anger at being shot down and the whole *bloody* mess.

Every forty or fifty yards he rested for some minutes. He was rising after one of these halts when he saw the soldiers. Already he had taken on the caution of the hunted animal so he was on his knees, his head lifted just above the scrub and turning, eyes searching. There were eight soldiers marching up the track in file about two hundred yards below and to his left. They wore shirts open at the neck, baggy trousers wrapped round below the knee with puttees, boots on their feet. They carried rifles slung over their shoulders. He kept very still, only his eyes moving, following them as they trudged steadily aross his front and away to his right to disappear around a curve in the hill. Smoke still rose in a thin wisp beyond them where the wreck of the Swordfish smouldered. He thought it must be a good quarter-mile away.

He had not realised he had come so far, though every muscle in his body confirmed the distance when he lifted his burden again and went on. He and Tim had still not gone far enough.

He was meandering along the face of the hill now, not climbing, midway between track and crest. Higher on the hill the scrub broke into scattered clumps with wide stretches of bare, rocky ground. He did not want to be caught on one of those. Here he was winding between the clumps and always able to drop into cover. He stumbled along with his head turned, looking back, and so he saw one of the Italian soldiers returning.

Mark crouched, slid Tim off his back, then slowly raised his head until he could see above the scrub. The man was sauntering easily down the track, retracing the soldiers' line of march. Mark thought, Returning to some base, to a telephone or wireless to report? While the others poked through the wreckage of the Swordfish – or searched for Tim and himself? He waited until the man had gone around a bend in the track and then struggled on.

There was a bulge in the hill about three or four-hundred yards ahead. He hoped that once they had got around it they would be out of sight of searchers coming from the Swordfish. He covered fifty yards or more but then, when he was resting, saw the soldiers again. There were two above the track and five below it. They carried their rifles with the barrels pointing down into the scrub ahead of them and they were searching through it.

Mark swore. Now he had to keep out of sight, moving on hands and knees, crawling with Tim on his back and Tim's boots dragging behind. He had to stay in the scrub and skirt around the patches of open ground. It took him a long time to work around the bulge in the hill, until he could rise cautiously, look back and see only scrub, know he was hidden from the soldiers.

He dropped down again. He had glimpsed, far below him and beyond the track, the village set in a steep cliff by the sea. He wondered if anyone down there would see him if he stood up to walk? He could make better time that way and he had to if he was to stay ahead of the search.

He heard engines then, faintly at first, but they grew louder and then stopped. He chanced a look round and saw two trucks on the road. Their open bodies were packed with soldiers who began to drop out over the sides and tail-boards as he watched. An officer wearing a tasselled forage cap climbed down from the cab and started shouting orders, waving his arms and pointing. The soldiers moved off along the track and out of sight, splitting into two parties as they went. Mark could guess what was happening: they were joining the others to extend the sweeping line. There would be thirty or more men in it now. The two drivers stayed with their trucks, squatting side by side in the shade of one of them, smoking. They faced up the hill towards him and would see him if he stood.

So he had to go on crawling, shoving through the scrub, cursing and sweating, Tim's weight growing heavier and heavier. He fell into a narrow little ravine, only two or three feet deep, in the bottom of which ran a trickle of water. He crawled through that, up the other side and on. His only plan was to try to keep ahead of the search, which he knew was impossible but stubbornly kept at it.

Until he had to stop. He could hear soldiers calling to each other, very close to him. The sun was overhead, he was exhausted and had to rest. He could not fight them all. When they came up to him he would have to surrender.

He thought of Katy. She would not be waiting for him through his years of imprisonment. She had her own life to live. He and she had finished.

He saw the head of one soldier bobbing above the scrub, turning, questing, then another. A whistle shrilled and for a moment Mark thought one of them had blown it because he had seen Tim and himself sprawled beneath the scrub – or perhaps had heard the sobbing rasp of his breathing. But then the whistle shrilled again and Mark realised it came from further down the hill. The heads bobbed away, disappeared.

Had they called off the hunt, just when they were set to walk onto him? They had not; he saw the soldiers gathering on the track, sitting with legs stretched out wherever they could find shade. They were eating; Ward could see bread and more than one wine bottle: lunch break. The officer sat apart from the others on a canvas chair, eating from a small camp table.

Mark knew he had only been given a brief reprieve. He could stretch out his lead while they ate but they would soon make that up. He would be a prisoner long before nightfall –

Not if he could help it. He surveyed the land behind the Italian soldiers. No, he bloody well wouldn't be taken.

He took up Tim again and started to crawl back the way he had come. The men on the road below were quiet for a moment, intent on eating. Tim said quite clearly, into that silence "The squadron's caught them on the hop this time. Good old *Eagle*. We'll be halfway home before –"

Mark nearly let him slip down from his back, hissed up at him, "*Shut up, Tim!*"

That had no effect. Tim rambled on, incoherent for the

most part but now and then phrases came clearly: "What say to another beer? These *bloody* desert strips!"

Mark kept on crawling through the scrub. Tim was delirious. His babbling sounded loud to Mark but although the soldiers were hardly more than a hundred yards away, all of them seemed to be talking now, and they did not appear to have heard. No one shouted or came running up the hill. After a time, Tim was silent.

Mark stopped twice to rest and each time peered down at the track, saw the soldiers still lounging there. He was about to rest for the third time when he recognised the narrow little ravine before him so he kept on and slithered down into it, coming to rest by the stream that ran down its floor.

He laid Tim down. The stream was barely a trickle from one small rockpool to another, a staircase of them descending the hill. Mark wondered anxiously if the water was drinkable, but then decided he would have to drink it anyway. He put his face to one of the pools and sucked. The water seemed fresh, was cool as he splashed some on his face. He untied the handkerchief from Tim's wrists and used it to bathe the observer's face. He thought Tim was breathing more quietly now, but the cold water did not wake him.

He heard the soldiers climbing the hill and calling to each other. He crept up the side of the ravine and saw them strung in a long line again, moving forward and continuing the search. But their backs were turned to him; they were going away. Now he was hidden in the dead ground they had already swept over.

He stretched out beside Tim and closed his eyes. He ached from head to foot, was coated in a paste of dust and sweat. His hands and knees were torn and bloody but he didn't care. The bastards hadn't got him. And they wouldn't. He closed his eyes against the sun. Its heat and his exhaustion worked together and soon he dozed.

He woke with a start and found that he and Tim now lay in shade. The sun was sinking and the scrub that fringed the edge of the ravine cast long shadows. It was late afternoon. The snarling of an aero-engine had wakened him and he lifted himself on one knee until he could see a seaplane skimming low along the side of the hill about a mile away. The seaplane was looking for him, he knew, and wondered why they hadn't used it before? He decided that the British raid in the early morning had disorganised the base and its aircraft were only now becoming operational again.

He cursed as he saw the seaplane working back along the side of the hill towards him. He grabbed Tim and hauled him to the side of the ravine until they both lay in the shadow under the fringe of scrub. He resisted the temptation to look up when the seaplane swept low above him because he knew his face would show white. For that reason, too, he had thrown his jacket over Tim's head.

Tim started shouting as the engine boomed overhead but it quickly receded and Mark lifted the jacket. Tim pawed at its leather and blinked at him. Mark said, "Hello, old cock. How d'you feel?"

Tim mumbled, "What's going on? My bloody head –" He stared around at the scrub.

Mark thought with relief, He's all right. He said, "We copped it. Flak. Came down on the island and Ethel was a total write-off. You got a bump on the noggin and you've been out all day." He told the rest then, explaining how they got where they were.

The seaplane returned, sweeping low. As the drone of its engine faded, Mark raised his head to see it circling far along the hillside, then it lifted over the crest and was gone. Minutes later a whistle shrilled faintly in the distance and the trucks on the track below him started up and drove away. He said, "I'll bet they're going to pick up the search party. Called it a day, I suppose, after the observer in that seaplane reported he couldn't see anybody."

The trucks did not return but later a file of soldiers trudged wearily up the track and turned off it to go down into the village. There were eight of them.

Mark thought that these would be the party he first saw, and that the village must be their base. They disappeared among the scatter of little, white houses then showed again on the shore. They went to a house on the left of the village and passed inside.

It was dusk. Mark knelt below the edge of the little ravine and watched the village through a gap in the scrub. Tim lay by the side of the stream and asked, "Anything happening?"

"Fishing boats coming home. Four of them. Three fairly big, one small." They had all come in under sail, drifting in slowly with a faint, barely fair wind. The sails came down as they closed the shore and the men in the boats stepped over the sides into the sea and waded in, pulling the boats well up onto the shore. A line was made fast to each boat but Ward thought they must have been secured out of habit because the sea was calm and the sky clear; there was no threat of a storm that might wash the boats off the beach and out to sea.

He watched the smallest boat as the fishermen passed to and fro unloading their catch. He was working out what he and Tim would need, thinking that there might be a sentry at night because the soldiers were presumably there as some sort of coast watch. He was trying to solve problems and to anticipate them. One problem was that Tim still could not walk. He had broken or sprained his ankle, either in the crash or when Ward hauled him out of the Swordfish. He was also in considerable pain from bruising or internal injuries and winced whenever he moved. He did not complain but Ward worried.

When night fell the white houses were a grey mass in the cleft below him, pricked here and there by lights that went out one after the other until there was only one, on the left edge of the village. That was the house the soldiers occupied, the guard-house.

Mark slid down beside Tim and asked him, "Are you tired? Need to sleep?" He was remembering Campbell and the effects of concussion.

"Lord, no. Wide awake."

"O.K. You call me in one hour from now." Mark fastened his leather jacket around him and laid down. It was pleasantly cool now but later they would be very glad of the flying-jackets. He closed his eyes and went over his plan again in his mind. He thought it might work. There was only one way to find out. He slept.

When Tim woke him the night was chill, the sky clear with a dusting of stars and a sliver of moon. Mark knelt at the stream, drank from his cupped hands then splashed water on his face. He rose to his feet, looked about him carefully then stretched his tall frame. He could see the white houses clearly and the boats beyond, drawn up on the shore with the sea washing at their sterns. He asked, "Anyone moving?"

Tim answered, "One man. I think only one. I've seen someone patrolling in front of the houses."

So there was a sentry. There would be, of course, because the soldiers had hunted for British airmen all day and had not found them.

Mark said, "Let's have your knife."

Tim dug it out of his pocket and passed it over. "What do you want it for?"

Mark answered evasively, "In case I need a knife." He wanted a weapon and hefted the big claspknife, its handle filling his palm, heavy. He shoved it in his own pocket then unzipped his flying-boots and took them off.

Tim asked, "What are you going to do?"

"Take a look around and see what offers." Mark dropped his boots beside Tim. "You keep awake, and be ready to move."

Tim said wrily, "I'm as ready as I'll ever be." Then as Mark moved away: "Look out for yourself."

Mark lifted a hand but did not turn. He walked down to the road, crossed it, then angled to his left. He worked around the back of the village in a wide circle then closed in on the house at its left edge where a vertical chink of yellow light still showed: the guard-house.

He moved slowly now, eyes lifted, searching, until he saw the black thread of the telephone wire looping from pole to pole down to the house. The poles were ten feet tall but between them the wire sagged down almost to the height of his head. He reached up, eased down a loop of it and cut it with his knife. He cut it again twenty feet further on and wound that loose length around his waist.

He went on, edging away from the guard-house and sidling into the shadow of the next cottage along. He waited a while there, listening. There was no sound from the guard-house but he could hear the slow footfall of the sentry. Mark eased to the corner of the house, peered cautiously around it and saw the soldier. The man was walking along the front of the houses and some ten yards from them. As Mark watched, the sentry halted, stood for a minute or so staring out to sea then turned to retrace his steps. He carried a rifle slung over his shoulder.

Mark withdrew into the shadow cast by the house and crouched in its darkness. He listened to the slow footfalls returning and wondered that no dog in the village had barked. He had never killed a man before, did not wish to now, but – he would not be a prisoner.

The sentry came into sight but did not look in Ward's direction, walked slowly on to the guard-house. The vertical crack of light widened as he opened the door and peered in. Then the light was snuffed out, all but that vertical chink, as he closed the door again. He turned and walked back along his beat.

Mark waited until he had passed, then followed, silent in his stockinged feet, stalking the sentry along the front of the houses. He trailed the man by ten yards to begin with but steadily closed that distance. As he passed the boats he saw their sails and oars laid across their thwarts.

When the sentry was almost at the end of his beat, Mark was barely a stride behind him. The man halted, began to turn and Mark reached out, grabbed the front of his jacket and rammed the point of the knife under his chin. The sentry sucked in air. His mouth was open but he made no sound. He could not see the knife but knew what it was, felt it pricking into his skin. He saw Mark's face with the tight mouth and black brows, close, looming over him.

Mark said nothing; there was no need. He marched the man back towards the village, never relaxing his grip or the pressure of the knife, until they were in a gap between two of the houses. He took the Italian's rifle away then and stood it against the wall while he held the man pressed against the white stone by the knife at his throat. Mark pulled his handkerchief from his pocket and jammed the grubby ball of it into the sentry's mouth.

The Italian had got over his first shock. His eyes were watchful now, not wide. He would fight his way free if Ward gave him the chance. Mark did not, but pushed him to the ground, knelt on his back and tied his arms and ankles with a length of the wire, used another short length to fasten the gag in place.

He picked up the rifle, left the alley and walked back along the front of the houses. Despite the coolness of the night he was warm and sweating. He went to the guard-house, reasoning that there would be a sergeant or a corporal in there who ought to be wide awake – but would he be, after a day spent on the hill? And the sentry had peered in at the guard-house door – to see how long he still had to patrol before waking his relief?

Mark went quietly to the door. It stood an inch ajar, letting out that narrow slit of light. He held his breath and set his eye to that crack but saw only the end of a table and the far wall. He pushed the door gently, slowly, and it opened without creaking. A man sat slumped in a chair at the table, wrapped in a brown blanket. Presumably it was the guard commander but his badges of rank were hidden by the blanket around him. His booted feet were outstretched and his head leaned on the high back of the chair. He was snoring.

There were three beds against the left-hand wall, two of them occupied by blanket-wrapped forms, one empty. The sentry's? That other would be the commander's bed, against the back wall. And the rest?

Mark held the rifle ready as he edged his head around the door. Suppose one was awake? But they slept, four of them lined along the right-hand wall. So that was all eight accounted for: one outside and seven in here. Rifles stood against the wall by each bed except the sentry's. Mark's gaze slid back to the table. There was the clock in the centre of it, facing him. On the end of the table near the commander stood a field telephone, but Mark had already cut the wire to that.

He moved to the table, knowing what he wanted. Among the litter of mess tins was a foot of bread, a sausage nearly as long and the colour of a boot, a hunk of cheese. He thrust this all inside his jacket. There was a stone wine jar with a cork jammed in the top of it and he carried that with him as he backed out of the room.

Outside, he set down the jar and the rifle, then cut another length of wire. He closed the door gently and slipped a noose of the wire around the handle. There were hooks in the wall to hold open in the day the shutters that now were closed. He looped the other end of the wire around one of the hooks, drew it tight and made it fast. He tied the shutters of each window with wire. The place was not exactly a prison now, but at least he would have some warning if the Italians awoke.

He picked up the rifle and jar and walked back around the village. He found Tim where he had left him, sitting by the stream. Tim's whisper came: "What happened?"

"We've got a boat."

"What about the sentry?"

Mark told him, kneeling by the stream and emptying the dregs of the wine from the jar, washing it out then refilling it with water cupped in his hands. It took some minutes and his terse account – "Then I found the sentry and tied him up, went to the guard-house . . ." – was done long before the jar was full. Tim watched him and asked only one question: "Didn't the sentry put up a fight?"

"I suppose he thought it wasn't a good idea."

Tim was silent after that. This new, ruthless Mark Ward was a stranger.

They weaved slowly down to the village, Tim limping with one hand around Mark's shoulders, the other holding the jar of drinking water. Both were in stockinged feet, their boots tied together and hanging around their necks. This time Mark took a short-cut through an alley between the houses.

They had stepped clear of the front of them when a dog whimpered close by.

They froze. The dog yelped then went on whimpering until a man's voice growled and it was silent. Tim and Mark drew breath but then the door in the nearest house opened and a man stood on the threshold. He was not five paces away and they could see him clearly, an old man, in trousers and a shirt, skinny and stooped, barefoot.

He stared at them. The rifle was slung over Mark's shoulder but he did not touch it. He smiled at the old man, lifted one hand in salute then started forward again, Tim limping along with him.

As they shuffled down to the shore, Tim whispered, "What's he doing?"

"Don't know. Just take it steady, as if you didn't expect him to do anything."

"What if he wakes them all and they try to stop us?"

"Nobody's going to stop us." Not now, with the boat only feet away.

That tone of cold certainty silenced Tim.

Mark put boots, jar and rifle into the boat, set his shoulder to the bow and shoved but it did not move. Tim, balancing on his good leg, added his weight and now the boat slid astern. Mark kept it moving, feet digging into the sand and shale as he strained at it, Tim hopping alongside. Then the stern took the water and she floated.

Tim clambered in over the bow with Mark's help and dragged himself aft to the sternsheets. Mark shoved again until the bow was free and the water up to his knees, then he climbed aboard. There was no wind so he shipped the oars, turned the boat around and began to row.

Tim said softly, head turned on his shoulder to look back, "That old boy's watching us."

The man had moved out from the shadow of the house and now stood at the water's edge. Mark said, "Let him." No one would catch them now. He wondered if this was the old man's boat, and they were taking away his livelihood. His or another's; he had not protested. Were the natives of

167

these islands Greek? Did he hate the Italians, have a liking for the British? Mark was sorry if he had done the old man harm, but he had to get away.

Would he have killed the sentry, if put to it? Jamie had said, "You're a hard man. I've seen it . . . men who did it with their bare hands." Mark shied away from that, but a determination to escape still ruled him. Perhaps the sentry had seen it in his face.

It drove him throughout the next day, after the storm had hit them. The wind raged for twelve hours. They barely survived, with the one big sail reefed down to a quarter of its size and the pair of them bailing. The storm left them both exhausted and Tim Rogers very ill. Mark saw no searching aircraft and concluded that either the storm had prevented the seaplanes from flying or the Italians had not bothered to continue the hunt.

He headed southward, for Crete, but in the evening of the second day he sighted a ship. He watched as she came up, a tramp steamer, heading to pass close by the boat. He had trailed lines over the side, and if she was Italian he would keep up the pretence of being a fisherman. There was little of the food and water left because he did not feel he could refuse Tim's thirst, but he still would not give up.

The ship was a Greek tramp, bound for Lávrion in Greece. She took them aboard and Mark could finally relax, collapsing on the bunk they gave him.

Before sleep claimed him he remembered the planned attack on Taranto. He must have missed it. It was an odd feeling; these weeks and months past he had watched the steady approach to the attack, its growing inevitability, the tunnel narrowing down towards its dark ending. Now all that was changed. Did he feel reprieved – or cheated?

He wondered how the attack had gone and how many of his friends had survived. He thought about Katy, her photograph in the pocket of his shirt. And then, because he was weary, he slept.

2

A Walk in the Rain

They were aboard the Greek ship for two nights and a day as she chugged her way slowly between the islands. On the afternoon of the second day she berthed at Lávrion, thirty miles south of Athens, and soon afterwards a doctor came to the cabin amidships where Mark sat worriedly by Tim's bunk. The doctor made a quick but thorough examination of Tim, and an even quicker one of Mark, then nodded his satisfaction.

Mark had wondered if they would be interned and now the ship's captain brought an army officer and two soldiers to the cabin. All four crowded in, to the doctor's annoyance. Captain, doctor and officer were all men in middle-age, paunchy. They argued incomprehensibly among themselves, the officer pointing at Mark, the doctor at Tim, pale and drawn. The captain pointed his black cigar at each in turn.

Mark could guess at the captain's argument: he wanted the airmen off his ship. He had saved their lives and cared for them, brought them safely here, but he was not running a hotel or a hospital. The army officer seemed ready to go along with that but the doctor was against it, and if he was not winning the argument it seemed he was forcing a draw. There was a great deal of shrugging and spreading of hands, then finally the officer went ashore but left his two soldiers on guard outside the cabin. The doctor clapped a pudgy hand on Ward's shoulder and told him, "You all right. O.K. Consul come. Yes?"

Mark answered, "Yes. Thank you." So he wasn't being hauled off to some internment camp straight away.

The doctor left then and Mark sat on the single chair beside the bunk. Tim said he was better. "My ankle doesn't hurt. I think I could walk. I'm just so bloody tired." He dozed off again a few minutes afterwards. Mark reflected wrily that Tim had been dragged, concussed, from a smashed Swordfish, carted around the island like a sack of old clothes and then survived two days in an open boat. It was hardly surprising that he felt tired.

The consul arrived an hour later in a great hurry and out of breath, the army officer puffing along behind. The consul was stocky, neat in a dark grey suit. His thinning hair was carefully parted and brushed. He carried a trilby hat in his left hand, shook Mark's hand with the other. "Hello there. Ferrers. I'm in business here but I also act as consul on the side. Never had anything like this before! However –" he took a breath, "– there's an ambulance waiting on the quay to take your friend to hospital. You've been released to me, in my custody for the time being – that is, until they decide what to do about you."

Mark saw a ray of hope. "You mean we might not be interned?"

"Ah!" Ferrers winked. "Not sure, old chap, but I'll explain later. Here's the stretcher."

Two uniformed men carried Tim ashore and Mark followed them down the gangway. He leaned into the ambulance and gripped Tim's hand. "Take it easy, old cock. I'll be seeing you."

Tim returned the grip. "Thanks. If it wasn't for you I'd be a prisoner or burned up in Ethel."

"Not you – born to be hung."

Tim, embarrassed, looked across at the doctor sitting opposite him in the ambulance, then back to Mark. "Listen. What I said about you and Katy before we took off on this raid – I'm sorry – shouldn't have said it."

But he had thought it. And now? Mark said, "I don't blame you. I tried to make a joke of it, and it was a bad one. The truth is that Katy's going back to the States and we both decided it would be sensible to make a clean break." Not the whole truth, but enough. And what had happened over

Maltezana showed he'd made the right decision. His life wasn't worth a damn. No airman's was.

Tim said, "Pity. I thought you two might –"

But the doctor was peering impatiently at his watch and Mark wanted no more of this conversation. He stepped back and grinned, "Don't get them to let you navigate this thing or you'll never reach the hospital." The doors closed and the ambulance drove away. He watched until it reached the end of the quay, turned around the corner of a warehouse and was lost to sight.

The Englishman, Ferrers, broke in on his thoughts: "He's a close friend?"

Mark shrugged, "He's a good bloke; one of the best."

He stooped to climb into the consul's car as Ferrers shook hands with the army officer then got in behind the wheel and drove away. As they left the quay and wound through the streets of the town he said, "I can't tell you anything definite about internment. By rights the Greeks should hold you but they're friendly to us and *not* friendly towards the Italians. Mussolini has been making threatening noises for some time and the feeling here, the fear, is that there could be a war, and soon. But as far as you are concerned we'll just have to wait and see. I've telephoned Athens and told our people there that you're here. Meanwhile, if there's anything I can do – well, just say the word."

"Thanks. That's very good of you." Mark paused, then said deliberately casually, "I was friendly with a couple of people in Alex, an American war correspondent, Bert Keller, and his photographer. I understand they're in Greece now. Is there any way of tracing them?"

"You mean you want to see them?"

Mark shook his head quickly, "No, I'd just like to know how they are. That's all."

Ferrers glanced at him, puzzled. This young man had been plucked from the sea, was bedraggled, unkempt, but he had not asked for a drink, a meal, a cigarette – only wanted news of two friends. Well – "I'll telephone the U.S. embassy in Athens. I should imagine they'll have the answer."

The consul lived in a cool, whitewashed old house inside a walled garden on the outskirts of the town. His wife was Greek, a dark, handsome woman in her forties. Her English was careful but good. Ferrers explained casually to Mark that it was her family's business in which he worked, and Mark gathered he was a director or partner. Mark had a bath and they gave him some clean clothes of Ferrers that were very short in the arms and legs so that Mrs. Ferrers gurgled with suppressed laughter and the consul grinned openly. "We'll buy you some hand-me-downs tomorrow that will be a better fit."

Then he said, "I spoke to the American embassy about your friends. They said Mr. Keller and the young lady went north about a week ago and should be back in Athens any day now." He waited, quizzically.

But Mark only said, "Thanks. I just wanted to know they were all right."

They sat down to a meal then, and later, over the coffee and brandy that Mark suspected was brought out in his honour, Ferrers asked, "Well, can you –" he corrected "– are you allowed to tell us what happened?"

Mark grinned. He was relaxed now. This was like dinner with his parents or in other houses of the Ward clan, a long way removed from the open boat or the flight-deck of *Eagle*. "Don't see why not." He told them about the raid, the smash, and the escape. He lived through it all again vividly in his mind, but told it in short, arid sentences of understatement. Nevertheless, they read between the lines and he saw it in their faces. He was afraid they might consider him some sort of hero – he knew where the real heroes were and they weren't sitting around a table like this. He felt an impostor.

He asked casually, "Has there been any news of other operations?"

There had, and Ferrers told him about them, but none had been an attack on Taranto. Mark wondered if it had been a complete fiasco, a failure at the outset, and so kept quiet by the Navy? He could not believe that. So it had not after all been launched – yet.

Ferrers said, "Harking back to your American friends: I hope they *are* on their way back to Athens. The weather has broken in the north and there's heavy rain. It started yesterday, on the twenty-sixth, and it's still falling. The roads up there are terrible."

So this was the twenty-seventh of October. Mark had lost count of the days.

Katy. Soon to be in Athens, which was only thirty miles away.

When he went to his bed and turned over to sleep he thought about her.

The car was an old Ford, shabby inside, but it ran well and did not let in the rain. It lurched and slid on the road, greasy with mud washed down from the hills. Twice it skidded off, bumping along the shoulder until the driver wrestled it back onto the road. Bert Keller sat in the front beside the driver and Katy shared the back of the car with their stacked valises. At the beginning of their trip, when they left Athens, the luggage had been strapped to the grid on the back of the car, but when the rain started yesterday they had shifted it inside.

The frontier with Albania lay a mile or so behind. In the last week they had driven along the frontier from east to west. They found it thinly guarded everywhere and had to look ten, fifteen or even twenty miles back into the Greek countryside before they found troops in strength. Bert had explained the situation: "They've pulled back from the border and manned defensive positions in the mountains. If it comes to war the Greeks are going to fight on their own ground, where it suits them. I think they're right. And those Greek soldiers look good." They did, bronzed and tough, confident.

Now Katy stared out through the scratched glass of the Ford's side window and saw the land dropping away from the road to a choppy, white-flecked, grey sea. Out there, twenty miles away and hidden by the veil of falling rain, lay the island of Corfu. The legs of her khaki drill slacks were damp from their last exposure to the rain, when Bert and she had got out to look at the frontier post, but her sweater and open-necked khaki shirt were dry. The trenchcoat that had saved them lay on top of the valises and dripped water on the floor. Her boots were caked with mud but at least she had greased them well beforehand, so her feet inside them were dry.

She asked, "Do you still think there might be war?" She wanted to go home, away from it all, and soon she would.

Bert shook his head and when the sodden brown and grey hair flopped across his brow he pushed at it impatiently with one hand. "Not on your life. The weather's broken and Mussolini has lost his chance. He'll have to wait until it clears, maybe till the spring. Nobody is going to mount an attack in this."

The driver nodded agreement and Bert chuckled. "See? Kristos goes along with that."

Kristos was a young officer in the Greek army, assigned to them as guide, interpreter – and to steer them away from areas the Greeks did not want them to see. He had been given the job because his English was good. Before joining the army he had lived with an uncle in London for a year. He was handsome and dark with a thin Clark Gable moustache. He turned to smile at Katy. "No war now."

He swung back quickly to the road as the Ford slid again, skating on mud. It bumped and skittered along on the verge while he spun the wheel frantically and pedalled the brake. Bert and Katy grabbed at handholds and clung on. Then the car stopped dead with a shuddering crash that shook the teeth in their heads. Kristos was thrown onto the wheel, Bert against the dash but his forearm cushioned his face from the blow. Katy banged into the back of Bert's seat and ended on one knee in the well between rear and front seats.

She said, "For God's *sake*!"

The engine had died. Kristos pushed himself back from the wheel, rubbed at his bruised chest and opened the door. It let in a cold draught and driven rain that fell on Katy's face. Bert got out on his side and the two men splashed to the front of the car and stooped to examine the damage. Katy watched them, hopeful but apprehensive. There was something not right about the nose-down attitude of the car.

Bert came splashing back to confirm her fears. "Busted front suspension. This baby goes nowhere, except on the tail of a truck."

"Oh, hell!" Katy stared out at the empty darkening countryside.

Bert said, "I could put it stronger than that but I'll wait till you're not around."

Kristos straightened and stood looking around him.

Katy picked out the map from where it was slotted between two of the valises and bent her head over it, peering, then called, "We look to be miles from anywhere!"

Kristos came round to them. "Yes. Long way. But there is a light, a house." He turned, pointed and they saw the yellow glow about a quarter-mile from the road, could just make out a building at the head of a shallow valley. "There might be a telephone."

"It'll be a roof over our heads, anyway," said Bert. He opened Katy's door and one corner of his mouth twitched up in wry humour. "And it's a nice night for a walk in the rain. Pass the luggage out."

They unloaded the valises and Kristos locked up the car. They spent some minutes first pulling on trenchcoats and then casting up and down the road until they found a track that seemed to lead towards the light. They started along it, Kristos in the lead and carrying Katy's valise easily besides his own. A stream rushed down the valley floor only yards below the track, to plunge into a culvert under the road. The track was just wide enough for a cart, flattened rocks under a skin of mud. They struggled up it until the light was revealed as a small, uncurtained window in a low, square house. When they were close Kristos shouted and the door was opened, letting out a pathway of light as they trudged up to it.

There was an old man called Constantine and his wife, but no telephone. After Kristos explained the situation there was a welcome and a fire, oil lamps for light, a small room for

Katy, another for Bert and Kristos. Constantine told Kristos he had four sons but all were away, three married and with their own places now, the youngest doing his military service. The old man's wife served a meal of thick soup or a stew, it fell between the two, and strong cheese with coarse bread and retsina from a stone jar.

After that they all went to bed; Constantine took it for granted, expecting to be up with the dawn. Katy was in bed, her torch tucked handily under it and her lamp turned out, when Bert tapped at the door and called, "Are you decent?"

"Since when did you care? Come on in."

He leaned in at the door. "Just checking that you're O.K." He always did when they were in the field.

"I'm fine."

Bert nodded, "Seasoned campaigner now. Look, tomorrow we'll beg or borrow a car and head for Athens. Are you still going home?"

Katy answered definitely, "Yes."

"Uh-uh! Well, this place is a wash-out, in every sense of the word – there'll be no action till maybe the spring. So I'll make for Alex again because something might break there before too long. Talking of Alex –" He was only a silhouette against the firelight from the kitchen but she knew he was watching her, "– what's with you and that Navy flyer, that Ward guy with the hard look?"

Hard? She remembered Mark's body on hers and answered shortly, "Nothing. There's nothing between us."

Bert started slowly, "I kinda thought –"

She cut him off abruptly, "You thought wrong."

"Did you have a fight?"

"No, we didn't." They had talked like civilised, sensible people, hadn't they? "Look, Bert, it was just one of those things. We had some fun, I liked him and I – think he liked me but he went back to sea, I came to Greece and I'm on my way home. End of story. Don't make it sound so serious!"

Bert scowled at her. "That so? I'm too serious? Listen, kid, when I wasn't much more than your age I met this girl but she had to go to the West Coast with her family; it was 1917

176

and I was shipping out to France to cover the action there. So we said good-bye. Finish? End of story? No. Because I met her in 1939. And she said she'd never stopped thinking about me but now – well, she was twenty years older and it was just too late. She said, 'We've been such fools.'" He choked, broke off and put a hand to his face.

Katy said softly, "Oh, Bert, I'm sorry."

He lowered the hand. "Aw, hell, that's a pack of lies I dreamed up because you said I was too serious. She married a feller owned a drugstore chain and wound up happy as Larry. But suppose –"

He saw the blur of the boot she threw and caught it two-handed against his chest. "O.K.! But remember, just suppose –" He tossed the boot back to fall beside her bed. "G'night."

"Good-night, Bert." She smiled and shook her head as he closed the door and left her in the darkness. Then the smile faded. What had happened to the girl photographer who'd crossed the Atlantic to seek a handsome army officer who up to then had hardly given her the time of day? The answer to that was: plenty. She had found that the man she was looking for did not exist, had been created by distance, time and her own imagination. She had seen the real man's notebook and a scrap of his shirt, all that was left of him after a mortar bomb. She had seen Mark too, that time he had come back from the raid on Bomba. She had seen too much and she was going home.

Or she had backed off, frightened of getting out of her depth?

No. She had taken a rational decison, done the right thing, for her sake and for Mark. She believed that. So she turned over, but it was a long time before she slept and then it was restlessly, waking now and then to hear the drumming of the rain.

In the south the sky was clear above Athens, with a sprinkling of stars. In the city a government aide woke Metaxas, the Greek dictator, and told him the Italian minister wanted to see him. It was close to three in the morning.

Metaxas was a small man. He pulled on a dressing-gown and slowly descended the stairs. He was ill, but mentally alert, apprehensive. The Italian minister, Grazzi, handed him the ultimatum Metaxas had been fearing for some time. It demanded that Italian troops be allowed to occupy several strategic installations in Greece and it would expire at six a.m., just three hours away.

The demands were, intentionally, impossible to accept.

Metaxas said heavily, "So it is war."

Mark woke to knocking on his bedroom door and lifted himself onto one elbow. "Yes? Come in."

Ferrers entered and switched on the light. "Sorry, old chap." Mark was squinting against the glare. "But I thought you'd want to know. The embassy at Athens just phoned. About an hour ago –" he glanced at his watch, "– at three a.m., the Italians handed the Greeks an ultimatum that runs out at six. The Greeks say it means war."

The consul wore pyjamas, was bare-footed. Although in his forties he looked old now, his face haggard. He saw Mark staring at him and said, "It's a terrible shock. Like this, in the middle of the night. We were expecting it, of course, dreading it – sooner or later, but –" He shook his head, scanty hair untidy. "My wife – very upset, of course."

Mark asked, "Is there anything I can do? If you need any help –"

Ferrers said, "No. I have some phone calls to make, that's all. It was just that we thought you'd want to know – and I wanted to talk to someone." He smiled faintly. "I'm feeling better already." There was something reassuring about the calm, black-haired young pilot.

Ferrers turned to go, then paused. "Oh, I remembered to ask about you. They said you'd have no problems now and they'll probably have you back in Alexandria in no time. Now I'll let you get to sleep. Good-night."

The light went out and the door closed. Mark stared up at the ceiling. Katy would be on her way back to Athens now. Maybe in a day or two he would have to go there to the embassy. So what? He knew she was all right and that was all there was to it.

She woke again to the drumming of the rain, turned over – then was still, listening. The drumming was close but there was a more distant sound, faint under the rain but only too familiar now. It was the flat crackle of small-arms fire, rifles. And she recognised the rattle of a machine-gun.

It stopped.

Had she been dreaming of the desert and imagined she'd heard it? She knew she had not. She was naked in the bed but pulled her underclothes out from under the pillow and carried them with her in one hand, the torch in the other as she crossed to the wall. She tapped on it with the base of the torch.

Bert's voice came, muffled, from the next room: "Whassamatter?"

"I heard firing."

"Firing?" A pause, then: "Are you sure?" Bert was always reluctant to get out of bed.

"Certain. Get dressed." Katy was nearly ready, dressing rapidly by the light of the torch laid on the bed. She pulled on socks and boots, laced them, snatched up her trenchcoat and the torch and left the room.

In the kitchen the fire was black and dead. She looked at her watch, saw it was a minute to six then switched off the torch and crossed to the grey square of the window. It was still dark outside but she could see the falling rain. Bert and Kristos came into the kitchen, both dressed and carrying torches, Kristos with his pistol belted around his waist. It was he who opened the door and led the way outside. The three of them stood before the house, shoulders hunched under the rain, staring down towards where the road lay hidden in darkness. The low grinding of engines came to them faintly and Bert said, "Trucks." And: "You're sure about the firing?" Then, before she could answer, he suggested to Kristos, "An exercise? Or some platoon testing weapons?"

Kristos answered, "I don't think so."

Light glowed in the house behind them and spilled out of the open door. Constantine stood in the kitchen, wearing a nightshirt buttoned up to his skinny neck and holding a lamp above his head as he peered at them. Kristos called softly, angrily to him and Katy guessed he said: "Put that light out!" But the old man would not take orders from a stranger in his own house, argued and demanded an explanation. Kristos had to go in, take the lamp from him and extinguish it. He spoke a few words firmly to the old man then rejoined the other two. "I told him to dress. I'm going down to the road to look."

Bert said, "We'll tag along."

"Stay behind, please. Thirty – forty metres, no lights." Kristos started down the track and Katy saw him unfasten the holster and take out his pistol. They gave him the lead he'd asked for and then followed. He went slowly, cautiously, halting often to listen and peer into the night.

So also did Bert and Katy. The grind of engines in low gear came clearly now – and voices, but still only distantly.

Then one voice yelled closer, challenging. Kristos stopped. There was a double spurt of flame as his pistol fired twice and the *crack! – crack!* of it hammered at their ears. The flashes blinded them for a second, then they saw him running back and he shouted, *"The Italians!"*

The night was slashed with flame in a dozen places and the crashes of the fusillade deafened them. Kristos flung his arms wide, his head jerked back and he fell face down in a rain puddle, the water splashing high. Bert stood staring but Katy snatched at his arm and shouted, "Get down!"

They sprawled in the mud and there was more firing until a blast on a whistle cut it short. Bert gasped, "The creek! Get in there for cover!" They crawled towards it through the mud, almost blind as a rifle fired again then a voice bawled angrily. Bert said, "This way." He turned and lunged forward, disappeared from Katy's sight.

She heard the slither then the splash and called softly, "Bert?" But there was no answer. She edged forward, found the lip where the ground fell steeply to the stream, saw it glinting silver below her. She lowered herself over, feet first, felt rocks under her boots and water freezing around her legs, found Bert head down in the stream, drowning in it.

She stooped and hauled him out, her arms around his middle so he hung over them like washing, a dragging weight. Straining and gasping with the effort, she floundered along the side of the stream with him like that for a few yards until the bank retreated and there was a space where she could lay him down clear of the water. She heard him coughing and retching then, and thought, Thank God! But Bert did not reply when she spoke to him.

He had to have help. She thought she could hear movement on the track and remembered the wild volleys. But Bert might die without the aid she could not give. He had fallen on his head, she did not know what injuries he might have suffered and he was not a young man. He had said to her wrily, "Nice night for a walk in the rain."

She stood up and shook out her short, blonde hair so the soldiers might see that she was a woman. She held her left hand open above her head, the right holding the torch away from her body but down level with her waist. She switched the torch on so it glared up at her face and shouted blindly again and again, *"Americano! Americano!"* She did not know the Italian for "surrender".

A rifle flamed, then another. She heard the burring *crack!* as a shot passed close. Then the torch was smashed from her hand, she fell back and the darkness wrapped her round like a shroud.

Ferrers told Mark, "Breakfast as soon as you're ready for it." He set the cup of tea down on the bedside table. "A fine day, but the news is bad. The Italians jumped the gun. Mussolini issued that ultimatum as a pure formality and his army crossed the border at five-thirty this morning, half an hour before the ultimatum ran out." He sucked in his breath, angry. "On the other hand, although they've met little resistance, they are only advancing slowly. The few troops along the border are making a fighting retreat but it's the weather up there that's slowing the Italians down to a crawl. It's appalling. Mussolini couldn't have chosen a worse time."

The consul paused at the door and now he smiled. "I saved the good news. First: I rang the hospital. Your friend Rogers had a good night, his ankle is not broken and he should make a good recovery. I also telephoned the American embassy in Athens a few minutes ago. The army officer the Greeks sent along with your friends phoned in from the frontier yesterday afternoon and said they were starting back. So they're well out of it. I thought you'd like to know."

Ferrers went out to the kitchen, slipped an arm around his wife's waist and told her, "He's looking fit as a fiddle, in spite of all he's been through. What it is to be young."

She smiled at him. She thought Ward a well set-up young man, not handsome, but if it had been left to her she would have found him a fine girl long ago.

Mark wondered how Katy was, what she was doing. He could picture her clearly. But she was bound for her home in the States and in a day or two he was going back to *Eagle* – and JUDGMENT.

He was certain of that.

3

Countdown: Then There Were . . .

Mark did not go to the U.S. Embassy. Ferrers drove him to Athens where a Royal Air Force transport aircraft returning to Egypt, found room for him. He waited a week in Alexandria until *Eagle* returned from operations in the Aegean. He rejoined her then, and was made welcome in the wardroom: "Good God! Look who's here!" "Talk about the bad penny turning up." "Where's Tim Rogers?"

He told them his story but only sketched in the escape: "– when it got dark we pinched a boat."Later he asked, "Any word on Taranto? I didn't hear any news in Greece."

"We had to put it off, old boy. *Illustrious* had a fire in her hangar and five of her Swordfish finished up as burnt-out wrecks. Some of the others were saturated by the overhead salt-water sprays they had to use to put the fire out. It took days to repair the damage, strip the Swordfish right down then dry 'em, clean 'em and put 'em back together. Bad luck."

Postponed. Mark thought that was the correct word. Not cancelled. When the moon and the weather were right then the attack would go in. And soon.

He left the wardroom and descended to the cavernous hangar with its harsh light. Hardy's wide figure sat, like Humpty Dumpty on his wall, on a staging as he worked on the engine of a Swordfish. Doug Campbell, hands dug in the pockets of his shorts, stood below the staging, talking up at Hardy. He turned, broke off in mid-sentence as Mark came up, and said delightedly, "Here's Mr. Ward!"

Hardy swung down to land lightly on the deck while the skinny figure of Laurel squirmed out from under the tailplane and hurried to join them. Laurel did the talking, of course: "Lord love us! Can't believe it! Doug was just telling us you'd come aboard, sir. What the hell happened to you? When you didn't come back that morning we thought, well, all right, they've been overdue before, but then --"

Mark let him run on as Hardy nodded and Doug Campbell laughed. They were genuinely pleased to see him and he was touched. The fitter and rigger eyed him from head to foot as they had always scrutinised Ethel when he landed her on. He supposed they were looking for holes, or bits of him missing, and he grinned.

Campbell, tired of waiting for Laurel to run out of breath, broke in, "What about Mr. Rogers, sir?"

That got silence, and they watched Mark, serious now.

He reassured them: "He did something to his ankle in the crash, and collected a few bumps and scrapes, but they told me he'd be as good as new. I expect he'll be in hospital for a bit, though, and we won't see him for a while."

"What crash, sir?"

So then he had to tell his watered-down story all over again. When he finished, Laurel said, "Well, you do see life."

Mark changed the subject: "They told me in the wardroom there'd been some excitement aboard *Illustrious*."

Laurel nodded vigorously. "Ah! The fire. Nasty, that, but it might have been a lot worse."

Hardy said slowly, "I think we've got trouble of our own. Remember early last month when the Eyeties bombed us and near missed us?"

Mark nodded. *Eagle* had been escorting a Malta convoy.

Laurel muttered, "Cured my constipation, that did."

Hardy said, "Seems those near misses shook the old girl up and now our fuel system's falling apart."

Lower deck gossip was confirmed later that day. *Eagle* needed extensive work in the dockyard and it would be a week or more before she was fit for operations again. Mark thought the delay made no difference; he had a growing feeling of bleak inevitability. He laughed and joked with the others in the wardroom, played the piano. But the feeling was there. The tunnel was closing in.

When leave ashore was granted he climbed down into the liberty boat with a crowd of brother officers, had a drink at the Cecil and a meal at Pastroudi's. It did not seem the same and at first he told himself this was because he had always had Tim Rogers for company on his runs ashore. Then he thought, with brutal honesty, that was nonsense. He was trying to fool himself and failing. The truth was – Katy had gone. To hell with it.

Because of his feeling of inevitability he was not surprised when, after he had been two days back aboard, Ollie Patch, who had led the Flight in the attack on Bomba, said at breakfast, "We're sending five Swordfish to *Illustrious*, plus crews." Mark knew why, knew also that he would be one of the pilots. In the forenoon he stood on the flight-deck and watched the Swordfish slung over the side by the big crane aft of the bridge and lowered to the lighters waiting below, to be ferried across to the other big, new carrier.

He went down to his cabin before lunch and as he opened the door saw a trousered and shirt-sleeved figure, the face hidden by a book, sprawled on the bunk that had been occupied by Tim Rogers. Mark thought, They've shoved some replacement in already and never said a word to me. Bloody cheek! Then Tim put down the book and Mark stared at him, said quietly, "Oh, it's you."

Tim sniffed. "I'm glad your eyes are all right, seeing as you're flying."

Mark was very glad to see him. "What are you doing here?"

"They passed me fit and I said I wanted to fly with you. They thought, as we'd been together a bit now, that might be a good idea."

Mark reflected that Tim could have kept his mouth shut, stayed ashore and missed this big one. But he'd volunteered – to fly with Mark Ward again. "Just when I thought I might get an observer who knew which end of the chart was up. Did the doctor say you were fit to drink?"

Tim swung his legs off the bunk and stood up. "In moderation."

"With me paying, it will be. Come on."

In the forenoon of the next day they crossed to *Illustrious* with the other chosen aircrews, fitters and riggers. At eleven thirty-six hours she slipped and proceeded astern of *Warspite*.

There would be Eagles at Taranto.

Before his first patrol from *Illustrious* Mark went down with Tim Rogers to the huge but crowded hangar-deck to look over and check the Swordfish he had been given. Laurel and Hardy were working on it and the rigger said, "Looks all right, don't she, sir? We reckon she's a good 'un. Right?" Hardy grunted agreement and Laurel rattled on, "What're you going to call her, sir?"

Mark had not thought about this, but did not need to: "Ethel."

Laurel pursed his lips doubtfully. "You don't reckon that might be unlucky, after what happened?"

Mark glanced at Tim. "Well, we're here."

Laurel shrugged. But he knew that Ward could be a deep bloke, and while he'd not been talkative before he was even quieter now. "If you say so sir."

Mark said shortly, firmly, "Ethel."

Illustrious and the Mediterranean Fleet sailed as part of a complex operation, MB8, to cover the passage of four convoys and culminating in JUDGMENT, the attack on Taranto. One convoy was to Malta from Alexandria, the second in the reverse direction. A third carried supplies to Greece from Egypt and the fourth consisted of empty ships on the return journey. Whenever convoys sailed the Fleet had to be at sea in case the Italians came out from Taranto. The enemy presence in force there bedevilled all Cunningham's operations and that was the reason for JUDGMENT.

The air attack was timed for the night of the eleventh. With the Swordfish transferred from *Eagle*, *Illustrious* carried a striking force of twenty-four. Then one suffered engine failure and crashed into the sea on the ninth, another on the tenth. In the forenoon of the eleventh Mark was climbing to the flight-deck when Tim Rogers shouted from above him, "Keith and Going have ditched!"

Mark ran up the last ladder and out onto the deck. He stood by Tim and stared out but there was nothing to see. The Swordfish had crashed twenty miles away, far over the horizon and Tim had simply repeated the report passed down by word of mouth from the bridge. But they both stood there, waiting, anxious, until they heard that *Gloucester*, a cruiser escort, had picked up pilot and observer. There had been no airgunner aboard.

Mark went down to the hangar-deck to look at Ethel, and passed on the news, good and bad. Laurel muttered, "Something bloody funny goin' on. Three down in three days. It makes you wonder if there's a jinx on this flaming operation. Fire in the hangar, then *Eagle* has to drop out, and now this."

Mark grinned at him, "Balls. No jinx. There's something wrong but we'll find it."

They did: pollution in one of the fuel tanks in the hangar, possibly breeding from the time of the fire and the drenching with sea-water. The fungus inside looked like spaghetti. That tank was shut off and the fuel system of every Swordfish dismantled and cleaned.

Mark took no part in that labour of detection and correction but he had spoken with inner conviction. He knew that JUDGMENT would go on, with twenty-one Swordfish, or even less, if necessary. *Illustrious* had orders to leave the main Fleet on the afternoon of the eleventh of November and steam with her escorts to a position twenty miles west of the island of Cephalonia. She was to fly off her strike force at eight that evening.

Briefing.

The wardroom was crowded with pilots, observers and other officers, lounging in chairs or propping up the bulkhead. *Illustrious* was a big ship but she was full to overflowing. There were cabins for only a few of *Eagle*'s air crews. Mark, like the rest, kept his kit in the cabin of one of *Illustrious*' pilots and slept on a camp bed out on the open-sided quarter-deck.

Sleeping in a passage below decks would have meant people bumping into him as they passed. The quarter-deck was breezy but the flight-deck covered him overhead.

Now he leaned against a table in the wardroom, long legs crossed, dark eyes sombre and intent under thick brows. Tim sat by him at the table, notebook before him, pencil in hand. The big claspknife lay on the table. When Mark returned it to him Tim had looked at it but taken the knife without asking how Mark had used it.

The Observer Commander, Beale, was on his feet and they listened to him. The attack . . . it would be made in two waves, the first flying-off at eight in the evening, the second an hour later. Mark was in the second wave, which meant an extra hour of waiting. Courses to be flown . . . position of the ship when they returned – Mark thought, If and watched Tim busily scribbling notes. Enemy defences . . . 240 anti-aircraft guns sited around the harbour and a lot more heavy machine-guns. Add to them the guns of the fleet, six battle-ships, nine cruisers, forty-eight destroyers . . . Tim Rogers had stopped writing and pulled a face at Mark, who tried to grin.

Barrage balloons . . . *balloons?*

Mark peered at the reconnaissance photographs with the others: beautiful clear prints. They showed the ships – and the white blips of the barrage balloons spread across the harbour. The wire cables that tethered them to the pontoons formed a steel fence. The Swordfish would have to fly through it.

Dinner. An awful excitement he could feel like a shiver, a sense that tonight they might make history. This attack by the Swordfish was being attempted because it had to be. Nobody knew if it could be done. Aircraft had sunk ships before, at sea, in port, by day and at night, but could they attack a great fleet in a heavily defended port – and hurt it? Sink some or even one of the ships? Could any of those aircraft penetrate the massed defences? And if some did, how many of them would escape? You could expect casualties to be heavy, even in a surprise attack, but this night there would be no surprise. Italian sound-locating equipment would pick up the Swordfish long before they were in gun range.

Nobody knew the answers to the questions. There was no past form to go on, no previous, similar operation. This was a first. Tonight they would write the book. Tonight they would learn the answers.

Mark's sense of inevitability, of following a long, pre-ordained path, was strong. The operation that had been only a vague possibility in those far-off summer days, was here now and real. Events followed one another with the regularity of a ticking clock. He walked and talked on the flight-deck with Tim, stood at his shoulder on the goofer's platform abaft the bridge and watched the first wave of twelve Swordfish fly off one by one into the night. He and Tim went below and dressed in their flying-kit: navy trousers tucked into flying-boots, leather sheepskin-lined Irvine jackets zipped up, Mae West lifejackets strapped on, leather helmets, gloves. Tim picked up the big bag that held his chart-board and instruments and they climbed the ladders to the flight-deck. Once again Doug Campbell would not be going with them: his cockpit was needed for the long-range fuel tank.

By the light of the moon they made their way through the nine Swordfish ranged aft. Their Pegasus engines bellowed, with blue flames licking from the exhausts. Their wings were still folded back for close packing on the flight-deck so that they looked more like huge four-poster beds than aircraft.

The air felt chill. Mark climbed up Ethel's side and slid into the cockpit. Hardy leaned over him, helped him secure the locking-pin of the Sutton harness, then laid a broad hand on Mark's shoulder and bawled into the Gosport tube, "Good luck, sir!" His round face was serious. Mark looked past him and saw Laurel standing on the deck below, peering up worriedly. The two mother hens. Ward felt a surge of affection for them and nodded, grinned, took the tube and fastened it to his helmet so he could speak into it. Hardy climbed down and Mark worked through his pre-flight checks, squinting at the instruments in the orange light of the cockpit, ran up the engine and tested switches. Finally he called Tim: "Can you hear me?"

"As if you were only a few feet away."

He was, with just the big dustbin of the overload tank between them.

Mark looked down at Laurel and Hardy, spreadeagled now on the deck and holding the ropes of the chocks wedged under Ethel's wheels. Their faces were grey blobs in the darkness, turned up to him. He lifted a thumb to indicate to them: ready.

Illustrious was making twenty-eight knots, the funnel smoke a thick stream and veering around as she turned into wind. The sea was black and silver under the moon and laced with green phosphorescence. The flight-deck lights came on, twin lines of them seeming to close in as they ran away towards the bow and the night sky lifting beyond. A green light flashed from the bridge then another blinked on the flight-deck and the first Swordfish rolled forward and sped away, lifted off. That was Ginger Hale, leading this second wave, a great man to go to war with: cool, skilled, brave.

Mark waited, alone and lonely now. Campbell, Laurel and Hardy, the other air crew, were all miles away. But he was calm. The green light blinked at him, Laurel and Hardy snatched away the chocks. Ethel rolled forward, briefly halted as Laurel and Hardy spread the wings and slammed home their locking-pins. Mark tested the aileron controls. Green light again. He let Ethel run forward, accelerating down the narrow lane between the lights, then lifted her off, heavy with the three-quarter-ton weight of the torpedo under her belly, but climbing away into the night.

He found the others already in the air and joined the circus of shadowy Swordfish with blue formation lights marking their big double wings with the struts and bracing wires between. They circled widely above *Illustrious* and Mark turned his helmeted, goggled head to look down at her. The escorting destroyers were shadows on the sea, his eyes led to them by the white arrows of their wakes. The carrier was picked out by the twin ribbons of her landing lights.

Mark counted heads as another Swordfish clawed its way up to those already circling: seven.

Where were numbers eight and nine?

Below on the flight-deck a cursing crowd of fitters and riggers worked furiously to disentangle two Swordfish with their wings locked together. When that was done the aircraft had to be checked to see if they had suffered damage, if they were still fit to fly on the operation. At the end of it there was relief and frustrated bad temper equally shared.

Ethel droned on, gently banking, through the night sky, Mark counting the shadows and the pairs of lights again but getting the same answer. Until at last another came slowly up: eight.

Still waiting, circling, for five minutes – ten. Mark was uneasy, sensing that something had gone wrong. Where was number nine? Broken down? Flopped in the drink?

Tim Rogers said, "Signal from the ship: Carry on."

So nine was not coming. They were down to eight.

A blue torch blinked from the Swordfish of Ginger Hale, the leader: form up. Mark eased Ethel into the formation: two "vics" of three Swordfish, and one of only two. The course was north-west for Taranto and they climbed steadily to three-thousand feet then levelled off. Mark tilted back his head now and again to look at the clouds above him. They steadily thickened to a solid ceiling.

It was then that Tim shouted, voice blaring distorted in Mark's ears: "– Almighty. Look . . . Queenie . . . her tank . . ."

Mark's head jerked around and he saw Queenie, L.5Q. She carried bombs, not a torpedo, so her overload tank could be strapped under the fuselage. Now one of the straps had broken and Mark looked just in time to see the other strap give and the tank fall. Queenie followed it, skidding sideways and down, was lost to his sight. Without the overload she did not have the range to carry out the operation and would have to return to *Illustrious*.

Now they were only seven. Lucky seven? What price the jinx now? They had set out from Alexandria with a striking force of twenty-four that was now reduced to nineteen. That was a loss of almost a quarter and they had yet to come under fire – the twelve in the first wave were still an hour from Taranto.

It did not matter. He had that feeling of inevitability again. The attack would go on.

They did not talk for a long time but that was not unusual. Mark's mind was on his flying and Tim worked on his chart. Despite the Irvine jackets, the boots and gloves, they were very cold in the open cockpits. It was lonely in the night. There were the other Swordfish lifting and falling gently, as on a carousel. There was the Gosport tube, but in the night and the cold, between the cloud ceiling and the sea, with the battering slipstream and the engine's roar, there was loneliness.

Tim Rogers broke the verbal silence: "The first wave should be close to Taranto now."

Mark looked at his watch. "Yes." He wondered about the twelve Swordfish an hour or so ahead. Williamson led them and his plan was to attack from two directions. Half of the planes were to drop bombs on the inner harbour to create a diversion, also to lay a line of parachute flares along the eastern shore. All six Italian battleships were moored at that eastern end of the harbour, near the town. Williamson meanwhile would lead one flight of three torpedo-carriers in over San Pietro island and then the Taranto breakwater before turning north onto their targets. The other flight of three torpedo-carriers would cross the submerged breakwater north of San Pietro, fly across the harbour and then turn south. The two attacking flights would have the battleships between them and that should help to confuse the naval gunners. Mark thought: If any of Williamson's Swordfish ever got as far as the ships . . .

4

Taranto

The freighter had sailed in convoy from Benghazi bound for
Catania in Sicily but she was detached before arriving at that
port and sent instead to Brindisi. This pleased the captain and
most of the crew because Brindisi was the ship's home port and
they would be able to see their families. On the morning of the
eleventh, however, a wireless signal re-routed the ship again,
this time to Taranto, amid general cursing. The naval party
aboard did not curse because they were all from the north of
Italy anyway. The prisoner they were there to guard did not
curse either. Jamie Dunbar did not want to go to Italy at all.

That evening he and a young *tenente* of the Italian navy leaned
companionably on the rail below the bridge as the freighter
passed in through the entrance to the great harbour. To starboard the long breakwater ran out from Cape San Vito, to port
lay San Paolo island. Two guardships, each with a gun forward
and aft, were moored in the half-mile-wide entrance, with an
anti-aircraft battery mounted on a lighter. Jamie could just
make out the silhouettes of the guns in the dusk.

The *tenente* said softly, "*Mare Grande*. The great harbour
of Taranto."

Jamie looked out across the four-mile-wide expanse of
water and said, "We've got a pond like this in Hyde Park."

The *tenente* smiled, seeing the joke. He was correct but
friendly towards Jamie, who was polite, and with an effort
of will, obedient. He was looking for a chance to escape but
the *tenente* had not given him one. He and the six seamen and
the petty officer in the naval party had been aboard a destroyer
sunk at Tobruk. They were returning to Italy for leave and
redrafting to another ship, so they were given the task of
escorting this prisoner.

There was no doubt which was the prisoner. The *tenente* was casually immaculate in his uniform but Jamie wore an assortment of clothes found for him in the hospital. The big Italian patrol sent out, nervously, to seek their own dead and wounded outside the wire at Sidi Barrani had found him. He had lain unconscious near the craters made by the mortar bombs. The medics with the patrol had cut and ripped away his clothing to locate the score of small shrapnel wounds and stop their bleeding. They had carried him back behind their lines near-naked under a blanket.

The freighter steamed slowly across the *Mare Grande*. Jamie could see cruisers anchored inside a protective screen of barrage balloons swaying gently in the wind above the harbour. Beyond the cruisers and closer inshore were six great battleships.

The freighter slid on over water like glass and the *tenente* said, "We anchor off the Commercial Basin for the night." In fact they moored to a buoy, then the watch on deck lowered a boat and let a ladder down the side. Jamie watched them from the corner of his eye; you never knew what little piece of knowledge might be useful. Possibly the *tenente* guessed this. He glanced at the men working by the glimmer of screened lamps and a three-quarter moon; the harbour and town were blacked-out, scarcely a pin-prick of light showing. "The captain goes ashore to report and receive his orders. I think, tomorrow, you go ashore."

Jamie thought, Damn-all chance of getting away so far, and a sight less once I'm dumped in a prisoner-of-war camp.

The *tenente* slapped Jamie's shoulder gently, sympathetically, "Come. You go below now."

Jamie was locked in his cabin for the night. First he swore out of frustration but when he'd got that out of his system he sat on his bunk. He had to think of some way of smuggling his few illicit possessions ashore. He had collected them – stolen would be a more accurate term – in the course of the voyage. He had taken anything he could, like a jackdaw, because – like the little pieces of knowledge – he did not know when they might prove useful. There was a packet of biscuits, a table-knife, a box of matches. They were tucked down into a crevice behind the bunk.

He looked from the scuttle, with the deadlight screwed down over it so no light would escape, to the door. If he unscrewed the deadlight the scuttle was still too small for him to slip through. The door was ordinary, with a lock he was certain he could force with the table-knife, but a sentry armed with a rifle stood outside. There were louvred ventilator slits at the top of the door. If Jamie stood close against them he could see the sentry, just, through their angled slats.

All of this he knew only too well. Tonight, as on other nights, he could see no way of escaping. He climbed bad-temperedly into bed and tried to read the newspaper they had allowed him, but he could only pick out a few words of Italian that he knew. He swore again, threw it aside and settled down to sleep. They had disconnected the switch so that his light stayed on. He turned his back to it and closed his eyes.

The thought came suddenly: He and Mark Ward had got on the last time they met. If only that big, black-haired devil were here, then together they'd be able to get out of this.

Bert Keller asked, "How about you? 'Nother *bianco*?"

Katy shook her head. Her glass of white wine still stood half full.

Bert waved a lean hand at the waiter behind the bar: "*Strega*."

"Signore." There was a quick smile from the fat, greying Italian too old for military service; he liked the affable Bert.

They sat at a table in the bar of the hotel, Katy chic in a navy-blue suit and a white blouse that set off her tan. Bert said lugubriously, "Boy! How unlucky can you get? I could turn in an actual eye-witness account of Mussolini's invasion of Greece but the bastards won't let me file the story."

Katy said calmly, "Count your blessings. Anyway, how much did you see with your head stuck in that ditch?"

Bert looked his old self again: lazy, rumpled, his long face creased in a sardonic grin. Not like on the night she had dragged him from the stream and feared he was dying. When the bullet smashed into the torch she was holding, it numbed her arm to the shoulder for hours, but first the shock of it had sent her sprawling beside Bert, winded and half dazed. Some time later she became aware of soldiers around them, their rifles menacing. There was an officer, young and excited, volubly taken aback at finding a blonde, frightened and very emotional American girl on this black night of rain. She was soaked, plastered with mud, and her hands shook but now her fear and anger found a target. She dressed down the subaltern as if she were a general. Maybe something of her naval captain of a father had rubbed off on her. "We're neutrals, you trigger-happy clowns! Americanos! And this is an old man, a famous newspaperman! If he dies I'll see you shot, goddamn you!"

So four of the soldiers dumped Bert on a stretcher and then the little party headed for the rear: Katy, Bert, the stretcher-bearers and two soldiers with rifles slung on their shoulders as escorts. All Katy remembered of that march through the night was the firing and the continual banging of grenades from the direction of the house. Both faded behind them as they slipped and slid down the track to the road. They trudged back along the edge of the road until they came to an ambulance.

The light was growing now: grey under low clouds, streaming rain. Trucks ground up the road and soldiers, heavily laden with packs, ammunition and rifles, tramped in straggling files on either side. The puttees wound around their calves were daubed with mud and their boots were great shapeless lumps of it. They were excited, keyed-up, but already their feet were dragging. They had found the marching in this weather and this country hard going. They did not look like a victorious, invading army.

The ambulance took Bert and Katy to a field dressing-station where a doctor tended to Bert and said he would be all right. There was also, soon, an intelligence officer who interrogated Katy and was sceptical of her story that they were U.S. correspondents. Their passports were back in the house, Katy told him. He did not believe that, either, and there was a shouting match which ended when Katy told him icily, "When I get to our embassy in Rome I'll see you busted down to a buck private! Now go to hell and leave me alone!"

He went away, muttering under his breath and uneasy, leaving Bert and Katy under guard. When he returned later in the day his manner was still distant but he brought their passports and luggage, or what was left of it. He said the soldiers who had found Kristos, Katy and Bert had assumed from Kristos' uniform that he had come from a military strongpoint. Since old Constantine's house was nearest, they had attacked it and bombed their way in. Regrettably there had been some damage but that was the fortune of war.

The valises were bundles of seared rags, Katy's cameras handfuls of junk, but the passports, though stained and battered, were intact. She thought bitterly that the paper always seemed to survive, remembered it blowing among the dead in the desert.

She asked about Kristos, Constantine and his wife, and when she and Bert could be returned to Athens. The officer answered that Kristos was dead but the old couple had been found hiding near the house and allowed to seek shelter with another Greek family along the road. He did not know what arrangements would be made for Katy and Bert but was certain they would not be passed through the lines into Greek-held territory. He seemed to derive some satisfaction from that.

He was right. The Italians shipped them back to Italy on the first returning transport. It berthed in Taranto and they had been there almost two weeks now, while Katy made her arrangements and Bert wheedled, argued, trying to change her mind. As he would to the end.

He sprawled in a deep chair away from the bar now, one arm dangling loosely like that of a rag doll, a cigarette between the hanging fingers, smoke rising in a thin thread. He said, "I fixed my passage back to Cairo this afternoon – as far as Istanbul, anyway. The ship sails tomorrow in the forenoon and she has plenty of room aboard. Not many passengers these days, with the war." He paused a moment, watching her, then asked, "But you've had it?"

Katy replied patiently, "I've told you: that plane leaves for Lisbon the day after tomorrow and I'll be on it. I've done my time."

"Time, hell! You know I just have to say the word and

they'll extend your contract and keep you on the assignmen with me."

Katy shook her head. "No. Remember, we cabled th States that I was finishing, going home, the first day we g back here." Bert studied the *strega* in his glass and Katy sai "Bert. Look at me." And when he met her eyes she aske "You didn't send that cable, did you?"

Bert cleared his throat, "Look, honey, I thought if you ha a week or two to think things over –"

"Bert, you really are the goddamn limit." She was shakin her head again but she was smiling.

Bert said cautiously, "You're not mad?"

"More than a little. But I sent my cable the day you tor up yours. You can wire another one if you want them to sen a photographer to join you in Cairo. I'm going home."

That was final, and Bert grimaced, accepted it. "Guess lost that one. Well, I can understand how you feel. Ah! It's hell of a life. I do it because it's my job, all I know. When get too old they'll shackle me to a desk, but till then . . . He was silent a moment then looked her in the eye. "It's bee great having you along. Leaving aside that you saved my li back there in Greece, you've always pulled your weight. I'r going to miss you."

"Thanks, Bert." She knew he was sincere. But he had sai he'd "lost that one". So what now? She could guess. He' try again. She knew him so well. Oh, Bert, I'll miss you.

Bert took a mouthful of the *strega*, swallowed and sighed "Heard from that young feller?"

Katy could not help laughing at his tongue-in-cheek inno cence. "Here in Italy? How would I hear from a British Nav flyer? Pigeon post?" Then the smile faded, "Anyway, that finished."

"Yeah, you told me. I remember now."

"Damn right you do. I've told you a dozen times."

"Guess you have, at that."

"So leave it alone."

"O.K." He was silent for a minute, then: "I never though I'd get to like some Englishman who studies to compose fo the philharmonic and then makes a good living instead out of writing vaudeville songs. Still, you wouldn't think it to look at him: big, strong young feller. You couldn't call him a good-looking guy, more of a hard nut, but –" He found her eye on him and broke off there. "O.K., O.K."

The sirens wailed.

Katy shivered at the sound and exchanged glances with Bert. The waiter called rapidly across the bar, his voice almost drowned by the sirens and the loud chatter as the other customers crowded quickly out of the bar. Bert said, "I didn't catch that."

Katy had: "He says it is necessary to go to the air-raid shelters."

Bert grumbled, "To hell with that! I hear there hasn't been a real raid on this place yet and I'm not surprised. There's more 'n a thousand guns of one sort or another around this town." He raised his voice: "Hey, Mario! Leave that bottle o' *strega* an' put it on my bill."

The waiter was already struggling into his jacket but as he passed them on the way out he set the bottle on the table. Bert stood up and looked around the empty bar with only one light burning above him now. He cocked his head on one side, listening. The sirens had moaned into silence and now there was quiet. He said, "Sounds like one more false alarm. But if something does happen, I want to see it, so I'm going up to my room. Join me?"

Katy sighed and shook her head but she was smiling as she rose to her feet. "You never give up."

Bert grinned at her, then with bottle in one hand, glass in the other, and cigarette in the corner of his mouth, he headed for the stairs. "Bring your glass. You might need it."

Katy said drily, "Look at you go. Booze and cigarettes – the fully-equipped war correspondent." But she picked up her glass and followed him.

Upstairs in his room, Bert edged cautiously through the darkness to the table by the window then carefully set down bottle and glass. Katy waited just inside the door and saw the red glow of his cigarette black out as he stubbed it in the ashtray. Then he pulled the curtains aside and moonlight flooded into the room. Bert opened the French windows wide and set them back against the wall. "Just in case there's any firing. That might save the glass."

Katy crossed the room to stand beside him and Bert said softly, "Will you look at that?"

The huge harbour lay before them and the six battleships were anchored less than a mile from the shore in a wide-spaced, staggered line following the curve of the bay. Bert counted them off from his right, as he remembered them from the daytime: "*Duilio, Cesare, Littorio, Vittorio Veneto, Doria, Cavour.* The first two and the last two are big enough but those babies in the middle, *Littorio* and *Vittorio Veneto,* they're monsters."

From the balcony Katy could see, beyond the battleships and in the middle distance, the mile-long curve of the Tarantola mole sweeping out from the shore to her left. Further out still and to her left stood Cape San Vito with another breakwater running out from it. The half-mile wide entrance to the harbour lay between the end of that breakwater and the island of San Paolo. Then the island of San Pietro lifted at the centre of the bay and to her right was the jutting arm of Cape Rondinella. Unseen, but closing the gap between San Pietro and Rondinella was a submerged breakwater. Moonlight glinted on the silver skins of the balloons riding high in a long line across the bay between the battleships inshore and the islands.

Bert muttered, "Boy! What a view."

In spite of the great ships, squat fortresses of steel with their long guns, Katy thought the scene was deceptively peaceful and it would seem pleasant to pull up a chair and sit here in the window in the stillness of the night, looking out at the moonlight on the bay, and the ships. It was a picture postcard scene, such as a tourist would send home.

Home.

These ships were the tools of a war that was spreading like a plague. Mark Ward had sombrely suggested that it would, when she first met him in Alexandria. Hitler and Mussolini, propagators of the plague, would demand, threaten and grab until they were stopped. That much was clear to her now. She knew that when she was in America she would still be looking back at the war, that it was slowly but surely following her, and that she would wake each morning and wonder if this would be the day it caught up with her.

She heard Bert grumble, "Where in hell did I put that bottle?"

There was a tiny lick of yellow flame on the dark hump of Cape Rondinella over to the right of the harbour. It was the merest wink and for a second Katy was unsure whether it had been some trick of the moonlight reflecting on the window of a house. Then the report of the gun came flatly, distantly across the harbour and the orange burst of the shell flared in the sky out over the sea.

Bert ceased his fumbling search for the bottle and grabbed Katy's arm, "Hey! Get back in here! Looks like, maybe –"

His words were lost in thunder as they retreated into the room and the batteries opened up. At first there were only the guns on the Cape, on the island of San Pietro and the lighters moored in the entrance to the harbour. Even though they were four miles away, their noise was deafening, the flashes of muzzles and the bursting shells dazzled the eye. But then like the swift spread of a forest fire the batteries all around the inland shore of the harbour joined in – and the guns of the ships. Now there was not just the sound of thunder but a shuddering of the air and the building beneath the feet of Katy and Bert. The glass of the French windows exploded from the frames and cascaded, shattering, to the floor.

The sky over the harbour was one great curtain of red, green and orange light but now it was touched by a paler radiance that seemed to come from directly overhead. Bert put his mouth to Katy's ear and shouted: "Somebody up above us is dropping flares!"

That white glow grew as one minute, then another ticked by, but it did not pale the coloured inferno over the harbour and the ships. Bert said again, his head close to Katy, "I dunno who's up there but he'll be coming down pretty damn quick!"

Katy did not doubt it, thought she saw it happening and said, "Look!" Bert did not hear her, but she was pointing, so he too saw an aircraft fall from the sky, seemingly out of that inferno. Katy gripped his arm and they tensed for the crash but slowly the tiny toy-like aeroplane pulled out of its dive and levelled off above the sea. It flew in towards the shore, very low above the surface of the harbour, slipped between the steel cables of the barrage balloons and came on with shells bursting all around it. When it seemed they would lose sight of it they unthinkingly edged forward into the window again, almost out onto the little balcony. From there they saw the aeroplane lift slightly so it just cleared the long Tarantola breakwater, then banked to the left. When it straightened out it looked to be heading straight for them.

Katy realised she was receiving the scene not as a continuously moving film but rather as a rapid succession of separate photographs as the plane was lit by shell bursts or flares then lost in darkness. And it was a mile away. But she saw it clearly, old-fashioned and lumbering, like a box-kite hauled along by the spinning propeller in the nose. A British Swordfish. The sort of plane Mark flew.

Bert croaked incredulously, "I can't believe it! They're using those things! They haven't a snowflake in hell's chance!"

A torpedo dropped away from the Swordfish and in that same instant the biplane curled over on one wing and crashed into the sea. Katy was praying. She felt Bert wince and it was not because of her fingers digging into his arm.

There was a dull, heavy explosion out in the harbour, heard even above the hammering guns. Bert said, "Torpedo. Maybe it hit one of the ships. Or maybe just grounded on the bottom of the bay."

Now he pointed. Two more Swordfish were lurching in, low over the sea, lifting above the Tarantola breakwater as had the first. Then they too banked to the left, dropped torpedoes and swung away. But they were luckier, headed towards the mouth of the harbour and disappeared into the night.

Two more explosions. Then more, seeming to come from inland. Bert said, "They're bombing."

Another Swordfish came curling past the end of the break-water to the left, and far to the right yet another suddenly appeared, flying on an opposite course. They closed on the same ship, rocking and weaving through the barrage, held briefly steady and straight until the torpedoes fell away, then turned out to sea. One of them flew right over the ship and Katy caught her breath as both Swordfish seemed on the point of colliding – but one crossed above the other.

Bert was counting the British planes: "Six." This one also came out of the darkness and the looping tracer away to the right, launched its torpedo and swung seaward, was hidden again, like the other two, by flame, darkness and smoke. Then like echoes came the sullen explosions.

Katy could feel the smoke in her nose and throat, smelt it, acrid and reeking. She put her handkerchief over her mouth as Bert had covered his. Her senses battered, she was finding it hard to think, was unable to measure time. How long had the attacks gone on – ten minutes? An hour? She stood in the window as the guns pounded on and the shrapnel from the bursting shells rattled on the roofs around them and rained on the promenade below. After a time the firing eased. After a longer time, it ceased.

Bert took a pace out onto the balcony and Katy went with him, staying close. In the quiet, Bert said, "I guess those fliers have done a helluva lot of damage." It was difficult, however, to see for certain. The flares had burned out long ago and light from the three-quarter moon could not pierce the cloud of smoke that covered the harbour. He went on slowly, "Two of those ships look as if they're listing."

The quiet was only comparative now that the guns were silent. Fire-engines and trucks raced or ground through the streets. There was a din of bells, whistles, sirens out in the harbour and an ebbing and swelling undercurrent of men shouting. Katy stood by Bert and, with him, listened, tried to see through the smoke.

Until the guns on Cape Rondinella fired again, and she knew there was to be a second wave to the British attack.

5

The Tunnel

Jamie woke when the first gun fired and turned onto his back, lay staring up at the deckhead with its prickling of rust through the paint. Then the ship seemed to shake as the barrage opened up in earnest and Jamie felt he was inside a drum being violently beaten. He slid out of bed and dressed. He didn't want to be running around in his underpants if the ship was hit by a bomb.

He guessed that the Royal Air Force was raiding Taranto. A fine thing if I'm blown up by my own air force. Bloody funny. He guessed also that the tremors running through the ship's frame every few seconds would be the firing of the gun she carried aft on the poop. And every now and again as the barrage briefly eased he could hear a patter like rain above his head – he realised that this was shrapnel from the bursting shells, falling on the deck.

There was a distant, thumping explosion that he felt rather than heard, sending a shudder through the ship again. A huge bomb? Then distant, squeaky shouting. It had to be horrific up top. They were getting hell up there. And he was locked in here, below decks –

He only paused for a few seconds to think about it, to acknowledge that this was a million-to-one chance. He had no real kind of a plan at all. But this might be the only chance he would ever have. The sentry outside was trapped below decks as surely as he was and would be staring, like him, up at the deckhead, wondering when the blow would fall, waiting –

Jamie dug down into the crevice behind the bunk, fished out the biscuits and stuffed them in his pocket, then found the table-knife and the matches. He snatched up the newspaper, twisted it into a long stalk then lit the end and held it below the ventilator slats. There was another heavy, dull explosion and he felt it shiver through his shoes. He hammered on the door and bawled, "Fire! Fire! . . ."

The smoke from the smouldering paper was wisping out of the ventilator. Jamie pressed his face close against the slats, the smoke wreathing around him setting him coughing and bringing tears to his eyes. The sentry was suddenly before him, seen cut by the slats into horizontal strips, wide, dark eyes peering nervously in at Jamie's contorted, weeping features.

The man turned and shouted, almost screamed as his voice rose, and at his call the petty officer came running. He may have been in his own cabin or at the head of the companion-way watching the air raid. Jamie heard his pounding boots, saw his bulky figure loom behind that of the sentry. Jamie let out one last choking wail then bent his knees, shuffled aside from the door, and straightened. He stood pressed against the bulkhead, left hand outstretched to hold the last of the burning paper under the ventilator so that its smoke would seep out, but not close enough for the paper to be seen. He checked that the knife was handy, loose in his jacket pocket.

There was a high, rapid interchange of voices outside, rattle of a key in the lock and then the door swung open. Jamie did not wait for one of the men to enter. The door opened away from him; he had positioned himself on the opposite side to the hinges. As the opening gaped he swung himself around and into it, leaping over the coaming with arms thrust out. He caught a fleeting glimpse of the Italian P.O. right in front of him with the sentry peering over his shoulder. Then Jamie slammed into them both with the burning newspaper still in one fist. They staggered back, stumbled and fell, the three of them crowded close in the narrow passage, the sentry's and P.O.'s legs tangling. They sprawled on the corticene of the deck but Jamie was on top, thrust himself up, turned and ran. He left the remnant of burning paper with them.

He knew exactly where he was going, had followed the same route many times with the *tenente*. At the end of the passage he went up the ladder two treads at a time. As he reached the head of it the sentry's rifle fired behind him and the slug ricochetted off the steel sides of the companion. He shoved open the door, passed through, and looking back and down saw the P.O. at the foot of the ladder. Jamie slammed the door and yanked the clips on hard. They would give him a few seconds.

He ran on without hesitation. The night was thunderous with the tumult of the barrage and lit by the multi-coloured bursts that filled the sky over the great harbour. He would not be noticed. The gun on the poop fired, a lick of flame and a *crack*! of report that deafened him. He was only a score of yards from the men working it but they had no eyes for him.

He swung over the bulwark and went down the Jacob's ladder, feet fumbling for the wooden rungs as it swayed and wobbled. But he dropped down it quickly, to where the ship's boat was made fast, and –

The boat was full of water, only its timber buoyancy keeping it afloat and he guessed that it had been holed by shrapnel. He looked up the ladder, but he was not going back. To hell with that. He stepped down into the boat and felt it subside under his weight. He was a fair swimmer but not when fully dressed. He tore off all his clothes but his underpants then rolled over the side and swam away from the ship.

He knew where the shore lay but could not see it. His position was too low in the water. He did not know if he was heading for safety or not. He swam slowly and steadily, pacing himself, as the barrage died away and comparative silence fell over the harbour. There were still sirens, bells, whistles, shouting.

He swam for some time, he thought about fifteen minutes, before he saw a ship ahead of him. As he closed in on it he saw the boat alongside. This one lay at the bottom of a proper accommodation ladder, like a wooden fire-escape angled down the ship's side to end in a small, square platform at water level. He swam to the boat and crawled in over its stern.

He sat in the sternsheets for a time, getting his breath, and told himself wrily that this was where the hard part started. He did not know how far it was to Greece or Malta and his only experience with boats had been an occasional afternoon spent sailing off Alexandria. This trip would be different. Rather longer. There were oars in the boat but were there food and water? He had nothing but his pants. Well, he would steal what he needed. First he had to get out of the harbour. He moved forward in the boat and seized one of the oars. Which way should he go to get clear?

A voice cracked sharply above him. He looked up and saw a squat, dark figure at the head of the ladder. The man ran down its steps, agile as an ape despite his bulk, and halted on the small platform. His head thrust forward as he peered at the boat where it lay out from the ship at the end of its painter, at Jamie now sitting on a thwart and holding one of the oars ready to ship it in the rowlock. The man spoke again, harshly, incomprehensibly, then pulled a pistol from his jacket pocket and pointed it.

Jamie glared at its muzzle glinting blue-black in the moonlight and said irritably, bitterly, "All right! Of all the bloody luck!"

The man started, then growled, "Hey! You English?"

"Yes."

"Are you a spy, or somethin' like that?"

Jamie noted the accent and thought: Italian-American. He said, "No. Prisoner of war."

"What in hell you doin' with my boat, hey?" The stabbing of the gun muzzle emphasised the man's anger.

"I was going to Malta or Greece." Jamie cautiously, surreptitiously, shifted his grip on the oar, fingers reaching along it to find a better balance for what he intended.

The man stared, "In that boat? With oars? In your shorts? Don't try to kid me." He reached down with one hand to grasp the painter.

"Don't try to stop me." Jamie held the oar two-handed, pointed at the man's chest and made ready to hurl it like a harpoon. He thought the other man was unlikely to be a crack shot with the pistol and he was off balance now, crouching to hold the painter, the gun muzzle wavering.

The man was still, watching the oar, then his eyes lifted to Jamie's face. "You really mean it." He did not expect an answer, and said, "O.K." He shoved the gun into his pocket and hauled on the painter. "You come aboard. We're sailing for Istanbul in the morning."

Jamie didn't believe it, didn't trust him, kept his grip on the oar as the boat slid in to bump its prow against the platform. "You're Italian."

"Naw!" The man shook his head. "Turk."

Jamie said, "You've got an American accent." Then he realised the illogicality of that remark.

The man shrugged heavy shoulders, "So what? My brother, he's American citizen. I tried it over there but I like to run my own ship. This is mine. I'm captain. C'mon." He led the way up the ladder.

Jamie stepped onto the platform and called up after the Turkish captain, "Suppose the Italians search the ship?"

The captain paused and looked down at him. "They won't find you. Been done before. People want to come in, people want to go out, and no questions."

"Why are you doing this?"

"I don't like Hitler, Mussolini." The squat man grinned, showing big, square teeth. "And you'll pay me. Right?"

"Right. Once you get me to a British consul."

Jamie followed him up the ladder, trying to remember anything he'd ever learned of the process of repatriation from a neutral country. But if it came down to money then maybe he could work his own repatriation and be smuggled – into and out of – Turkey. And there was always that nurse in Cairo . . .

The second wave of seven Swordfish flew on course for an hour below the thick cloud ceiling, then it thinned, became ragged, ended. They climbed up through a clear sky to eight-thousand feet.

Twenty minutes later Mark saw the cone of fire that was Taranto, sixty miles away, but he watched it for another minute before he realised what it was. The sky was clear ahead, and the cone stood on the horizon, shaped like a Red Indian tepee and made of a patchwork of red, white and green light: brilliant, scintillating, shifting colours. He spoke into the Gosport tube, "Did you ever see the like of this?"

"What?"

Mark did not answer but waited for Tim to put aside his chartboard, stand up and peer around the overload tank.

Then Tim said, "Good God!"

"It's a barrage."

Tim was silent for a moment, digesting that and seeing the implications. Then: "They're expecting us. It looks as though Williamson's first wave stirred them up."

There had never been any hope of having the advantage of surprise, they knew that. Just the same – Mark said, "Right bloody welcome."

Tim did not answer and Mark could guess at his thoughts: was it possible for any aircraft to survive such a barrage? Williamson's squadron had flown into it, but had any of them come out?

Ethel was flying at a hundred knots, trundling along parallel to the coast and about fifteen miles out over the sea. Mark watched the cone of fire as the seven Swordfish slowly approached it, and after a while it died down. He wondered then if the Italians had still been firing at the last of Williamson's squadron? That would fit with the timetable. Then the cone brightened again and he thought, They've heard us. That's for us.

Soon afterwards they were almost opposite Taranto and the fireworks were fifteen miles away to Mark's right. Hale then led them around to starboard, onto a north-easterly course, directly towards the flak. Mark saw a signalling flicker of blue light from the after cockpit of Hale's Swordfish, and then two of the others banked away, leaving the formation and heading off on their own: the flare droppers. The flares would help, but there was a big three-quarter moon up behind Mark's right shoulder. He could see all he needed.

He recognised what he saw; he had pored over the photographs long enough. Ahead and just off to his right was the big, round basin of the outer harbour, four miles across. Dead ahead was Cape Rondinella with the northern shore of the basin running away behind it and lit along its length by the gun flashes of the batteries sited there. To the right lay San Pietro island in the centre of the mouth of the basin and also spurting flames. Further still to the right was the jutting headland of Cape San Vito, the southern end of the basin.

Hale's plan was to lead his torpedo carriers around the northern shore, past the balloon barrage, then turn to starboard when he came level with the battleships, all anchored at the eastern end of the basin. The ships would then be beam on to the attacking Swordfish and so offer the biggest targets. Furthermore, some would be overlapping so there was a chance that a torpedo passing ahead or astern of one would hit another anchored behind.

That was the simple theory. The practice would be less simple. Mark realised that he and Hale and all the others would have to take the position of the battleships on trust because the bursting flak and the drifting smoke hid them. Some of the smoke would have come from the fires he could see burning some four or five miles away. There was one just off to the right of Ethel's nose – would that be the seaplane base? There was another blaze round to the right and he would bet that was the oil-storage depot. But most of the smoke came from the shells that had exploded over this landlocked circle of water during the last hour. More than fifteen-hundred guns had been firing for that time and the smoke still hung. Mark thought he could smell it.

They were closing in on Cape Rondinella now.

Tim Rogers reeled in the wireless aerial, winding the wheel down by his knee. Then he tidied up the cockpit, tucking the Bigsworth chartboard away, securing any loose gear or instruments so nothing would get lost or fall out. He checked that his parachute pack could be easily pulled out of the rack where it was stowed – it could well be needed. But if they were hit on the run-in when less than a hundred feet above the sea, he might just have time to snap loose from the jock strap before the sinking aircraft pulled him down.

He stayed on his feet to be able to see better, the webbing canvas of the jock strap running like some umbilical cord from the harness at his middle to the anchorage in the floor. He leaned out over the right-hand side of the cockpit so that he could peer around the big dustbin of the overload tank, see where they were going, and what awaited them.

Mark knew what Tim would be doing around this time, just before the attack: tidying up like a busy housewife. Time for one last joke? "Don't forget to put the milk bottles out."

Was that a chuckle from Tim? Over the Gosport tube it sounded like an emptying bath. Tim said, "You remember: One-three-five degrees. That's your course for home on the way out of here. In fact, you might as well set it now."

"Roger. One-three-five degrees." Mark set it on the compass ring and locked it, wondered as he did so how many pilots ahead of him had done the same, only for it to be a waste of time because they lay now at the bottom of the harbour. He said, "I take it you've finished for the day, then."

"That's it," Tim agreed, eyes behind his goggles staring out at the great box of bursting flak spread over the harbour, a box that seemed to grow bigger as they drew nearer. "I'm just a spectator from now on."

Mark thought, End of conversation. The torpedo attacks on the ninth of July off Calabria, the others at Bomba and Tobruk, had all been preparation for, and leading up to, this raid. He and Tim had taken the course and now it was examination time.

Ethel crossed the coast north of Cape Rondinella and came under fire from the batteries there but the bursts were ahead of her and low. He wondered again if the gunners were overestimating the speed of the Swordfish. Now there were houses below. There was no smoke beneath him here and the moonlight showed rectangular gridworks of streets and here and there a garden or a park, then what could be a factory building with a tall chimney casting a long shadow. The last lot of flak had been left behind and they were gradually losing height now, coming down slowly from eight thousand –

There was the first flare, burning brilliant white in the east and hanging over the town about four-thousand feet up. And now the second . . . As Ethel droned on Mark saw the line of flares extended one by one above the eastern shore like a string of jewels. Already he thought he could make out the outline of a vessel but by the time the Swordfish were down near the water the flares would have sunk lower and would be silhouetting every ship in the harbour.

He could not see the balloons. He searched for them, eyes narrowed, shifting, but did not find them. Where the *hell* were they? He knew they floated there, the bloody balloons with their mooring wires like cheese-cutters that could slice Ethel in two.

The torpedo Swordfish were in line ahead now; Mark had automatically eased Ethel into her place in the line. Hale led them at the front of the file. Mark saw his leader's blue formation lights blink off and on and then the nose of Hale's Swordfish tipped down.

It was every man for himself from now on. Mark eased the stick gently over to the right and forward until Ethel was howling down in the torpedo dive. He could feel the shiver of the airframe, the slipstream beating on his face. Now they were into the flak. He had grown to know the red, blue and green comets now since that first terrifying baptism of fire off Calabria, the way they came up in slow streams at first but then quickened to flash past with a shriek and *bang!* Now he could smell them and the stench of cordite was rammed into his lungs with the pressure of the dive, caught at his breath.

The flak was thickening, with hundreds of guns hurling up shells and tracer all around the bay, from the inner harbour as well, and from San Pietro island away to the right. He threw Ethel about, from side to side, to try to avoid the flak but there was no avoiding it, no way past, they had him boxed in –! Then the port wing was hit, a huge chunk bitten out of it in a burst of orange light and he felt the shock of it through Ethel's frame, a kick on his seat and a shudder in his hands.

He decided he had to get out of this or they'd be blown to

bits. He wrenched Ethel to starboard. She was still diving, and now banking away from the box barrage filled with hurtling shrapnel and flames. She curled in a spiral as he held her in that diving, banking turn, until they had turned full circle and the altimeter had wound back almost to the stop. He could see the glint of red light on the water of the harbour below and now he straightened Ethel up, hauled back on the stick to pull her out of the dive. For one long, heart-stopping second he thought his flying skill and experience had betrayed him and would kill him, that he had left it too late and he was going to fly her into the sea. He glared down into the black water through the blur of the spinning propeller as the nose lifted slowly, so slowly, but then the oily glitter slid away under him and he was staring instead at a ship in the distance ahead.

He eased the stick forward again to bring Ethel into level flight. He had judged it finely, but correctly. He was very low, only ten to twenty feet above the sea, but he had stolen in under the flak. The brilliant, flaming globes still slid up into the night sky as if running on strings, but they burst high above him. The ship he had seen in the distance was now close, too close, and off to his left. He would never line up on her in time to hit her. She was firing a score of guns, the muzzle flashes twinkling along the length of her, but they weren't firing at him. He leaned to his left, twisted his head around and saw another Swordfish to port and astern of Ethel, skimming the surface of the harbour and headed for the ship.

Mark faced forward. There was a second ship beyond that first one and a shade to the right of it. Ginger Hale's theory of the targets overlapping was being proved right, by God! And this other ship was a monster! From his memory of the photographs and his judgment of where she lay she must be –

He was suddenly aware of Tim's voice croaking in his ears: "Can you hear me? Are you all right?"

Tim had clung to the sides of the cockpit as Mark plunged Ethel seaward in that diving spiral so that she seemed to be sliding down on her starboard wingtip with the bursting shells and entangling lines of tracer all about her. Then Mark was pulling her out of it, the world ceased turning around Tim and he was thrown forward against the petrol-reeking overload tank. He peered around to the right of it, saw the big ship, recognised it, and yelled the information into the Gosport tube again and again – but Mark did not answer. Tim could not reach forward to tap Mark's shoulder as he could usually have done, because of the overload tank bulking between them and he beat on it with his fists in impatient rage, useless because he knew Mark would not hear that hammering, either.

Now, at last, Mark answered his shouting: "What is it?"

"I've been bawling at you for the last five bloody minutes!"

"Sorry. Didn't hear you. I've been busy up here."

"Ship just to starboard. A big 'un. *Littorio*. Or one of them, anyway." The reconnaissance photographs had shown two battleships of the *Littorio* class in the harbour.

Mark answered, "That's right. I see her. She's ours." He banked, very gently, until Ethel was flying straight at the *Littorio*, the water blurring close under him like black glass. Others had seen her. A Swordfish was just lifting over her bow after completing an attack. Another was closing her, flying two, maybe three-hundred yards ahead of Ethel and to the left. And now came the flak, the ship's gunners seeing the two Swordfish and concentrating their fire on them. But the old-fashioned biplanes flew on through the bursts, slipping from side to side to confuse the aim of the gunners.

Christ! Mark sucked in air as a third Swordfish sailed out of the night and slid past the nose of the plane ahead of Ethel, looking to almost rip the propeller away. But it sailed on across Ethel's front, was hit, faltered, fell and smashed into the sea.

Mark winced and trained his eyes ahead to where the other Stringbag kept steadily on. He thought, Looks like Tiffy Torrens-Spence; can't see the number on the fuselage but – beyond Torrens-Spence was the ship. Nothing else. She seemed to stretch as far as Mark could see on either hand, her upperworks, bridge stacked on bridge, rising to reach the sky. She was ablaze with muzzle-flames – but not using her searchlights. He thought, One piece of luck. A searchlight's brilliant beam shining straight into his eyes would have left him flying blind.

Torrens-Spence — Mark was certain now that it was the Irishman — dropped his torpedo and climbed, swung away.

Hold her steady.

Get in close, as Tiffy had.

There was a safety range normally on the torpedoes so they would not explode before running three-hundred yards and the dropping aircraft would have that much of the running time to turn aside and fly clear before the torpedo struck. But tonight, at the insistence of the air crews, the armourers on *Illustrious* had run off nearly a third of that safety range, to be sure that no torpedo would fail to detonate because it was dropped too close.

So hold on.

Now the ship was huge in the torpedo-sight set before the cockpit: monstrous, like a street of tall houses or a block of flats. She was a great floating platform for the dozens of guns she carried and all but the biggest, the fifteen-inch in their turrets, fired at Ward.

Now!

Mark's gloved left hand thumbed the release button and he felt the lurch as the torpedo fell away. He swung Ethel to the right and pulled back the stick to get her climbing. She clawed her way up from the sea to clear the ship's two forward turrets with only feet to spare, and Mark saw a man on the deck of the ship by the foremost turret. Undoubtedly it was a man in a white uniform and Mark thought incredulously: What's that bloody fool standing there for? Doesn't he know it's dangerous with the air full of shrapnel?

Then shells burst around him and he felt the jar as Ethel was hit once more, but she flew on. He jammed her nose down so she was skimming the surface of the sea again, banked right then straightened out, heading for the mouth of the harbour four miles away. Shells were bursting ahead and above. Ethel juddered, a hammer blow shaking her. Underneath! Mark yanked back the stick, lifting her again and realised he'd put her wheels into the sea but she hadn't cartwheeled; he'd got away with it.

He still kept her down to try to stay under the flak. There

was something ahead, low in the water, and above it – He threw Ethel to the left as he saw the balloon like a silver whale floating ahead and above him. The balloon was tethered to an anchored lighter and Ethel tilted on one wing, banking over the lighter's blunt bow. He thought he saw the wire, like a black pen stroke on the night, pass just outside the starboard wing.

Level again. Low again. He flexed the fingers of each hand in turn. It had seemed impossible that they would get in through the fire of the massed guns, but they were here. Now they had to get out. There were ships spread across the harbour ahead: these would be the cruisers shown in the photographs. Beyond them the batteries on San Pietro island and Cape Rondinella were marked in the night by prickling flames that sprouted tracer and bursting shells.

He swung to port, away from that threat and headed instead for the harbour mouth. He knew it was a half-mile wide and midway between the island of San Pietro and Cape San Vito. He remembered there ought to be a floating battery of anti-aircraft guns mounted on a lighter in the entrance and two guardships moored in it also, and now he saw them, or rather the repeating flames at the muzzles of their guns. The lines of fiery coloured globes arched out towards him but slid past on either side. He was flying down between the lines.

And now the tunnel of his dream was real: not a narrowing passage between crowding clouds but a dark way through a sky filled with flashing, blinding explosions. It was a dark way that did not end in a window of light but in blackness. He held on as the bursts crept in on him, nearer and nearer, as the blackness came closer, at first slowly like the shells but then rushing up at him. Until he caught a glimpse of the squat, low vessels that carried the guns, slipping past either wingtip then astern of Ethel, and he flew her on into the darkness.

6

Homecoming

When the guns on Cape Rondinella opened fire, Katy thought, Oh God! Not again.

But once more flares glowed into brilliant life, one by one, to hang in a long, spread backdrop of light against which the battleships would stand out in relief for the attackers from the sea. Bombs fell on the ships in the inner harbour behind, and so out of sight of the watchers in the hotel. And then came the torpedo-carriers.

This time they all attacked from the north, diving in through the deep umbrella of bursting shells and tracer then pulling out of the dive to trundle along so low that, from the hotel window, their wheels seemed to roll on the surface of the sea.

One was hit as it dived and curled away as if destined to crash into the sea. Katy watched with hands to her mouth and then saw it reappear, running in low under the flak and following the path of the leaders. Another skidded off course, put down its nose and smashed into the sea. But those that came after let go their torpedoes and went swerving and wavering away, the wide biplane wings wobbling, heading for the mouth of the harbour and the sheltering darkness.

Were there five – or six? She was not sure, had lost count of them and the explosions of the torpedoes. The guns kept up that thundering barrage for a long time after the last of the Swordfish had gone and the flares had died. Then it became ragged, so they could hear individual guns, slowly faded, stopped.

Bert remembered Katy and turned to her where she stood shaking by the window. He stepped back into the room with his shoes crunching on glass. He lifted a chair left-handed and set it behind her. "Here. Sit down."

He laid a hand on her shoulder and her knees gave way; she sank down on the chair. His voice sounded strange to himself, as if it came from somebody else a long way off. He imagined that would be caused by the battering his ears had suffered. He cleared his throat. "Where did I put that bottle?" Had he said that before? It rang a chord of memory.

The bottle was not on the table. He stooped to peer about on the floor. The glasses lay there, smashed, the fragments and the stems of them reflecting the red light that washed in through the rectangle of open window. But there was no bottle. Then he saw that he himself still held it, by the neck in his right hand.

He offered it. "Here. Take a slug."

Katy put her hands around his on the bottle and her mouth to its neck. She gulped the *strega*, not tasting it, but then pushed it away, gasped and coughed. Bert drank himself then dragged up another chair and folded his bony frame onto it. He dug into his pocket and brought out his packet of Camels, stuck one in his mouth and thumbed the lighter into flame.

Katy said warningly, "The blackout."

"What blackout? The whole damn town is lit up." But he cupped the cigarette in the palm of his hand as he sucked at it greedily.

They stared out, silent. Escaping steam whistled out in the bay, klaxons blared and the huge pall of smoke eddied on the breeze. A sailor appeared on the wide promenade before the hotel and waved his clenched fists at the sky, shouted in impotent fury. Bert suggested, "A liberty-man who missed the boat back to his ship? Or got leave to sleep ashore? He should be glad of his luck." He listened, then, "Do you understand what he's saying?" And when Katy shook her head: "Just as well. He's calling the Royal Air Force sons of bitches and a whole lot worse."

But both he and Katy knew those aircraft were not R.A.F., they had seen those big biplanes too often to be mistaken and they believed they knew the ships they came from. They did not know *Eagle* was in the dockyard at Alexandria.

The Italian sailor walked away. Up on the balcony they sat on as slowly the pall of smoke thinned until they could make out something of the ships in the harbour. One of the monsters was down by the bows and her long forecastle awash, another had been beached, while a third was being towed towards the shore but was already low in the water.

Bert marvelled, "They got *three* of them! Three of the big ships of the Italian Fleet put out of action for months or maybe years! Nobody ever fought or won a naval battle with *aircraft* before."

He looked at Katy and saw she was not listening. Two of the Swordfish had been shot down, for sure. God only knew how few, if any, would get back to their ships. He thought, C'mon! You're the smart guy always has the words to fit the picture. But all he could find to say was: "Don't worry."

Katy had made up her mind. She was certain Mark Ward was safe, but she had to know. She would always have to know. "I'm going to Alexandria with you."

The harbour with its explosive midnight sun lay astern and Mark's eyes adjusted; the blackness changed to a moonlit night over a sea glinting silver in the pale, cold light. He set Ethel climbing steadily and on course. He looked back only once when Tim Rogers called, "You never saw anything like that!" For some seconds Mark leaned sideways to look past the overload tank at the cloud of smoke covering the harbour and the flashing, flaming box barrage that filled it. Then he looked ahead and settled down for the flight.

He had a lot to think about: the flying, of course, watching his heading and the instruments, trim and fuel. But behind that –

Accepting that he was alive. That he had penetrated that hell of gunfire, made his attack and then escaped. That he had faced the tunnel and laid the ghost that he had conjured up himself.

He found he could think very clearly as Ethel droned along,

lifting and falling gently, obedient. He knew that his survival was no guarantee of immortality; it did not mean that from now on he could survive anything. Tomorrow he could ditch over the side, or far from the ship, and be killed. He also knew that tomorrow he would be wrapped again in the pilot's mental protective coating that made him believe, however dangerous the mission, that some other poor bloke would catch it, not himself.

He had faced death, knew it was inevitable sooner or later, and meanwhile he must live. You only had one time around. You must not waste it.

He circled once over *Illustrious* as Tim used the lamp to send their recognition signal. He saw the answering light blink from the bridge, ordering, and took Ethel in towards the round-down of the stern. The two lines of lights came on along either side of the flight-deck but this was no tunnel. He watched the batsman's torches and set Ethel down gently, beautifully.

She ran on to the lift, the deck-handling party shoving at wings and fuselage, to be struck down to the hangar. Laurel showed on the deck below the cockpit, the wind flapping the overalls on his thin frame, "All right, sir?" He gulped with relief, laughing up at them. "Mr. Ward? Mr. Rogers?"

Then Hardy stood behind him like a wide shadow but solid, grinning at Ward. "It looks good, sir. Only one missing out of the first wave and five of your lot are back already."

Welcome home. A strange ship but home for now. Mark clambered down with Tim and went to debriefing. Then to the wardroom that was crowded, noisy, with an atmosphere of celebration, of a victory won, though its full magnitude would not be known until reconnaissance photographs were taken in the light of day. All had landed on who were going to land on and *Illustrious* was steaming swiftly away from possible dawn reprisals. Two Swordfish had failed to return so another four men, friends, had vanished from this close club of the wardroom. But far worse had been expected; they had steeled themselves for losses of a dozen or more crews.

Mark drank a whisky and soda and there were sandwiches,

a big cake. He was ravenously hungry. He had been flying for over five hours in the noisy, wind-buffeted open cockpit, lonely, with only his fears and his courage for company.

Now he was dog-tired, a tall, black-haired young man with a drawn face. He sat down in an armchair, alone in the crowd, and wrote a letter. He wrote slowly because he was tired, carefully because this was important, but without hesitation because he knew exactly what he wanted to say. He did not need to take the photograph from his shirt pocket because he saw it with his mind's eye. When the letter was finished he went aft to the quarter-deck and his camp bed there. He lay for a minute staring out at the sea and the stars with the wind brushing his face and stirring his hair. Then he slept, at peace.

Doug Campbell, telegraphist airgunner lay in his hammock aboard *Eagle* at Alexandria and stared up at the deckhead, inches above his face, and wondered about all of them.

Katy packed her kit in a few minutes by the light of her torch, following a now familiar routine. Then she wrapped her slim body in her trenchcoat against the cold breeze from the shattered window. She sat in an armchair because her bed was strewn with broken glass from the bombing; her short blonde hair was gritty with dust. It felt as it had in the desert but she would shower in the light of morning. Katy was ready to go back to Alexandria.

She did not know if this would ever be America's war but now it was hers and her life would be joined with that of a young pilot. She had seen the slow, lumbering biplanes fight their way through to an incredible victory. She was Katy Sandford and would fight her way through. It would be a long, hard and bitter struggle but she and Mark Ward would face it together. Katy curled up small in the chair and slept.

Curtain

Sarah stirred in her chair and the golden labrador opened its eyes, watched her. The old man had stopped talking. She remembered that he was an old man, talking of lovers long ago. She looked down at her notebook, the few notes she had made at the start of the interview, and the rest of the page still blank. She did not need notes and closed the book, took a breath and said softly, "Thank you."

Mark Ward nodded, "Any of that of use to you?"

"Yes." Those words she had written a year ago: *There is a raw energy to the music, a drive and a passion, but at other times a haunting loneliness. There are passages that leave the listener feeling suspended between heaven and earth, lost and remote. What fashions a man that he should write such music?* She thought she understood them now, the man behind the music – and the woman. She had not been told a parable. He had said, "This is how it was, how we were." She could draw what moral or lesson she wished. Her life was her own.

The sun's rays slanted in at the window now, casting long shadows. Sarah looked at her watch and saw she had over-run her time by several hours. "I have to go now –" She stopped as the labrador scrambled to its feet, head turned to the door. Then she heard, muted by the length of the hall, the crunching of a car on the gravel in the drive and an engine that cut out.

Ward lifted his long frame from the chair. "That will be my wife, driven up from the station. She parks the car there and goes up by train; doesn't like fighting the traffic in London these days." And as he led Sarah down the hall: "She asked me to apologise for her absence. Some relatives of hers flew in from the States on their way to the continent and decided to stop over for a few hours. She felt she was duty-bound to go up and have lunch with them."

Sarah followed him and the labrador out to the front of the house. Another Mini now stood behind hers, the driver closing the door and turning to the house. This was a woman in her sixties, small, still quick, smiling. Sarah saw in that smile the laughter of the girl in the yellowing photograph.

Ward introduced them, then Katy said, "I came down on the train with Jamie."

Ward grinned, "How is he?"

"As always. Laid back. Grousing about the younger generation and in particular his grandson. You know Jamie."

"Yes, we know him." Ward glanced at Sarah.

She slid in behind the wheel and started the engine. Rob Dunbar would be waiting in London. Katy stooped to put her face to the open window. "We'll see you again."

Sarah met her eyes in an exchange of woman's knowledge, "I hope so."

Katy laughed, "I'm sure."

Sarah let in the clutch and they waved, the tall man and the slight figure of the woman at his side, until the Mini turned out of the drive and Sarah went her own way. But for a second she heard the thunder of the guns and saw the night sky flaming above Taranto.

Factual Note

The Swordfish damaged in the accident before flying off (page 191) was repaired and took off later. L5F, Lts. E. W. Clifford and G. R. M. Going, could not catch up with the second strike, which had left Taranto by the time they arrived, but they carried out their mission alone and returned to *Illustrious*.

Although only briefly mentioned in this book, because I was trying to tell a story of two young people, the aerial reconnaissance photographs taken by the Marylands of 431 Reconnaissance Flight, R.A.F., flying from Malta, played a crucial part in the planning of the attack on Taranto.

In the short term that attack gave the British Forces in the Eastern Mediterranean a breathing space, time to build up their strength, and a spectacular victory when any victory was desperately needed.

In the long term the twenty-one Swordfish which flew from *Illustrious* added a new dimension to the war at sea. They proved beyond doubt what could be done. The Japanese raid on Pearl Harbour, and the great carrier battles of the Pacific, followed. But those Swordfish showed the way.